HOLLOW ROCK

BY
GARY BARGATZE

Warfield

Happy Hollow

Hurricane Creek

Upcoming Titles in the
Your Winding Daybreak Ways Series

McGill

Cabedelo

Thunderwood

Babylon, A Human Requiem

For more information about the series, visit the author's

website www.garybargatze.com

HOLLOW ROCK

GARY BARGATZE

———————————

RIGOR HILL PRESS

RIGOR HILL
PRESS

Grateful acknowledgment is made for permission to reprint lines from:

"Pony Blues" written by Charley Patton, © 1997 EMI Longitude Music. All rights administered by Sony/ATV Music Publishing LLC, 424 Church Street, Suite 1200, Nashville, TN 37219. All rights reserved. Used by permission.

"Pea Vine Blues" written by Charley Patton, © 1997 EMI Longitude Music. All rights administered by Sony/ATV Music Publishing LLC, 424 Church Street, Suite 1200, Nashville, TN 37219. All rights reserved. Used by permission.

"Green River Blues" written by Charley Patton, © 1997 EMI Longitude Music. All rights administered by Sony/ATV Music Publishing LLC, 424 Church Street, Suite 1200, Nashville, TN 37219. All rights reserved. Used by permission.

Your Winding Daybreak Ways and *Hollow Rock* are works of fiction. All incidents and dialogue, and all characters with the exception of some well-known and public figures, are products of the author's imagination and are not to be construed as real. Where real-life historical or public figures appear, the situations, incidents and dialogues concerning those persons are entirely fictional and are not intended to depict actual events or to change the entirely fictional nature of the work. In all other respects, any resemblance to persons living or dead is entirely coincidental.

ISBN-13: 978-0-9909499-9-2
LCCN: 2015918809

Editorial Credit: POP Editorial Services, LLC
Cover Design by Alan Pranke
Typeset by B. Cook

Printed in the United States of America

For my mother and father,

who loved us unconditionally

HOLLOW ROCK

1

WE STEAMED INTO the city just as the blues began oozing up out of the juke joints into the white establishments lining Beale Street. It was a rare occasion when my father invited my mother and me along on one of his political trips. But he said he felt I was old enough now to share some of his boyhood memories of growing up in Memphis before hopping a freight at sixteen and never looking back.

Despite having to meet the demands of the weeklong Governors' Conference, my father found time some afternoons and evenings to escort my mother and me around the city. While evenings were family affairs devoted to fine restaurants, opera houses, and theaters, the afternoons were "bachelor outings" highlighting the seedy underbelly of the city. Mama would have thrown a conniption if she'd known the Governor, as she called him, was dragging me down to Beale Street and introducing me to block after block of drinking, gambling, prostitution, and voodoo.

But my initiation into manhood was never my father's intent. He just loved music and sought the latest sounds in the honky-tonks and gentleman's clubs thriving in the hurly-burly of what respectable folk called "that iniquitous thoroughfare." We saw duets, trios, bands, and even a brave choir from Beale Street Baptist. The groups were performing recent compositions of everything from hillbilly to jug, from ragtime to lively spirituals. But it was the ragged, guttural, personal lyrics of a lone guitarist sitting on a straight-back chair in a dimly lit corner of a squalid speakeasy that spoke to me as no other music had ever done before. And by the time we boarded the train for Nashville at the end of the week, I knew how I wanted to spend the rest of my life: writing songs, traveling the circuit, and playing the blues.

There was one other noteworthy aspect to our trip to Memphis. My mother and father didn't fight the entire week. I don't know whether they'd declared a truce or were inhibited by curious reporters and hotel staff, but they showed each other considerable respect. This was not the first time they'd observed an armistice. And during each of the previous cease-fires, I'd get my hopes up that the fighting was going to end for good. But just as I'd begin believing the fantasy, all hell would break loose again followed by bitter skirmishes lasting weeks on end.

And this time wasn't any different. All the hoping and praying hadn't changed a thing. My prayers for a peaceful holiday season had been answered with a resumption of hostilities featuring my mother's customary threats and my father's political calculations. I heard everything through the open door they no longer bothered slamming shut.

"I'm through with your dalliances and empty promises to turn the page. I've told you a thousand times, Jim, the young men will be your downfall. One way or the other, it'll get out—you can count on it. I'll stay here 'til after New Year's and then I'm taking Todd and we're leaving Nashville for good. I'd pack up and leave tomorrow, but I think we owe Todd one last family Christmas."

"I hope you're not serious, Margaret."

"Dead serious now, Jim. You promised me there'd be no more lovers if I followed you to Nashville and became first lady of Tennessee. We hadn't even been here six months when the strangers started showing up after dark. Can't deny it, Jim. The same pattern as before."

My father paused, crafting a response. "Just for argument's sake, let's say you picked up and left with the boy. How'd we explain your leaving to the press?"

"That's something you'll have to work out, Jim. I didn't cause this mess."

He paused again. "Well then, let me run this by you. How about we say you're suffering from an illness requiring a suspension of your official duties for a spell? Explain you'll be heading back to the farm to rest and recuperate?"

"I see a big problem with that already," Mama said coldly.

"What's that?"

"I've made up my mind I'm not going back to the farm. I'd be seeing you every week or so. It'd just be picking at the scab."

"For God's sake, that'll blow everything up! I can see the snarky headline now when the rumors make the rounds: 'Hurricane Peters Out.' . . . It'd be the death knell for a second term and for all I've been trying to do to help my people pull themselves up. It's all about payback, isn't it, Margaret?"

"Furthest thing from my mind, Jim. It breaks my heart thinking about the early days and what might have been. No.

It's about survival and sparing Todd from the fighting, from the spectacle of seeing his father cavorting around the mansion with young—No. It won't be long, Jim, until Todd understands what's going on. I thought long and hard about it before deciding to leave and start over far from the limelight, away from all the deception, the lies."

"Again, just for argument's sake, where would you and the boy go?"

"Far enough away to breathe again but close enough for Todd to have a father."

"Anyplace in mind in particular? Warfield? McGill? Hurricane Creek?"

"No, I was thinking farther west. Across the river, maybe McKenzie, Camden, or Hollow Rock. I don't want you getting any ideas I want an arm and a leg to keep your secrets. I don't want anything of the kind. Just a small stipend until I can get work and make a simple life for Todd and me."

"Get work doing what, Margaret? Think of your age . . . bumping up against forty-five next year."

"Doing what makes me happy, Jim: teaching. I think you'll agree I have a knack for it. Remember when you were a student at Miss Owings? You said I changed your life. And you know teacher's just love hearing that."

Sunlight broke through the clouds for an instant as my father reminisced, "I'd fallen in love with your beauty, with the song in your voice. I hung on your every word. Learning was so exciting, so easy back then, and I hated leaving you for West Point." The clouds overwhelmed the sun again as an edge returned to my father's voice. "If you're hell-bent on following through on this, there's nothing I can really do to stop you. But in return for helping you find a place and paying the rent, I need you to show me some flexibility in how I explain this debacle to the newspapers. I frankly don't know just yet how I'll deal with this, but I need your word you'll show me some flexibility. Agreed?"

"Within reason, Jim. Agreed."

After a long silence honoring an undeclared cease-fire, my father broached the subject of Christmas. "Since you want to make this a happy family occasion, how do you propose we finesse the holidays? Invite folks in to take some of the focus off us?"

"I'd prefer a low-key holiday, Jim. We don't need any more stress than what we already have now. And I suspect our guests would quickly pick up on the tension between us."

"Okay by me," he said and then paused briefly signaling a transition to another holiday topic. "So what do you want to do about gifts? You want anything in particular?"

"Oh, I don't know. Perhaps some jewelry. Earrings, a brooch, or even better, a locket to carry some of the good times close to the heart. . . . And you, Jim?"

"Can't think of anything. How about my leaving it up to you?"

"You sure?"

"Sure." I could hear the sunlight returning to his voice. "But if you really pressed me, I'd say you couldn't go wrong with some quality cigars." And then the clouds returned. "What do you think we should do about the boy? . . . I don't have anything in mind, but since it's our last Christmas together, I think it should be something special, Margaret, something to take the sting out of upending his life here. Any ideas?"

My mother didn't hesitate. "He's already told me, Jim. He said he wants a decent guitar. I don't know why. We all like music but none of us is musically inclined. I'd have followed up, but I had guests arriving for a luncheon."

"I suspect I know."

"Well, why then?"

My father must have thought better of divulging details of our forays onto Beale Street. Instead he said, "How about we keep that for another day. Does he want anything else?"

"You know he's never really asked for much. That's all he mentioned."

"Well, I'll ask around and make sure we get the best we can find."

The informal truce held throughout the holiday season. And as I expected, Christmas Day was theater of the first order. I wouldn't call it farce but more dark comedy because of the vindictive subtexts lurking just below the polite veneer. The curtain opened with the obligatory appearance at West End United before heading back to the mansion to exchange gifts in the private quarters.

As was customary, we always exchanged several inconsequential but useful gifts before turning to the grand finales. We always allowed my mother to open her big present first. Father extended his hand. "Here you go, Margaret? Hope you'll like 'em."

She carefully unwrapped the first of the two professionally

decorated boxes and slowly lifted the lid revealing a set of gold diamond earrings. "They're beautiful, Jim! You really shouldn't have."

"Nonsense!" my father interjected and smiled. "And here's a second."

My mother turned the long, thin box over several times in her hand. "I hate to open it. The paper's gorgeous."

"Go ahead, Mama, open it!" I urged. "The suspense is killing me."

She toyed with the bow for a few seconds before finally beginning to unwrap the small box. Again, she slowly raised the lid and peered in. "Oh my, Jim!" She lifted a gold cable chain out of the box and held it out admiringly for us to see. "I wish you hadn't. It's beautiful. Here, Todd, help me with the clasp."

And it truly was a remarkable piece of jewelry. Suspended from the chain was a diamond pendant—a single ribbon of brilliant gold looped and twisted into an elegant double heart pattern. One of the two hollow hearts sparkled with an array of shimmering diamonds, while the other added luminous depth and dimension to the design.

But having been privy to their recent conversation, I suspected my father was sending a final cutting message or two. My mother had asked for a locket to perhaps carry a small photograph of memories close to her heart. My father, however, opted for a hollow pendant incapable of holding anything. So for me the messages were clear. Choosing the pendant over a locket was his biting way of saying he didn't believe there were any truly good times during their marriage.

And the hollow double heart design signified his belief there was never any romantic love in their relationship either.

My mother never showed outward signs of anger or disappointment about the gift with its implied insults. She stuck close to the agreed-upon script. She handed my father his first gift. "Okay, Jim, it's your turn."

My father was never as appreciative of the fine art of Christmas wrapping as my mother. He tore into the paper and held up a highly decorative box brimming with fine cigars. "Just what the doctor ordered, Margaret. Thanks so much. There's enough here to share a smoke or two."

"And I'm sure you will," she replied and then quickly moved on before poisoning the contrived atmosphere with her response. "And here's another present. Useful but I think you'll like it nevertheless."

My father ripped the paper off the second gift and opened the box. He stood up, extended his arms, and held the lamb's wool cardigan up against his chest. "It'll sure come in handy these cold days, and it looks like it fits just fine. How do I look?"

"As handsome as ever," my mother answered. "Hope you like the color. If not, we can always swap it out for another."

"Wouldn't think of it. Fits well in the shoulders. It's top quality and besides, navy's my favorite color. Goes with anything."

Again, if I hadn't overheard their plans for a final family Christmas, I'd have found this exchange of gifts believable. But after hearing their plotting, I knew to look for implied insults in her gifts as well. And as suspected, my mother got two twists of the knife with the sweater and the Cuban cigars. But how on earth could she be sending a rancorous message with a top-of-the-line Alan Paine cardigan? Was it because she bought it rather than knitted it herself? Was she reminding my father how much love she'd invested in him over so many years?

I recalled my mother telling me the touching story of how she'd knitted my father a cardigan while he was away fighting in the Spanish-American War. She said it was long before there was ever any talk of marriage. She confessed she'd never been much of a religious person but when she'd knit, she'd think, 'Keep him safe.' And when she'd purl, she'd whisper, 'Bring him home alive.' She explained the cardigan was a simple prayer to someone somewhere who listened and intervened on her behalf.

And while I'd describe the message in the sweater as sentimental, the one in the cigars was blatantly vicious and sexual. She was attacking his manhood head-on. Oh, she bought his preferred Cuban brand, the *Hoyo de Monterrey*, but not his choice *vitola*. His favorite length was an eight-inch double corona, and she hurled her phallic slur with a robusto barely half the corona's length.

"Well, we've saved the best for last," Father said. He winked at me and added, "Todd, why don't you go over and check behind the sofa there and see what Santa brought this year?"

Although I knew what was probably hiding behind the couch, I knew I should act surprised. And sure enough, there it was—a mahogany Gibson six-string. I rushed back to my chair and began strumming randomly. "It's just what I wanted: wide neck, twelve frets at the body, just like the guitars we saw on Beale—"

I caught myself midsentence, realizing I'd just stepped in it—tipping my mother off to my whereabouts during the mysterious "bachelor outings." I quickly glanced over at my mother, who was quietly staring daggers at my father. I suspect she didn't explode this time because it was Christmas and it was now water over the dam. We were leaving Nashville for good just after New Year's.

My father shook his head and quickly changed the subject. "You're gonna need lessons, Todd." He looked over at my mother. "Once you find a teacher for him, Margaret, let me know how much it is a month, and I'll send the money out wherever y'all end up." He turned toward me and said, "Think of the lessons as part of our Christmas gift to you, Todd."

I walked over and kissed my mother on the cheek. "Thank you. The guitar means so much." I then moved over to my father and gave him a big hug. "And thanks for the lessons too." I sat back down and resumed strumming. My mother and father smiled knowingly at each other, satisfied they'd succeeded in at least softening the blow of their pending separation.

While they viewed the guitar as a gift associated with happiness, I saw it quite differently. For me the Gibson was a symbol of sorrow, a reminder of my parents' years of fighting and our last scripted Christmas together. I immediately sensed the heartbreak infused in the wood. I not only considered the instrument a Christmas present, but in another more perverse way, a gift, an opportunity already steeped with the blues. It would now be up to me to coax the suffering out of the mahogany with a pick, a slide, and some heavy-gauge strings.

2

UP UNTIL THE last minute I expected the Governor to call with a reprieve. Even though my mother had finished packing, I held out hope she'd somehow reconcile with my father before the caravan of moving trucks appeared at the rear of the mansion. I had mixed emotions about leaving. While I sure wouldn't miss my parents' fighting, I would regret leaving my school. And it wasn't because of a desire to delve deeper into Pythagoras or Dickens, but because of my classmates and my homeroom teacher, Mrs. Deane, with whom I'd fallen madly and adulterously in love.

But as the mantle clock chimed seven, my mother knocked, alerting me the movers had finished stowing our belongings and it was time to leave. I took one last wistful look about the bedroom, picked up my guitar case, and then dawdled downstairs to the dimly lit service entrance, where my mother, father, the lady's maid, Bessie, and our chauffeur awaited my arrival. I could see through the open door it was pitch black outside, thus fulfilling my father's request that we exit out the back entrance sometime after dark to avoid the press.

I gave my father a big hug. He held me out at arm's length and gazed into my eyes. "I'll miss you, boy. Study hard, and most of all, take care of your mother."

"I will. And next time I see you, I'll be playing my Gibson. I promise you that."

"Can't wait to hear you, Todd. You'll do me proud."

My father turned and embraced my mother for old time's sake. "Once you get settled, send me the information for the monthly payments."

She pushed back and replied, "I'll have that all figured out by the end of the week. I'll let you know then."

"And one other thing, Margaret. I got to thinking, if reporters show up snooping around your new place, just refuse to speak with 'em. Refer 'em back here to me. I'll take care of it. No sense having you dealing with their weaselly questions. They're just trying to pry a sensational headline out of you. They're all downright bastards."

"I know. It's better leaving all this unsaid. Just think what it would do to Todd."

"And not to mention my reelection chances. . . ."

My mother flashed a sardonic smile, turned, and exited onto the west portico without saying another word. But this time devoted Bessie didn't follow her. My father wanted the lady's maid standing beside him during our departure to symbolically fire a final parting shot: "Your decision to leave has consequences, my dear." And as we would discover later on, he was also telegraphing how he planned to handle the press when they learned of our scandalous departure from Nashville.

Following my mother's wishes, our chauffeur didn't stop until we rolled up in front of Mrs. Griffith's Hotel just after daybreak the following morning. The white frame structure was an elegant two-story Greek revival with banistered porches extending the length of both floors. As we dragged our numb bodies out of the motorcar, the resident hound began barking and raced down the front steps to greet us. A petite, silver-haired lady appeared at the top of the steps. She was vigorously wiping her hands on her blue feed-sack apron. "Welcome," she drawled. "Y'all made good time. Just leave all your things there. My husband will get 'em once he's finished shavin'. So come on in now and freshen up a bit while the chicken's fryin' and the biscuits brownin'."

As I inhaled my hearty breakfast of fried chicken, biscuits, and milk gravy, Mr. Griffith proudly explained the mythology behind the mysterious rock formation that lends its name to the town of Hollow Rock. "Geologists, astronomers, and even astrologers have inspected it. Mystified all of 'em. Never seen anything like it. Don't know what it's made of. They just all agree it's big. Some four hundred feet long, thirteen wide, and twelve high. Several of 'em say it's a meteorite. Doesn't seem to be attached to anything. Nowhere near any bluffs. Couldn't have fallen off anything like a ledge or somethin'. Kinda sits all alone in a large bowl in the woods. Old-timers tell us it was a lot bigger way back when but seems to be sinkin'. There's been some serious diggin' out there around it but they can't find a bottom. So, you see, it can't be an outcroppin'."

"Any idea how old it is?" I asked, excited by the prospect of living near a natural phenomenon.

"Eons, boy. Eons. My daddy said the natives used it in prehistoric times as a shelter and a ceremonial ground, and I know there's some truth to it. Every time they go diggin' out there, they turn up spear points, pipes, pottery, trade beads and such."

To my mother's chagrin, I interrupted Mr. Griffith. "Where is this place? I've got to see it!"

"Well, you walk south there to the railroad tracks. You'll see a path. Take a left and head east. When ya come to a clearin' on your left, you should see a trail headed north. Take it and the hollow rock will be on your right up by the creek. Can't miss it. Sits all alone in the trees. Big hole in the side of it that runs all the way through. You'll see. And with all the artifacts they've found you can just imagine while your walkin' around out there that hollow rock's been a popular place from time immemorial."

"Why's that, you think?" I asked.

Mr. Griffith smiled knowingly and replied, "First of all because of the hole. Prehistoric folk could crawl in for shelter especially during a winter like the one we're havin' now. And then secondly because of the creek runnin' just north of the rock. The branch supplied 'em water and fish while they were out on their huntin' trips. And you know what?"

"What's that?" I asked.

"Things haven't changed much over the millennia."

"How's that?"

"The hole, the woods there, and the creek still bein' put to good use."

"Railroading?" I guessed.

"Yep. It's a natural place for the locomotives to stop. Plenty of wood and water out there to fire the boilers and—"

Mr. Griffith hesitated, eliciting the desired response from

me. I was staring at him quizzically. "You know what I'm thinking, don't you, Mr. Griffith?"

He laughed, put his finger up to his temple, and replied, "Let me guess. I bet you're dying to know how the hole fits in with the railroadin'."

"Sure be nice, Mr. Griffith," I said lightheartedly, playing along in my role as student.

"Hobos, Todd. Many a Boxcar Willy's curled up in that hollow rock out there over the years. Ya see, there's a switch-yard just east of where you'll turn into the woods. So the junction there's like a depot for 'em. They spend a day or two out there waitin' to hop the next freight."

My mother jumped in with an embarrassing question that made me want to crawl under the table. "You say hobos, Mr. Griffith? Is it safe for Todd to be out there alone walking around?"

"Not to worry, ma'am," Mr. Griffith reassured her. "Ninety-nine out of a hundred of 'em are honest stiffs just down on their luck. Ridin' the rails to the next opportunity, ya see. We get 'em in here all the time. Give 'em a square meal, clean clothes, and a chance to take a hot bath."

My mother interrupted again. "That's really kind of y'all, taking folk in like that. Most people calling themselves Christians rely on the ministers and elders to see to those kinds of things."

"Might as well be honest with you about that, ma'am. Mrs. Griffith and I aren't churchgoers, but we call ourselves believers. There're a lot of good ideas in the Bible, and helpin' the needy is right up there at the top of our list."

My mother turned to Mrs. Griffith and then back again to her husband still seeking reassurances. "So . . . so y'all think it's okay for Todd to be wandering alone out there on his own?"

"I'll stake my firstborn on it," Mr. Griffith replied. "Despite the occasional hobo showin' up, the rock's actually a pretty quiet, respectable place. That is, except for the last Sunday in April."

"The last Sunday in April?" my mother asked. "What's different about the last Sunday in April?"

"Well, some five years ago my younger brother, Lance, organized an all-day celebration out at the rock welcomin' in the spring. I thought it would be a one-time affair, but lo and behold, here we are and it's still goin' strong every last Sunday in April. Downhome cookin' and dancin' to Mr. Buckley's band. He's the druggist in town, ya see, but we pull his leg accusin' him of takin' his music more seriously than he does his medicine. So y'all have been forewarned. Ya gotta keep that one Sunday free."

My mother flashed a relaxed smile for the first time in years. "I'll jot it down right after breakfast. I promise, Mr. Griffith. It sounds like fun. We can all certainly use a good time now and then."

Mr. Griffith nodded. "Yes, sir, we'll all stroll out to the rock together and enjoy the day. And believe me, we won't be alone out there either. Hundreds if not thousands of folks will be turnin' out for the shindig, hikin' over, drivin' in, or even hitchin' up a mule. One way or the other they manage to get there every year. They say they wouldn't miss it for the world."

I'd learned a long time ago that once my mother had successfully burrowed her way into a conversation, it would be next to impossible for me to get another word in edgewise. So after catching Mr. Griffith's eye, I waved my napkin of surrender and pointed to the front door, signaling I was excusing myself to explore the town. He nodded and winked as my mother shifted her narrative into a higher gear.

The plan was for us to stay at Mrs. Griffith's only a day or two until the movers had finished unpacking our belongings at a vacant cottage my mother had rented just around the corner on Mill Street. But everything, including the school where my mother would be teaching, was just around the corner in this postage-stamp village, which still trumpeted de Tocqueville's inadvertent visit here nearly a century earlier.

I grabbed my guitar case and lumbered out onto Main Street to explore my new home away from home. The businesses were primarily concentrated on the main drag. As Mrs. Griffith said at breakfast, "If you can't find what you're lookin' for on Main, then you probably don't need it al all." There was Hill Brothers' Market; W. A. Green's Dry Goods, Clothing & Shoes; W. B. Bowen's Hardware; Buckley's Drugs; and as a symbol of our changing times, Budge Prince's Blacksmith Shop sitting right next door to T. S. Jenkins' Auto & Truck Repair.

Once I'd surveyed the shops, I found the path headed east and then the old trail running north. And just as Mr. Griffith had promised, there it was on the right-hand side, rising up out of a mist that had settled over the creek and the bowl cradling the hollow rock. The fog worked its magic, unmooring me from my sense of time and place. The west wind whistled through the glazed woods, lifting the veil on the far-off past. While braves scoured the forest for charred but living trees, the squaws prepared a pit for this "thunderwood," which would soon fuel the sacred fire within the sacred circle. Three long wails. The deep vibration of drums and the rattle of gourds. The swaying of men and trees. Silent prayers to the Thunder Beings and then the whoops of renewal and redemptive joy. As the jubilation subsided, a glacial gust buffeted the brittle branches and lowered the veil over the hallowed rock again.

3

Reality tapped me on the shoulder, scaring the hell out of me. I whipped around reflexively. A tall, light-skinned Negro in his early twenties was standing there facing me. He flashed an embarrassed smile. "I'm sorry I made you jump like that. I hollered several times as I walked up, but you didn't react. You seemed to be studying the rock there pretty hard. You resting out here between freights?"

"No, no. My mother and I are moving in on Mill Street. Arrived this morning. Staying a day or two at Mrs. Griffith's until our place is ready."

He smiled broadly and extended his hand. "Well, welcome to town, ah . . . ah . . ."

"Todd Taylor," I responded. "And you are?"

"Jesse. Jesse Lockwood."

"Pleased to meet you, Jesse."

"Likewise," he replied. "Taylor, you say? Just pitching a long shot here, but you any relation to the governor?"

I smiled nervously and instinctively slipped the punch. "The governor's a distant relative." I then quickly changed the subject circling back to our earlier conversation. "What about you, Jesse? You live in Hollow Rock?"

"Used to. Up the trail there a half mile or so, not far from the roundhouse."

"Used to?"

"Yes, before I left for Jackson."

"You work there?"

Jesse smiled. "No, no. Still in school. Lane College."

"What are you studying?"

"Religion. Will be the first pastor ever in our family."

"I have to say, you've sure got the voice for it, Jesse—the kind of voice I'd imagined Moses heard at the burning bush. Deep, clear, resonating . . ."

Jesse smiled and then took his turn at changing the subject. "What about you? You working, Todd?"

I laughed uncomfortably. "No. Will be finishing up this year and next at Hollow Rock High. . . . Being honest with you, though, it's the last place I wanna be, cramming the nonsense in one ear and then having it seep out the other."

"Rather be working with your hands then?"

I laughed. "You might say it that way."

"I don't understand. What would you like to be doing then?"

I responded by raising my guitar case.

"So you wanna be a professional musician? How long you been playing?"

I lowered my head and muttered defensively, "Just got my guitar here for Christmas. A fine one. A Gibson six-string. So I'm just now starting to get the hang of it."

Sensing my uneasiness Jesse immediately went to work repairing the damage. "I'll betcha within a year you'll be playing with the best of 'em. So what kind of music you wanna play? Work songs? Dancing? Gospel?"

Regaining my footing, I answered confidently, "Well, yes and no. All that and a lot more all rolled into one. Work songs, gospel, chants, hollers, minstrel, and on and on."

Jesse smiled. "Rolled into one? I don't understand."

"I wanna play the blues."

"The blues?"

"Uh-huh. Heard 'em on a trip to Memphis. Takes a little bit of sauce from everything imaginable—hollers, chants, spirituals, work songs, you name it. You can find a lot of flavors in the blues."

"Why the blues, Todd?"

"Just everything about it. The rhythm, the sound, and most of all the stories—the tales of struggle, of suffering."

"I don't know if that's for me. Sounds depressing. Not like preaching the gospel where you have redemption, salvation, and joy."

"Oh, that's the magic of the blues, Jesse. The joy's there all right but it's in you as you listen to the stories. You feel their pain deep down in your soul, but you know these folks ain't giving up. You sense their courage and you realize their salvation's in the getting up, dusting off, and moving on. Yes, that's the magic in the blues. Hearing those tales of regret, of betrayal, and then finding the joy in sharing a kinship with the storyteller, realizing you're not alone with your feelings. I find that downright comforting."

"So you're just out here exploring?"

"Yeah. Mr. Griffith put me onto the rock here. And the

way he described it told me I had to pay a visit."

"You been inside yet?"

"No, just been walking around out here waiting for the fog to lift."

"Should be soon now, but ya don't have to wait to crawl in and explore the tunnel running one side to the other. Come on! I'll give you the two-bit tour."

Jesse led the way into the mist. "Okay, now. Ya might get a little dirty, but the tunnel's really worth the price of admission. Stoop down. Watch your head. . . . Okay, take a seat there facing the wall. We'll stay near the end here so you can see what it's like all the way through. See all the staining?"

"Yeah."

"It's soot from the untold number of fires built over thousands of years. See all the initials there? Folks trying to carve their way to immortality."

"Sure are a number of 'em."

"Yeah, and they run the length of the tunnel on both sides. But that's not all. Take your hand and rub the staining there."

"Unbelievable! There are hundreds more names hidden here under the smoke. You ever find any famous folks?"

"There are lots of legends associated with the rock, and that's the one farthest from the truth."

"What's that?"

"Hearing people talk, you'd swear anyone who's anybody has spent a night curled up in here."

"Like . . . ?"

"Well, you name 'em. But I'd say the most plausible are Crockett on his way to the Alamo, Andrew Jackson on his way westward to found Memphis, and rebel general Nathan Bedford Forrest, after a punishing raid on the Union depot down the road there at Johnsonville."

"And myths?"

Jesse laughed. "My favorite says the spirits of ancient tribes return here every year about this time, just as they did when living and roaming the earth. They come back to cleanse themselves, offer thanks to the Great Spirit, and celebrate the birth of spring. Over the years I've spoken with ten or so residents of the county—old folks allegedly still right in the head—who swear as children they saw the spirits out here flitting about in the mist building their sacred fires and worshipping. I'd totally dismiss their tales—I've been coming out here for years and have never seen anything—but one thing gives me pause."

"What's that?" I asked eagerly.

"If I didn't know better, I'd swear they were all in cahoots, but these folks were scattered high and low throughout the county and weren't acquainted with each other. As soon as I heard the same story repeated two or three times, I started asking each of 'em as I met 'em, if they knew a Mr. Jones or a Mr. Smith, and they'd say something to the effect, 'No, I've never had the pleasure of making his acquaintance.'"

By now, I could barely contain myself. "Telling the same tale? What about?" I asked.

Jesse appeared perplexed. "About themselves. Oddest thing. They'd be describing their early years, how in one way or another they 'went off the rails,' 'got sidetracked,' 'lost their way,' or something like that, and then all of a sudden out of nowhere they'd start cursing ever having been out here at the rock as youths and seeing the 'ghosts.' Mind ya, I just sat there dumbfounded. Then they'd pick up their stories explaining how they'd 'wandered in the wilderness for years' before finally 'returning to the straight and narrow,' 'seeing the light,' 'finding' Jesus,' or something similar to that. And then all of a sudden out of the blue they'd bring up the 'ghosts' at the rock again. But as if they'd totally forgotten their earlier cursing, they'd start 'thanking their lucky stars' or 'praising the Almighty' that they'd seen the 'ghosts' on that 'remarkable misty day.' Just the strangest thing. Can't explain it. But I have one piece of advice for ya, Todd."

"What's that?"

He laughed and replied, "If I were you, I wouldn't make it a habit of visiting hollow rock on days like this. Who knows what ya might see that'd 'flip your life upside down,' as one of the old fellas described it to me."

I drew my legs up close to my chest. Listening to Jesse's resonant voice echoing in the twilight of the hollow rock sent chills up my spine. He'd inadvertently introduced a feeling I'd never experienced—a fear of the future. On those rare but special days I spent alone with my father, he'd always find a way to weave one or two of what he called his "life's lessons" into our conversations. One of his oft-repeated bits of advice was "Boy, don't ever be afraid to take on something new. Run toward the opportunities. Run to 'em, ya hear?" So I had never feared the future. I repeatedly climbed the tower, pushed off from the platform, fearlessly released my grip on the bar, somersaulted high above the circus crowd, and confidently believed my catcher would arrive just in the nick of time to grasp my wrists and break my deadly fall.

I felt fortunate I had not divulged my encounter with the ancient spirits before learning how Jesse felt about others witnessing the supernatural out here. In light of his intense skepticism, I filed my story away, thus preserving our burgeoning friendship. And I also took comfort in knowing that the wandering tribe would always be there for me, primed for use in one of the blues I dreamed of writing before heading off to Memphis to launch my career.

4

Jᴇssᴇ ᴘᴏᴋᴇᴅ ʜɪs head out of the tunnel. "Well, won't ya look at that? Right on cue the sun breaks through. Come on, Todd, let's climb up to the crow's nest, enjoy the scenery and the sunlight."

"Okay by me."

"You'll have to leave your guitar down here in the hold."

"In the hole?"

Jesse laughed aloud. "No, the hold. It's a steep, slippery climb up the mast."

"Why all the sea talk, Jesse?"

He looked down smiling as he scrambled up the south wall. "I'll explain once we've reached the lookout up top."

When we topped the crow's nest, as he'd called it, I breathed a sigh of relief.

"There now. We've made it!" I shouted.

"Good job, mate!" he said. "Now I wouldn't do this for everybody, but here, take the seat of honor, right here in the captain's chair."

"Okay, Jesse. So tell me, what are these sea terms all about?"

"Nothing too complicated, Todd. When my mama and I moved back here to my grandparents' place, I found myself spending a lot of time alone. Being honest with ya, Todd, the white folk around here didn't take too kindly to my color and warned their children to stay away from me and our farm." I started to apologize, but he stopped me. "No way for you to know, Todd—to know how hard it is growing up isolated and not understanding what you've said or done to make other children shy away." Jesse shook his head. "Hurts. Really hurts. So I spent a lot of time out here alone, cooking up stories, and one of my favorites—a starring role as the infamous Captain Jesse Lafitte, plying the seas from the masthead here, first as fugitive smuggler, then as hero with General Jackson at Barataria Bay." Jesse pointed southward out over the imaginary bow. "The bay's not too far from our position here."

"So ya carried all that booty around all these years, huh?"

Captain Lafitte smiled and made a sweeping gesture with his hand. "Yes, and buried a lot of it too. From Grand Isle to Galveston to the Contraband Bayou to—" Jesse paused midsentence, lost in the moss-covered backwater of his youth.

I waited until he awoke from his reverie before gently asking, "Not prying or anything, Jesse, but how'd your grandparents cope with the neighbors' ill feelings about their color?"

Jesse's smile eased into soft laughter. "I guess I should explain. They're as pale as you, Todd. The masters were on my mama's side. Ya see, it was my papa's folks who worked the fields sharecropping, and before them, their parents were slaves. And it was some time after the emancipation my papa's family pulled up stakes and moved north to New York."

"Well, how'd your folks get together? They know each other as children before your papa left?"

Jesse laughed. "No. That's the amazing thing. Papa hadn't even been born when his family left Tennessee."

"So how'd all this happen anyway?"

"Blame it on hoboing."

"Hoboing?"

"Yeah, when Papa turned sixteen, he eased out the back-door determined to see the world."

A chill ran up my spine as I thought of my father's own flight from Memphis at sixteen. But I bit my tongue and stayed on track. "So let me guess, your papa stayed a bit too long in Hollow Rock?"

Jesse nodded and smiled. "Yeah. He was just stopping off to change freights at the junction, but his belly got the best of him. He went exploring for a hot meal and ended up on my grandparents' doorstep. And like just about everybody else in town, they fed him and some other 'tourists' that day. Wasn't long then until Mama was sneaking food out of the house and meeting Papa right here at the rock."

"That's amazing. You must have strong feelings then about these woods, about this place."

"Sure do, Todd. The rock's always been a safe harbor, a place to escape with the memories of my mama and papa."

"So go on. They get married here in Hollow Rock?"

"How could they? A slave marrying into a master's family? Even forty years after the emancipation, that could get ya lynched around here."

"So what'd they do?"

"Met up here one night and hopped a freight. Mama bought 'em separate tickets on a real train once they got to

Nashville and weren't afraid of being seen."

"Where'd they go then?"

"Up to my papa's home in New York. Got married and seven months later I was born."

I tried hiding my smile.

"Yeah, your arithmetic's probably right, Todd. The way I figure, I must've started my journey one warm spring day right here at the rock."

"So how'd your mama and you end up back here in Tennessee?"

"Not a happy story, Todd, but here goes. Mama said she and Papa moved into a downstairs apartment of his parents' house on the north side of the city in Harlem. They planned on staying just long enough for Papa to find a good-paying job, but we were still there thirteen years later, cramped up in two rooms, a kitchenette, and a bath."

"Really close quarters, huh?"

"Oh, it wasn't so bad for me because I didn't know any better. But now I can see what my constant presence did to their relationship. They were always at each other's throat about something. Papa losing jobs. Mama losing babies. Bare pantries. Empty coffers. Granddad's feelings toward both of 'em. The tension would build, blow, and then start rising again. But the pressure never returned to the starting point. Always seemed to get ratcheted up so the quiet times got shorter and shorter, until finally one day the lid really came off."

"What happened?" I asked impatiently.

"It's not what you'd think. No loud explosions at first. Nothing like that. No. Deceptively quiet. Like twin torpedoes speeding toward a battleship: a sighting, a thud, a flash, and then another. And the sickening realization, it's now over. Over."

"I don't understand, Jesse. Something drastic happened?" I whispered empathetically.

"Yes and no. As I said it was the beginning of the end, but you'd have never known it. I was in the back room with the door closed supposedly sleeping, but as usual I heard it all. Everything. Papa came in from his night job, a Sunday night. Ya see, he did the janitoring at Abyssinian Baptist all the way down on Fortieth a long way from Harlem. He hadn't been in the door no more than a minute when Mama fired the first shot. 'Your supper's on the stove there. Must be cold by now. You're almost an hour late. Run into an old lady friend?'

"I braced for the return fire, but something unusual happened. Papa didn't immediately respond. I heard him drag the kitchen chair out from under the table and collapse into it. Silence for the longest time and then he quietly asked Mama to join him. 'Come on over and take a seat. I've got something to tell you.'

"'What's that?' Mama asked. 'This better be good. And so you know, I haven't forgotten about your skulking home here late like a randy tomcat.'

"'For God's sake, stop it! This is serious.'

"'Okay, okay. Shoot!'

"'I'm gonna be leaving for a while.'

"'What do you mean, leaving?'

"'After years of trying, really trying, I've decided to take Papa's advice and make something of myself. I've joined the infantry.'

"'That's really swell now!' my mama cried. 'So what's to become of Jesse and me? You're leaving us here to fend for ourselves?'

"'Nothing of the kind. I'll be sending checks home monthly for the two of you. And since you won't have to pay rent, you'll have enough to get by on. Food, clothes, and the like. '

"'So when's all this supposed to happen?'

"'Right away. But I'll be close by. The signing officer said our Fifteenth Infantry Regiment will be training here and then taking up guard duties in and around New York.'

"'But be honest. You and I both know with the war raging in Europe and the Congress here declaring war, it's only a matter of time 'til you ship out. And it'll be the death of you, I just know it. But I'm telling you now, when your regiment pulls out of New York, Jesse and I are leaving too. Taking the first train out of here.'

"'Leaving? For where?' my father asked. His voice was laden with hurt.

"'Back home to Hollow Rock,' Mama said.

"'But you'd have my mama and papa here.'

"'It just won't work out. Barely does now. And once you leave. . . . No. We're headed back to Tennessee. No one there knows anything about us. Left home before anyone found out about you and me or Jesse. Everything will be better for us back home with my folks.'

"And Mama had it just about right. Papa received his basic training not far from the city; returned home to help guard the ports; and then left again, this time headed for South Carolina to complete combat training for an overseas assignment.

Papa wrote an occasional letter. Said he was none too happy with the treatment he and his men were receiving from the locals. Said there was lots of name-calling, threatening, and even some fisticuffs when they ventured off base for a night on the town. Said there was just little respect for Negro soldiers so far south of the Mason-Dixon line. Sad to say, Todd, it didn't get much better when the soldiers returned to New York in December just before shipping out to France. The regiment's commanding officer, a Colonel Hayward, had sought permission to participate in the send-off parade for the New York National Guard nicknamed the 'Rainbow Division.' But permission was denied. You know why?"

"You're not gonna say 'because of their color,' are you? Not that far north."

"But you have it, Todd. Listen to the snide response Colonel Hayward got back from his superiors: 'Black is not a color in the Rainbow!'"

"You think we'll ever get past this, Jesse?"

"No, not any time soon. Not in our lifetimes, that's for sure."

5

JESSE MOVED TO the other side of the crow's nest, stretched his legs out over the edge of the hollow rock, and continued. "Well, the short of it—Papa sailed for Europe and Mama and I took the next overnighter for Tennessee. They kept up their correspondence—Mama filling him in with our comings and goings and Papa keeping us posted with the latest from the front. When his letters arrived, Mama would tear into the envelopes, quickly scan the paragraphs to be sure he was all right, and then she'd read the letters aloud, pausing along the way to make observations or explain something to me.

"Being honest with you, Todd, I found his first letters pretty boring. Everyone around here was talking about the fighting, the bravery, and the dying, and Papa was telling us about digging latrines, cooking for the regiment, and sweeping out his officers' tents. But I sensed things were changing when I saw the look of concern on Mama's face and heard the fear in her voice for the first time. . . . 'Your father says here they've changed his regiment's designation from the Fifteenth Infantry to the 369th, that he's joining the French forces, and he's headed into the trenches.'

"Even though I would never have admitted it to her or anyone else, it seemed the more worry Mama showed with each succeeding letter, the more thrilling I found them."

"What'd he have to say?" I asked.

"He described going out on a raid his first night in the trenches. Said about twenty of them, a mix of French and American soldiers, climbed out into no-man's-land; slithered along in the slime on their stomachs as friendly and enemy fire whizzed by overhead; cut openings in the Germans' barbed wire; and then rushed their trenches."

"What happened?"

Jesse smiled. "Nothing."

"Nothing?"

"That's right. Nothing. Nobody was home in that part of the maze."

"They risked everything for nothing?"

"Yeah, I was disappointed too. But Mama was sure relieved."

"What else did he write about? Anything?"

"Well, after that raid we didn't hear from him for a while. Didn't mean nothing was happening—just the opposite. The more going on the less we heard from him. But we were still able to keep tabs on his regiment. My grandpa would send us clippings from the Negro weekly, the *New York Age*."

Jesse reached into his jacket and retrieved a folded piece of paper from his wallet and proudly handed it to me.

"Here's one of the front-page articles he mailed us. I suspect the fighting here happened a day or two after the raid."

I opened the yellowed clipping and began reading the three-column headline, which screamed: CRACK COLORED REGIMENT NOW FIGHTING WITH FRENCH DIVISION! The article, datelined May 9, 1918, Soissons, France, confirmed what Jesse's father said was going to happen—that he would be fighting the Germans from the trenches. I read some of the paragraphs aloud: "The men of the Fifteenth, now known as the 369th, are fighting in the first-line trench with the French to make the world safe for democracy." I looked up at Jesse. "That opening's got a nice ring to it, doesn't it?"

Jesse smiled and nodded. "I thought you'd like that."

I continued reading aloud. "'Our New York Guardsmen are the first Negro troopers from the United States to meet the Germans on the battle front, have become expert grenade throwers and are masters of the machine gun.' And a French general is quoted here saying 'after seeing these colored fighters in action, I'd judge them very stouthearted, but very rash.'" I looked up toward Jesse and handed him the article. "That's really something coming from a French general, praising your father's regiment like that."

Jesse smiled again. "I guess you can see why I kept the article some seven years."

"I'd have kept the clipping too. Something to be really proud of, to hold on to, show your own boys someday."

"Had another one Grandpa sent a few weeks later, but my roommate at Lane tossed it out with some old journals."

"Oh no. Do you remember what it was about?

"Well, I'd read it so many times I'd pretty much committed it to memory. 'Dateline June 11, 1918, Champagne Sector, France. Our New York Guardsmen have done us proud again in the Belleau Wood several miles northwest of Chateau-Thierry. Under heavy artillery and machine-gun fire, our troopers bravely advanced toward the German position despite suffering mounting casualties. Realizing the toll it was taking on the 369th, the French general ordered the American officer, Colonel Hayward, to "Retire! Retire!" The colonel snarled, "Turn back? Never! My men are breaking through their lines or they don't come back!"

"'With that Colonel Hayward tore the officer's insignia off his jacket, grabbed a rifle from one of his men, and turned to lead the charge. The Frenchman repeated his order, but the colonel responded, "My men never retire! They go forward or they die!" And with that, the 369th charged the enemy, who within minutes turned and ran for their lives. And with that vivid demonstration of determination and courage, the 369th rightly earned its nicknames, the Harlem Hellfighters and the Black Rattlers.'"

"Another proud moment for you, huh?"

"No doubt. And mostly because of where Papa came from. First he's hoboing, next he's janitoring, and then he's pushing the Germans out of France."

"You said you didn't hear from your father for a while and kept tabs on him through your granddad's clippings. So when did you hear from him next?"

"Not until August when the regiment went off line for rest and the training of replacements. Then we averaged a letter a week for the next month. Mostly describing what we'd already learned through my grandad's clippings, but more personal and in much more detail. The letters dried up again sometime in late September, when his regiment returned to fighting again alongside the French Fourth Army."

"How long did you have to wait for a new letter this time?"

"Well, we didn't hear anything for some months. Weren't really alarmed, though. We knew there was a big push on against the Germans' Hindenberg Line, and if something really bad had happened, Granddad would've let us know."

"The Hindenberg Line?"

"Yeah, it was the last line of German defenses on the western front. Heavily fortified, running across France several miles behind the active front, running south and then east from the North Sea to Verdun near the French-Belgian border. Daunting to say the least. Bristled with barbed wire and reinforced firing positions."

"Sorry to interrupt, Jesse. Go on. So when did you finally hear something?"

"In early December after the armistice. But it was different this time."

"How's that?"

"My granddad sent a small package, and it was addressed to 'Master Jesse Lockwood,' not to my mother."

"If you don't mind my asking, what was . . ."

"Here, I'll show you." Jesse reached into his pocket, pulled out what appeared to be a religious medal, and handed it to me. It was a bronze cross with triangular arms, narrow at the center and broadening out to squared ends. But the telltale signs that it was military were the crossed swords extending out between the arms. At the center of the small cross was the portrait of a young woman encircled by the words *République française*; and at the center on the reverse were the dates

1914–1918. The medal was suspended by a green ribbon with thin, vertical red stripes and two bronze palm branches.

"A medal your father was awarded?"

"Yes, but not just any medal. It's the French Army's Croix de Guerre, the Cross of War. Papa was only the fourth American to receive the honor. The other three were also members of the Black Rattler Regiment."

"That's really something, Jesse. How'd your father earn it?"

"Well, that takes us back to the other things Granddad sent along in the package: the French general's official order awarding the War Cross to Papa and my granddad's letter explaining everything."

"What'd your grandfather have to say?"

"He started off apologizing for not having written sooner; but he explained he didn't want us worrying. He said he wanted to try gathering all the facts before writing. Ya see, sometime in October the army had notified Granddad that Papa was missing in action and presumed captured. And it wasn't until sometime in November the army discovered they'd confused Papa with another P. Lockwood in the Hellfighters from Kansas, who'd indeed gone missing and was later released after the armistice."

"But what about your father then?"

"When the French shipped the citation over with the War Cross, the army noticed the medal was being awarded '*à titre posthume*'—posthumously. That's what led them to review the records, discover the mix-up, and mail Granddad the medal along with a second notification, the one which opens with the ominous phrase, 'We regret to inform you . . .'"

"I'm sorry, Jesse." I stopped there; I could tell he wanted to continue.

"All Granddad knew so far was that Papa had died a hero. He was determined to learn as much as possible so he could somehow soften the blow for Mama and me. So he went to work. He first went to the public library, where the staff tipped him off to a French bakery in Manhattan that might be able to help translate the citation. In the meantime he learned of an upcoming victory parade to honor the returning soldiers. He figured he'd try meeting up with some of the men from Papa's unit who'd fill in some of the blanks. And you know, between the bakery and the parade, Granddad was able to piece together a fair amount about Papa's last days.

"Let's see now, where'd I leave off with Papa's story? I don't want to confuse you."

"You said the letters dried up in September, when your father's regiment returned to fighting alongside the French Fourth Army."

"Yes. The Allies launched a massive counteroffensive on the Twenty-sixth. The French Fourth and the Hellfighters were to penetrate the German right flank and move on Mézières, a key rail supply line some fifty miles to the north. To meet their objective, they'd first have to fight their way through the villages of Ripont and Challerange. . . . Surprisingly, crossing the Hindenberg Line and moving northward toward Ripont were relatively easy. Papa's regiment met little resistance because unbeknownst to them, the Germans had withdrawn northward to set a trap on the outskirts of Ripont. You see, to reach the town you had to cross a narrow river bordered by marsh on both sides. So the Germans held their fire until thousands of Allies had waded into the swamp, and then they opened up with withering machine-gun fire and gas-laden artillery shells. Of the first few hundred Allies who'd penetrated the mire, only a handful reached the north shore unscathed. And from that point on, the Germans fought like cornered wolves, refusing to concede an inch without first exacting a toll in Allied blood."

"But the French and the 369th finally took Rip . . . Ripont, right?"

"Yeah. Took them into the next day to finally loosen the Germans' grip, and then they moved on up northward toward Séchault. The fighting along the way seemed to come in waves, letting up for a while and then all hell'd break loose again. But as they closed in on the town, the resistance really intensified and became deadly accurate. You see, the Germans had aviators buzzing overhead spotting Allied positions. And all my father's company could do was take cover in a trench and ride out the storm until nightfall, when the firing usually died down."

"How could they ever take the town with planes constantly marking their positions? Seems almost impossible."

"That's the problem Papa's company commander faced that night hunkered down in the trenches. But long before dawn he settled on a plan. He'd send two or three volunteers on a suicide mission. Order 'em to outflank the Germans, creep into town, and take out as many snipers and machine-gun nests they could before being killed or captured themselves. He figured his plan would weaken the German resistance just enough to allow the 369ᵗʰ to charge the town and overwhelm the remaining marksmen.

"So making a long story short, Papa volunteered, and just before sunrise he set out westward to outflank the German sentries. Since it was still somewhat dark and the terrain unfamiliar, Papa moved northward through a narrow clearing between a forest line and an intermittent stream. I suspect he figured he could fade into the woods if the Germans spotted his advance on the town."

"But if he was moving in a wide arc, how'd he know where the town was so he wouldn't go too far north?"

Jesse smiled. "Binoculars and the church spire. But funny you should mention going too far north."

"Why's that?"

"Because that was exactly the plan. Papa wanted to slip into town from the north, surprise them. Attacking from the rear has its advantages and its risks. . . ."

"Keep going," I urged.

"Well, when you're one against many, you've got to use the element of surprise to even the playing field some. But the big disadvantage, when things really get hot, you don't have an easy way out. You're sandwiched between main forces in the town and the reserve soldiers on the outskirts just up the road."

"Dangerous."

"Quoting the field commander, 'Beyond dangerous. Suicidal.'"

"Sorry to keep breaking in, Jesse. Go on."

Jesse nodded and continued, "When Papa sensed he was far enough north, he turned eastward and weaved his way through the underbrush to a hill overlooking the Séchault-Monthois Road and the town just to the east of it. He trained his binoculars on the narrow, cobbled streets. Surprisingly, no movement there. Looked like the Germans had already pulled out again. Probably moving northward toward Challerange to set another trap, but leaving a swarm of marksmen behind to buy time and inflict as much damage as they could. The only thing that looked threatening was a machine-gun emplacement some thirty yards south of Papa's position. The two gunners probably situated there on the outskirts to provide cover for the German snipers, when they finally had to make a quick retreat from the town."

"So he'd have to deal with the machine gunners first, right?"

Jesse nodded and moved his hand down toward his belt. "Yeah. Papa took out his bolo knife and eased toward them. He was in luck. They had their backs to him and were sleeping. He slipped up behind them and slit their throats. No warning shouts or screams from them. Just a faint gurgling. He cleaned his knife on one of the gunner's sleeves, stowed it, and then moved up near the town to wait for the German marksmen to start firing again so he could carry out his mission."

"Wait long?"

"No, no more than ten to fifteen minutes. First the booming of the artillery north of Séchault, next the scream of shells whizzing by overhead, and then the telltale crackle of sniper fire aimed at Papa's brothers scurrying for cover just south of town." Jesse put his hand over his brow, slowly scanned the treetops, and continued, "Papa peered through his binoculars. There. There on the second floor of that stone house. Smoke and the tip of a barrel. He raced across the road, ducked in behind a hedgerow, and then dashed up the backyard to an open door on the west side of the house."

"Did he rush in?" I asked.

Jesse shook his head. "No. Papa had to catch his breath first. Had to pull some grenades out of his pack. Had to picture what he was about to do. But within a minute or two he was ready. He took a deep breath and eased around the threshold. Silence. He'd guessed right. The snipers were upstairs focusing on the Rattlers. He quickly moved inside and out of the sunlight streaming in through the doorway. Silence at first, but then a whimper. Papa wheeled about and aimed his rifle at the shadows cowering in the corner."

"Germans?"

"No. The owner, his wife, and three children."

"What'd your father do?" I was riveted.

"He raised his finger to his lips and then pointed to the blue French helmet he and the 369th were required to wear. He was letting them know he was a friend who'd come to free them. But now back to business. He looked directly at the owner, pointed toward the second floor, and then held his fingers up in succession—one, two, three, four. The Frenchman held up three fingers. Papa knew immediately his bolt-action Lebel rifle wouldn't do. He'd never get off three rounds before one of the snipers put him away. So after signaling the family to huddle under the heavy dining table, Papa slowly mounted the stairs, moved to the doorway outside the snipers' nest, pulled the pins on two grenades, and tossed them inside in opposite directions. Then he raced down the stairs and out the door just as two explosions announced there were now three less German marksmen defending Séchault!"

"Whoa! What'd he do next?"

"Went fishing again, so to speak."

"Fishing?"

"Yeah. Waiting for the next sniper to open up from another house. He didn't have to wait long, either. But this time the firing came from the other side of the street."

"Any hostages in the house?"

"Couple of old folks—husband and wife—tied to kitchen chairs with bed sheets."

"What'd your father do?"

"As he had with the neighbors across the street, he raised his finger to his lips, pointed to his French helmet, and cut them loose with his bolo knife."

"How many snipers?"

"According to the peasant, only one firing from the casement in the main bedroom upstairs. Hearing this, Papa dispensed with the grenades. He figured he'd take the lone German out with his single-action Lebel this time. So he crept up the stairs, moved down the hallway to the open door, took several deep breaths to relax his nerves, and then swung into the bedroom firing a single deadly shot into the back of the sniper's head."

"Holy cow! What'd your father do then?"

"Papa eased out of the room, hurried down the stairs, and gave a thumbs-up to the couple as he raced out the back door."

"Back to fishing again?" I asked.

Jesse smiled. "Yeah, back to fishing. And as he waited for another bite, he could hear his fellow compatriot on the next street over doing his part to take the town back; hear him setting off grenades and firing his Lebel round after round. Papa smiled. He was looking forward to a rendezvous with him at the center church once they'd cleared the town."

"Only two volunteers?"

"Only two, and proud to say Papa was one of them!"

"Did they finally get to have that meeting at the church?"

"You're getting ahead of me, but yes. They spent another good forty-five minutes cleaning out the rest of the buildings before Papa signaled the 'all clear' with his thunderer whistle, and his companion responded in kind."

"Must've been some feeling they had. Imagine them walking toward the church, seeing each other, smiling, realizing they'd finished the mission and survived to fight another day. . . ."

Jesse nodded, but this time he looked away. "You got it just about right, Todd, except . . . except for the ending."

My heart sank. I knew something bad had happened. I responded haltingly, "I'm . . . I'm sorry. How'd I get it wrong?"

Jesse involuntarily shrugged his shoulders. "No worries, Todd. Just hurts when I think how close they came to pulling it off and having them hear everyone singing their praises, from the top generals down to the latest recruits in the regiment."

"What happened to them?"

"Well, you'd painted it just about right. The two of them met outside the center church and gave each other a big hug, but as they stood there celebrating, a single blue-steel barrel eased out of a corner window above the local market. The still steady finger of a dying sniper squeezed the trigger, dispatching a deadly round through Papa's neck into his comrade's heart. The heroes collapsed to their knees in a final embrace having earned their crosses that day."

I slid my arm around Jesse's shoulder without responding. And even until the last time I saw him years later on the battlefield, I never challenged a single word of his story. I'm sure it was possible the veterans of the 369th who met Jesse's grandfather at the parade could have spoken with the locals and pieced all of the details together. But I suspect with every telling the story had been burnished a bit—first by the Hellfighters serving in his father's company, next by his grandfather paying homage to a lost son, and finally, perhaps subconsciously, even by Jesse himself still yearning for the lost promises of a father's unconditional love.

As our friendship grew over the years, I never really gave it much thought after that. I had settled the issue early on. I had realized that after you'd stripped off all the varnish down to the bare wood, I was still holding a French War Cross in my hand that day at the hollow rock. So the bottom line for me was that Jesse's father was a hero regardless of the details of how he earned the cross that autumnal morning in the tiny liberated village of Séchault in the north of France.

6

JUST AS JESSE revealed his father's fate, the low sun slipped beneath the January tide and the west wind knifed through me. I shuddered.

"You okay?" he asked.

"Yeah, a little bit of winter and a whole lot of France."

Jesse nodded appreciatively and tapped me on the knee. "Whatdaya say we scramble down the mast, mate, fetch your guitar from the hold, and head on into port for some hot cider or lemon tea? I'd like you to meet my grandfather, Have him share some of his tricks and have you explain the blues."

"Tricks?"

"Guitar tricks. Techniques he learned over the years strumming all sorts of music: spirituals, ragtime, work songs, minstrel. Gramps played professionally for some thirty years before the arthritis settled in his fingers. Got to where his hands couldn't keep up with his mind anymore. I'm sure he'd love helping you learn the ropes, and I don't mean just today but while I'm away at school the rest of the year too."

I interrupted anxiously, "When you leaving, Jesse?"

"Tomorrow, late afternoon. Classes start again on Tuesday."

I lowered my head thinking, "How ironic. On the first day in my new home I find a great friend who almost immediately announces he's leaving town the very next day."

Sensing my disappointment, Jesse tried reassuring me. "Hey, Todd, don't look so sad. I'm not headed for Timbuktu. Just down the road to Jackson only an hour away. Be returning home some weekends to check on Gramps." Jesse paused there for effect, smiled, and then added warmly, "and to see you too, and see how you're progressing with those blues. So, mate, whatdaya say we start climbing down out of this gale?"

I returned his smile and saluted. "Aye, aye, Captain Lafitte. Full speed into port!"

As we began walking northward along the narrow path, I broke the silence. "Sorry, Jesse. Don't want to keep dwelling, but I was just wondering if you and your mother got to pay your last respects. Attend a wake, a memorial service, or the like?"

"It's okay, Todd, I appreciate the respect you've shown. But no, there was never a funeral to attend. Papa and his fellow hero were buried side by side at the American cemetery not too far from where they died. And it's sure one of the places I have on my list to visit someday."

"Perhaps we could travel there together and honor his memory," I suggested.

Jesse smiled. "A nice thought, Todd. Traveling there together, you and me. I hear the cemetery's impressive. Fourteen thousand heroes buried there."

I stopped suddenly. "Ya hear that? Listen!"

"You mean the chuffing and rumbling?"

"Yeah, and the snapping and hissing. What is it?"

"Remember? I told you we live near the roundhouse. Those are yard sounds."

"Well, if you hadn't been along explaining, I'd have sworn these woods were haunted by ghouls and demons."

Jesse kept walking as his voice reverted to the wistful tone I'd heard earlier when he was speaking of his father. "Haunted by ghouls and demons? No, not these woods. Not our woods here. Believe me. They're blessed by angels. I have the proof."

"Proof?"

"Yeah, I'll show you. Up there, a little past the trailhead."

When we reached the junction with the gravel road running to the roundhouse, Jesse stopped and pointed eastward. "The trail here marks the western boundary of Gramps's property. It runs east from here about a half a mile on both sides of the road. The house is up there just beyond the curve. We're almost there. Come on."

As we neared the bend, Jesse slowed and turned to his right toward a semicircular space carved from a stand of birches at the edge of the forest. He knelt down between two irregularly shaped flat markers and swept the light layer of snow away. He looked up and whispered, "Here's where the angels live, Todd. Gramps and I hammered these headstones out of the hollow rock and then chiseled them ourselves."

I moved closer and read the simple inscriptions, "Mama" and "Granny." I instinctively placed my hand on Jesse's shoulder. "My God, what happened?"

"You may have been too young to remember the pandemic."

"Pandemic?"

Jesse stood up and leaned against a nearby birch. "Yeah.

The Spanish flu. I'd hear Mama, Granny, and Gramps talking about 'the Spanish Lady' when they thought I was sleeping. The flu hit the East Coast first during the last months of the war and then slowly moved westward. Your parents probably hid the horrors from you. Thirty thousand dead in New York alone just like that!" Jesse snapped his fingers for emphasis. "Survivors said they knew the exact moment it struck them, and I heard Mama and Gramps trading stories of healthy victims suddenly toppling off their horses. Or of four ladies playing bridge and three of them dying overnight. No one knew what caused the flu or how it spread. That's what made it scary. It was like a hungry beast moving from city to city and house to house, moving ever closer to us. First, New Orleans, next, Little Rock, then Mobile, and finally Memphis. It was getting too close for comfort."

"When did it hit Memphis? I remember hearing stories, but I wasn't paying much attention to them."

"Late September 1918. And then it began spreading through the city like wildfire. I remember Gramps reading the newspaper headlines aloud for the first time in early October: INFLUENZA CRIPPLING MEMPHIS INDUSTRIES. He quoted the Health Department saying something to the effect, 'Scores were dead and hundreds lay dying.' From then on, it became a daily ritual. As soon as the *Commercial Appeal* arrived, Gramps would grab his glasses, call Mama and Granny to the dining-room table, and then announce the latest news about its spread. Strange, but looking back on it, I now understand how the fear of getting sick and dying could push the war reports right off the front pages and out of people's minds. That is, everyone except us folks who had fathers, sons, and husbands fighting and dying on the front lines."

"You could say the local battles trumped the far-off war, so to speak."

"Exactly. And that's pretty much how the newspapers described the pandemic—like a war. One battle after another. As things got progressively worse, they'd first reassure us that there was no need for panic and then they'd breathlessly launch into a reporting style that verged on emergency bulletins. One critical announcement after another. 'Doctors, Druggists and Nurses Overwhelmed by New Cases.' 'Officials Shutter Theaters, Dance Halls and Cinemas.' 'Schools and Churches to Close Temporarily.' 'Funeral Services Cancelled; Graveside Services for Family Only.' 'Hospitals Swamped; Central High to Become Red Cross Flu Center.' 'Six Hundred Percent Increase in Boston Death Rate.'"

"Besides closing everything down, how else did people fight the spread?"

"Oh, everything. Gramps said they were putting signs up in the cities: 'Spit Spreads Death.' And then to show they were serious about it they passed laws. Like the one that said if they caught you spitting in public, they'd fine you five hundred dollars or give you a year in jail."

"Pretty extreme, don't you think?"

"When folks feel their backs are to the wall and they're in a fight to the death, they'll do drastic things if they think there's even a slight chance it'll help them survive. Like what they did in Arizona, making it a crime to shake your neighbor's hand."

"How long did the outbreak last?"

"Well, the number of cases in Memphis really started dropping off sometime in late October. Schools and churches reopened and the newspapers returned to reporting the news coming from the front—good news with encouraging headlines like 'Americans Break Kriemhilde Line,' 'Germans on the Run,' 'Tens of Thousands Captured by Allies.' . . . I recall how we started feeling pretty good around here as Thanksgiving approached. The flu was dying out. The war was going well, and we hadn't heard the bad news yet about Papa."

I turned toward the graves and then asked as carefully as I could, "What happened to your mother and grandmother, Jesse?"

"Well, as the number of new cases and deaths declined in Memphis, everyone around Hollow Rock mistakenly thought we'd been spared. But the Spanish Lady wasn't through with us yet. I remember Granny and Mama giving all the credit to the tonics they'd started taking when the flu first hit Memphis. Granny sipping her Tanlac to 'build up her constitution' and Mama swearing by her Gude's Pepto-Mangan advertised as the 'Red Blood Builder.' But despite all the precautions, Mama came down with the flu first, and I'd swear learning of Papa's death had a lot to do with it. She was inconsolable at first, and then the lethargy set in. Wore her down, making her more susceptible."

"If y'all were staying out here to yourselves, how you think they came down with it?"

"As strange as it seems, I blame it on the church social we had to raise extra money for the real needy around here."

"Strange?"

"Maybe 'ironic' is a better word. You see, we thought getting Mama out of the house might help with her depression. And after all, we'd also be doing some good, doing the Lord's work. But no more than two days had passed before Mama came down with the shaking chills. Then the cough. Then it went to her lungs with the winter fever, and that's really what killed Mama."

"What about your grandmother? She get sick right after the social too?"

Jesse shook his head. "No, that's the other irony. The Lord let Granny live long enough to care for Mama and help dress her for her grave here. And then she got the chills, the cough, and the winter fever. We buried Mama one week and Granny the next, leaving Gramps and me here alone to soldier on."

"I'm sorry, Jesse. I don't know what to say."

He nodded and moved back onto the road. "You must be freezing by now, Todd. Let's get you inside, meet Gramps. We'll have something hot to drink and then start talking up those blues."

7

JUDGED BY DEMEANOR and stature I'd have never guessed this craggy, stooped scarecrow of a man would be one of the most resilient and loving people I'd ever meet. When bad things happened to Gramps, he never asked "Why?" but "Where to now?" For him, life could be a struggle, but it was never an all-out war. And contrary to popular thinking, adversity appeared to provide the resistance, which gave his spirit lift.

Like its owner, you couldn't really judge Gramps's house by its cover. As we approached the two-story white Victorian, the first thing I thought was Reverend Goodrich's admonition to his Hartford parishioners: "A place for everything; and everything in its place." But while the frame exterior and the landscaping were flawless and conventional, the interior was anything but. Jesse and I had just entered the front parlor, which Gramps had transformed into a creative maelstrom of wood, gut, and glue.

He was standing at a makeshift workbench staring at a billet of Appalachian spruce envisioning his next handiwork. Without looking up, he said, "Jesse, why don't you take your friend there into the dining room and give him a quick tour? I'll be in for introductions. It won't be long."

"I'll leave the tour for you, Gramps," Jesse responded. "Let you do the explaining, one musician to another. But while we're waiting for you, I'll heat up some cider for the three of us. Now don't take too long, you hear? I've got to get Todd back to Mrs. Griffith's before dark."

Still staring down at the block of wood, Gramps replied, "The dining room in two shakes of a sheep's tail. I promise."

Jesse turned and pointed to his left. "Follow me, Todd. We'll work our way back to the kitchen and get started on the cider. Now watch where you're stepping. The planes and saws are strewn everywhere. And I'm speaking from experience—they bite." We then weaved our way through several stacks of wood and an impressive array of tables, desks, and chairs, which Gramps had converted into specialized work areas supporting various stages of his creative process.

While Jesse fetched the cider, I stoked the fire in the stove and added several gnarled pieces of red oak. When he returned, I asked, "How long's your grandfather been making instruments?"

"You won't believe it, but he'd only dabbled until after Mama and Grandma died. And he really didn't get it into gear until he ended the touring because of the arthritis."

"And this doesn't interfere?"

"The arthritis interfere with the carving, bending, and gluing?"

"Yeah. Seems like a lot of delicate work."

"I know, but working with the wood doesn't require the speed and dexterity his playing required. And it's really been a blessing. Filled three large holes in his life. That's the great thing about Gramps. He gets knocked down, but he gets right back up, dusts himself off, and then moves on."

"What instruments does he make? . . . I think I saw parts of a fiddle out there in the parlor."

"Yeah. Fiddles, violas, and of course, guitars. Took a while but the word got out. Fellas in his old band got the ball rolling, and now he gets about four hours of sleep a night. Most of his work these days is commissioned. Folks as far off as Philadelphia and San Francisco, and not just band members playing popular tunes. We're talking about concertmasters in symphony orchestras. Some mentioning Guarneri, Amati, and Gramps in the same breath, describing his instruments as 'works of art.' Strange, isn't it?"

"Strange?"

"Yeah. How life works. Probably none of this would've happened if he hadn't gotten the arthritis and . . . and Mama and Grandma hadn't gotten the flu. I dunno. Seems like you need suffering to fire the creative spark."

"I dunno either. I've heard it argued both ways. Did madness spark Van Gogh's genius? Or was he successful in spite of it?"

Jesse smiled. "Well, since we're not going to settle it one way or the other today, let's grab the ciders and head on into the dining room. . . .You can see some of the instruments there and read Gramps's notes while you're waiting for the official tour to begin."

And what a tour it would be. I was shocked. I couldn't believe what I was seeing—every wall lined with violins, violas, and guitars. I suspect Gramps used the space originally as a showroom to market his instruments; but after much of his later work became custom-built, he transformed the room into something of a personal museum displaying examples primarily of his "early" and "middle" periods.

I'd probably examined three or four instruments when Gramps entered. "I'm all yours now, Jesse. Why don't you do the introductions."

"Gramps, this is Todd. Met him this morning out at the hollow rock. He and his mother are just moving into town. Staying at Mrs. Griffith's until their place is ready over on Mill Street. Todd will be finishing up at the high school next year and wants to become a professional musician. So I thought the two of you should talk." Jesse looked at me and continued, "Todd, this is Gramps, whom you've already heard a lot about today."

"Nice meeting you, Todd. I hope Jesse here didn't tell too many tales out of school."

"No, sir. Believe me, Jesse did you proud today."

Gramps put his arm around Jesse's shoulder and pulled him close. "I don't want to embarrass my boy here, but to tell the truth, I don't know what I'd do without him."

"I do!" Jesse teased. "As I told Todd earlier, you'd keep on keeping on, and you know it's true!"

Gramps glanced down and smiled. "I suspect so. My mama drilled it into me early on. She'd say, 'Boy, if you ain't living, you're dying. Didn't understand it at first but never forgot it." Sensing he was becoming too personal for his young audience, Gramps quickly changed the subject. "Jesse said y'all didn't have much time, so I guess we'd better get on with the tour."

"Really looking forward to it, sir."

Gramps pointed toward the doorway leading to the kitchen. "We'll start over on the far wall there. It sorta runs in chronological order. But say, before we begin, what instrument do you play?"

I was crushed. Before we'd even gotten started, this sixteen-year-old had to confess he didn't know much about playing or crafting instruments either. I felt the blood rushing to my head. "I . . . I . . ."

Jesse quickly stepped in and bailed me out. "Todd tells me he just got his first guitar this Christmas, Gramps. A Gibson. And he's determined to master it."

Gramps smiled empathetically and said, "And I'm sure you will, Todd. Sure you will." He turned and pointed to the wall. "You know what this is, Todd?"

I don't know how I had missed it. A row of six evenly spaced nails driven horizontally into the wall at shoulder height. And two feet below that row was another with six additional nails. Stretched between the rows were six strings drawn taut by bottles wedged between the strings and the wall. "Go ahead, try it." I moved over to the wall and waited for Gramps's instructions. "Left hand up by the top nails. No fret board, so you have to play the chords by feel. Right hand down below there near the bottom row." I placed my hands as best I could and looked at Gramps expectantly. "Now draw your right thumb across the strings," he said. Doing as I was told, I coaxed a wobbly chord from the taut strings. "That's it! Not bad, huh? Never thought you'd play a wall, did ya?"

I glanced over at Jesse and laughed. "That's amazing!" And then turning back to Gramps, I asked, "What made you think of building an instrument on the wall?"

"The honest truth, Todd: necessity. We didn't have much money growing up, you see." He then flashed a faint smile and digressed. "But I got lucky and married up. Jesse's grandma owned the house here and all the land surrounding it." He paused, reminiscing, but quickly caught himself. "Now where was I? So growing up poor meant you had to make do with what you had or what you could improvise. Always loved music and finally decided I wanted to play. So the idea just came to me out of the blue one day. And I wanna tell you, my papa was none too pleased with the racket and all the nails in the wall."

"What happened? Did he make you tear it down?"

"Never told me to. My mama thought it was clever. She was the musician in the family and defended me. So I hid behind her apron strings for a while until I saw all the stress it was causing between them. So I took it down on my own." He smiled slyly. "But fessing up, the tension between them wasn't the only reason I yanked the nails." He began walking and pointed to the next exhibit. "Ya see, I'd already concocted a plan replacing the troublesome six-string. I'd build an instrument I could play anywhere. Get out of the house. No more nails and no more noise. And here we are—problem solved." Gramps pointed to a primitive guitar he had fashioned out of a cigar box and a two-foot piece of mahogany. "I call it the 'Corona Model.' It's not the original. That's long gone. But this here's a reasonable facsimile, and as you can see this one has a neck and fret board too!"

"How old were you when you first started building your own instruments?"

I never knew whether he was telling the truth here or trying to make me feel better about my age, but he replied, "Let's see. . . . I didn't really start thinking of playing 'til I was fourteen. So I probably drove the nails in the wall sometime around my fifteenth birthday."

He began moving toward the third exhibit. "Now this one coming up's the only instrument I didn't carve myself." He pointed to a Martin 'D' and said, "Seeing I was trying every which way to play, Mama talked Papa into buying me this secondhand guitar, which had already seen its better days. Didn't matter much to me. For the first time I had a real guitar to play."

"Did you keep on building them then?" I asked.

"Funny thing. Those were the first and the last until a few years ago. Once I started playing in bands I never gave it a second thought. Bought every one of them brand new from then on. Looking back now I suspect there was a bit of pride showing through. My way of saying to myself, 'You've come up from nothing, so you deserve the very best.'"

Jesse jumped in. "No need apologizing, Gramps. You'd come a long way. I've seen Grandma's scrapbook. You were playing with the best bands in Tennessee."

He shrugged his shoulders, embarrassed, as he moved over to the next instrument. "Of all my children, Todd, this here's my favorite. Not necessarily the best, mind ya, but the first after Jesse and I found ourselves alone. You always take a little more pride in the first. A six-string dreadnought: twelve-fret neck, copied off my Ditson there." Gramps couldn't resist. He carefully lifted his favorite from its brackets, tuned it, and began playing "Amazing Grace." "Whatdaya think?" he asked.

I had never heard anything like it. If I had been blindfolded, I'd have sworn two musicians were playing. Mesmerized by his fingering and fearing he'd stop if I replied, I just nodded and motioned for him to finish the hymn.

He continued playing and said, "So I studied the construction of my bought guitars very carefully. First of all I learned the soundboard had to be spruce. Hear that? A strong, crisp sound. Nice overtones too."

I smiled and nodded again.

"But spruce won't do for the backs and sides. Gotta be mahogany. Gives them a sweet tone, especially fine in the treble and bass. Use mahogany a lot for the necks too. Strong and stable, cuts down on the warping." He ended the spiritual and segued into "Dixie." "So once you've carved all the pieces, you bond them tight with hot hide glue. Dries nice and firm. Helps transmit the sound. And after you let her rest for a while, you string her up with sheep gut." As he finished a resounding rendition of the South's anthem, he simultaneously concluded his demonstration with a flourish. "And after stringing her up, you tune her and then you let her rip!"

Gramps carefully repositioned the dreadnought in its brackets and extended his hand, signaling he was anxious to return to his work in the front parlor. "I'll leave you fellas on your own from here on out. The tour's pretty self-explanatory. There are notes for every exhibit, and you'll see a couple of my first violas and fiddles along the way too."

Jesse interrupted. "Sorry, Gramps. One more thing before you go. I know you're busy and everything, but I was thinking perhaps Todd here could drop by while I'm away at school. Check in on you and perhaps sit for a spell." Jesse smiled sheepishly. "And I thought in return you might help him improve his playing . . ."

"That . . . that would be asking too much of your grandfather, Jesse," I interjected. "He doesn't have the time, and I'm sure he'd quickly get frustrated with my fumbling about."

All the while I was protesting but hoping he'd accept the challenge, Gramps was gazing into my eyes and stroking his long gray beard. He then looked over at Jesse and probed, "You think he's serious about mastering his six-string?"

"I do, Gramps. I really do. I've spent the day getting to know Todd. I'd swear he's as serious about his playing as I am about my preaching."

Gramps turned and glanced down at my hands. "You willing to push on through even if you have to make them bleed?"

"Yes, sir," I replied earnestly.

"You see, getting a booming sound out of your guitar requires thick, tight strings that cut to the quick. And I'll tell you now, it ain't no picnic until you've got calluses piled high on your fingertips."

"I'll work morning to night, sir. I'll give it everything I've got. I promise I won't let you down."

Gramps extended his hand again, but this time it was accompanied by a faint smile. "In that case, Todd, I guess we have a deal. But mind you, I've gotta keep up with my building, so I suspect you'll be doing a lot of playing while I'm doing my carving, gluing, and the like. Okay by you?"

I smiled broadly and replied, "Okay by me. It'll be an honor, sir."

"Well, let's see. I wanna finish the fiddle I'm working on; have to ship her out to Kansas City midweek. So how about eleven o'clock sharp this coming Thursday? Bring your Gibson there and— Have you collected any sheet music along the way? Favorite songs? You see, I find it easier learning when you're practicing something you like."

"Sheet music? Nothing so far. Just doing some humming in my head. Tunes I'd heard on Beale Street in Memphis this past year. I hum them and then try playing them hit or miss."

"Can you hum a favorite or two out loud? Don't be bashful now. Loud and clear so Jesse and I can hear them."

After several aborted attempts, I looked over at Gramps and said, "Now don't you think I'm crazy. Just hold on a minute, and I'll try again." I kneeled down, opened my guitar case, and pulled out the Gibson. "One, two., three, four . . ." I pretended to start picking with my right hand and sliding a knife up and down the fret with my left. And magically I began humming in key and performing a respectable rendition of my favorite Beale Street song.

When I'd finished "playing," I looked up anxiously trying to gauge Gramps's reaction. But I didn't know what to think. Jesse and his grandfather were just standing there staring at each other. Gramps finally turned and, smiling skeptically, said, "Now that's the damnedest thing I've ever seen or heard, Todd. I've traveled far and wide, performing in lots of venues from fish fries to concert halls and playing everything imaginable—minstrel, vaudeville and cowboy songs, gospel and all sorts of dance music from polkas and mazurkas to minuets and waltzes. But this is the first time I've ever laid eyes or ears on something like that."

Jesse quickly went to work bailing me out again. "Was that the blues you were humming just now? The blues you were describing out at the hollow rock this morning?"

"Sure was."

Jesse looked over at Gramps. "Todd says it's just beginning to hit Memphis. He heard only one fella playing that style during a recent visit."

"I've heard of the blues, Jesse. They go back a long way. Some ten years at least. Even played Handy's "Memphis Blues" and his "Saint Louis Blues" in a minstrel band. But they sure didn't sound anything like what I just heard."

Trying to be polite while setting the record straight, I eased into the conversation. "Maybe I can shed a little light. My father was along on my Memphis trip. He loves music and keeps an ear out for anything new. We actually heard Handy's band playing his music in Church's Park on Beale Street. My father called them 'rag' tunes, said they had a ragged rhythm to them. But I remember our stopping in at Pee Wee's Saloon later that day. That's where I heard the tune I was just playing. Fella out of Louisville. Believe the name was Weaver. Yes, Sylvester Weaver. And he was playing his 'Guitar Blues,' picking with the one hand and sliding a knife up and down the strings with the other. As we left the saloon that afternoon, I remember how excited we both were having heard this new style live for the first time. And

I recall my father saying folks had started calling them the 'country blues.'"

Gramps nodded and then responded with a caveat. "Understand now I can help you with the basics for a wide range of music. But I want you to know upfront I've never tried flattening notes or playing with a knife like you just did with that Weaver tune."

"Fine by me, sir. I'll always be grateful for any help you can give me. The blues can surely wait a year or two—wait until I get back down to Memphis."

Jesse and I finished touring Gramps's gallery, dropped by the parlor to say "so long," and retraced our steps back to the hollow rock. "No need going all the way to Mrs. Griffith's, Jesse. I'll just head back down to the tracks, hang a right, and follow my nose back to town."

"I don't mind. . . ."

"No, you probably have a lot to do before heading over to Jackson. And besides, I've got to learn my way around town."

"Well, if you're into learning, then here's a shortcut. See that shag bark hickory over there."

I nodded.

"Well, just beyond the hickory, look closely. You'll see a narrow path heading off southwest. Not used much anymore. Hard to see with the blackberry thicket growing up all around it. But just follow it. You'll come out behind Buckley's Drugs. It'll cut fifteen minutes off the time and you can crawl home from there long before night settles in."

"Yeah, I need to be getting back. Mama will think a bear or something ate me. She's always been like that. It's a wonder she doesn't already have the sheriff out looking for me."

Jesse spontaneously glanced away toward the tiny cemetery near Gramps's house and murmured, "I know what you're saying. My mama was the same way. Hovering over me, watching every move I made. But strange how life is sometimes. It frustrated me when she did it. A young boy trying hard to grow up and cut the apron strings. I saw her standing in the way. But I miss it now. I realize it was just her way of showing her love."

I smiled empathetically and said, "Guess you're right about that, Jesse. I just haven't gotten past the frustrating stage yet."

Conveying more than I was ready either to consider or accept, Jesse replied, "Trust me, Todd. That day will come, and sooner than you think."

"I'd better get to moving," I said. "When you coming back home?"

"I'd say three weeks at the most. In the meantime you visit Gramps and practice hard. I'm expecting great progress out of you."

"Thanks for everything, Jesse."

"It's nothing. I'm just happy we met today."

"Me, too."

And after a few slaps on the back and a spontaneous embrace, I turned and raced back to the hotel for the expected inquisition.

8

My father's business and political rivals had grudgingly nicknamed him "the Cat." I say *grudgingly* because their antipathy was a venomous blend of one part envy and two parts hate. They had learned what my mother and I had known for years—he had a sixth sense that ensured he always landed on his feet. He could recognize danger, compress the time required to consider options, and then act decisively. Casual observers might say he had a hair trigger, but I can assure you there was always method to his perceived madness.

So it wasn't surprising that within days of our departure from Nashville my mother learned how the Governor planned on handling her "situation." I had pulled a chair up close to the parlor stove and was trying to tease out a Memphis tune, when Mama entered and tossed a thick envelope on a table next to me. "What you got there?" I asked.

She sighed and replied, "The Governor's plans for us. The postman hand-delivered it as I was coming up the walk just now."

I laid my guitar down, picked up the registered letter, and thumbed through the five single-spaced pages. I returned to the introductory paragraph, read it twice, and decided I'd rely on my mother's interpretation. I lowered the letter to my lap. "What's it saying, Mama?"

"Not much love there, Todd. All business. Drawn up by the Governor's lawyers. To make a long story short, it pretty much says he'll establish a substantial and irrevocable trust, if I agree to several conditions."

"Irrevocable trust?"

"Think of it as a pot of money the Governor's set aside and no longer owns or controls. He can't touch the money without my written permission."

"You said there were some conditions?"

"Yes. I have to agree first that he'd have free and open access to you. Second, that I'd give him an uncontested divorce at the time and place of his choosing. And third, that I'd never publicly or privately discuss his . . . his 'comings and goings' during our marriage."

"You all right with all that? You gonna accept his offer?"

"Honestly, Todd, do I really have a choice? It's what the Governor wants; and God help me if I tried standing in his way."

Having observed my father's modus operandi for years, we knew a substantial increase in support would begin flowing the moment Mama agreed to terms and would continue flowing until the day Mama passed away. We also realized there were at least three phases to any of his plans. Getting Mama's signature was merely the first stage. We'd have to keep reading the newspapers to learn the successive phases and how they played into his overall plan.

We didn't have to wait long for the first clue to his

thinking. Determined to get out in front of the story, the Governor's spokesman held a news conference. He revealed Mama had taken an indefinite "leave of absence" from her responsibilities as first lady and that she had left Nashville for an undisclosed location. The spokesman implied Mama needed rest and asked the reporters to respect her privacy during her return to private life.

The following week the spokesman was back at the podium to announce a Mrs. Burrows would assume the first lady's duties. Over the next few days the administration leaked details in dribs and drabs about this Mrs. Burrows. We learned her first name was Edna, that she was a widow, that her maiden name was Workman, which coincidentally was also the spokesman's family name, and that she had two sons, one of whom had married and was expecting his third child within a matter of weeks.

At this point the disclosures died down. But six months later the Governor's spokesman returned to the podium to announce a bombshell: the Governor and Mrs. Taylor had made the painful decision to "part ways" and the Governor would reluctantly be filing for divorce in the "coming weeks." The spokesman concluded this remarkable news conference with a sincere appeal for privacy and prayers for "both Margaret and Jim."

And then one year to the day after Mama and I had fled Nashville in the dead of night, the Governor and the spokesman's sister, this same Mrs. Burrows, stepped to the microphone to proudly announce their engagement and elaborate plans for a June wedding at the governor's mansion—with the public invited!

The political novice observes the Governor's moves and screams, "He's crazy! What's he thinking? He's up for reelection in two years, and here he is divorcing his wife and marrying another woman! There's no way in hell he can recover from all this. He might as well start packing. He's finished!" But my father's political rival smiles and disagrees with the novice's superficial reading of the tea leaves. "Just wait and see. You're gonna be surprised how all this plays out. The Cat's way smarter than that. A cold calculation informs each of his moves."

Truth be told here, the only difference between the novice and the political rival is while they both observe the Governor's moves as he makes them, the rival knows a hidden agenda lies just beneath the surface, orchestrating each of the Governor's actions. But from that point on, anything the rival suggests is mere speculation because he doesn't know the real motivation driving the Governor.

However, our being privy to the Governor's private life had always given my mother and me a leg up in understanding his motives. In fact, we had rarely been stumped after watching the first phase or two unfold. And that was certainly the case this time. Once we'd learned the widow Burrows was assuming Mama's responsibilities and she had two adult sons thriving on their own, it was relatively easy locking in all the pieces.

The Governor and his trusted spokesman, Workman, must have met to assess the potential damage from Mama's abrupt departure. Knowing his widowed sister was unemployed and now living alone, the spokesman most likely suggested Mrs. Burrows assume Mama's duties. My father must have agreed and then taken Workman's idea a giant step further, asking him the likelihood his sister would ever consider a marriage of convenience. The Governor most surely emphasized both he and Mrs. Burrows would enter the union with their eyes wide open—the Governor understanding the widow was marrying for financial security and she fully aware of my father's preference for partying through the night with handsome young men.

After this meeting with the Governor, Workman would have pitched both ideas to his sister at once; and after several days of careful consideration, she accepted the job offer and the marriage proposal. My father must have been elated. As far as he was concerned, it was a match made in political heaven—his marriage partner got her security, and he got the short- and long-term cover he needed for reelection.

I must admit my mother and I were puzzled at first by the Governor's willingness to raise the ante with an offer of both employment and marriage. But after exploring several hypotheses, we settled on the one most beneficial to the Governor. Employing Mrs. Burrows helped lessen the impact of the revelation that the first lady had suddenly left town. The message to the press would be: "Nothing to see here. Move along now. The administration has adequately addressed the situation and will continue firing on all cylinders as it has in the past."

But the Governor must also have realized that hiring Mrs. Burrows would do nothing to lessen the significant risk to his reelection chances if, for example, a disgruntled bureaucrat or two leaked corroborating information about the elaborate all-male parties he hosted at the mansion after hours. He surely understood that marrying the spokesman's sister would go a long way in addressing this long-term threat to his reelection. The marriage would provide him plausible deniability, especially if Mrs. Burrows strode to the microphone, waved her finger at the reporters, and denounced them for spreading these "false, scurrilous, and malicious rumors."

And my father's wedding ensured one additional benefit, which I found too painful to share even with my mother. The marriage sent a blunt message that in my father's eyes I was expendable, or at the least, an interchangeable part. Mrs. Burrows's sons would be the insurance policy securing his vast holdings and more importantly his legacy. If I didn't "work out," so to speak, my stepbrothers would be there to step in and manage my father's enterprise and fortune.

Once we'd deciphered the Governor's intentions, Mama and I rarely spoke of him or his administration. We got on with our lives—Mama back to her first love, teaching at the junior high school down the street, and I admittedly to sleepwalking my way through the last semesters of high school. As I explained to Mama a thousand times, it wasn't anything intentional. But every time I entered the classroom, a switch flipped, and the bluesman's wails drowned out the teacher's whispers.

And over those last trying months at home, I realized something remarkable was happening. Mama and Gramps were slowly coming around to my way of thinking, that the best thing for me was to move on and start doing what I'd dreamed of doing. Their parental nurturing had evolved into adult advice offered sincerely on a take-it-or-leave-it basis. They were signaling they felt they'd done their part and that it was now up to me to do mine.

I recall an extraordinary conversation I had with each of them just weeks before graduation and separated by a single day. If I hadn't known better, I'd have sworn they'd begun coordinating their mentoring. After a Sunday breakfast of pancakes and sausage, Mama said, "Grab your coffee, son, and come on into the living room." In the past, similar invitations signaled hour-long lectures on the benefits of finishing high school. But since graduation was now practically a *fait accompli*, I suspected an updated exhortation extolling the virtues of a baccalaureate.

Surprisingly, our discussion was about everything but a revised pitch for higher learning. After easing into our customary chairs, she smiled and immediately teared up.

"You okay, Mama?" I asked.

Continuing to fight back the tears, she nodded and murmured, "Just give me a minute. Everything's okay." She took several deep breaths to regain her composure and continued, "I knew this day would come, Todd. . . . First, I want you to know how proud I am of you. You've honored my wishes, staying here and finishing your degree. And second, I know you've got a lot of your father in you., especially his love of music and the itch to move on to Memphis. I've watched you practice until your fingers bled. So I also want you to know you have my blessing. I'll miss you, but I'll take comfort in knowing you're happy, healthy, and doing what you want to do. Can we ask anything more for our children than that?"

She moved over to where I was sitting, reached into her pocket, withdrew a small envelope, and extended her hand to me. "Think of this as a graduation present and . . . and . . . the down payment on a new beginning."

I nervously opened the envelope and discovered ten crisp fifty-dollar bills. "I don't know what to say, Mama."

Tearing up again and smiling, she responded lightheartedly, "'Thank you' will suffice."

I leaned over and gave her a big hug. "I love you, Mama."

"I love you, son."

She paused; and then reverting to her former role as overly protective mother, she continued, "I thought you could use the money for food and lodging until you catch on somewhere. And I mean it. I don't want you holing up in some filthy fleabag on Beale Street. I want you staying someplace clean and respectable. Like the hotel we stayed at with your father that time we went to Memphis. You remember?"

Lowering my head in embarrassment, I replied, "Yeah, Mama, I remember. It was the Peabody on Union Avenue."

She lifted my chin. "Now I know it can be pricey, but if you're running out of money, let me know, and I'll wire you more."

Doing my best to hide my frustration, I replied, "Hope to be working soon, and it won't be necessary."

She gave me a big hug, held me at arm's length, and gazed into my eyes. "One last thing, son. Promise me you won't leave without saying good-bye. More than once I heard your father say he regretted leaving his uncle's house without telling anyone. And it's always been a fear of mine—walking into your room one bright morning and finding the wardrobe and closet empty. No. I want to go with you to the station, buy you a round-trip ticket, wish you well, and then watch your train disappear around the bend. Grant me that, son."

I nodded, smiled awkwardly, and eased out of the room all the while thinking, "Patience. Patience. You have to tolerate brief lapses now and then."

The following morning I made my usual excursion via the hollow rock to check on Gramps and demonstrate my progress. I always made a point of stopping at the rock to reflect on my first visit there and offer up a simple prayer to anyone of a mind to listen.

"Todd, is that you?"

Startled, I wheeled about. "Gramps? What are you up to all the way out here? I'm supposed to be paying you a visit at eleven o'clock."

"Sorry. Time just got away from me. Been focusing hard on my prospecting and harvesting soundboards for three years hence."

"Prospecting?"

"Yeah, best time of the year to stake a claim. Find the saplings you wanna keep an eye on."

"But why out here?"

"Trees are thickest here—the ones bordering the hollow rock. Lots of shade; young'uns grow toward the light nice and slow. Rings are closely spaced, and the tighter the rings, the straighter the grain and the denser the wood. And density's the secret to making any of the soundboards really sing."

"And harvesting?"

"For sure. Always on the lookout while I'm out here prospecting. As they say, sometimes you get lucky and kill two birds with one stone. You can't see it from here, but I got my axe parked on the other side of the rock over there. So sometimes I cut one day and haul it back the next."

"What's this about three years?"

"That's the time it takes to air-dry billets real good. Improves the tone and stops the cracking. Never got into kiln-drying. Takes less time but there are a lot of ways to messing it up."

Since I was anxious to show Gramps my progress, I paused and then probed diplomatically, "So when you plan on heading back? I've got some surprises for you."

Gramps understood immediately and smiled. "Tell you what, young man, it's such a nice day, why don't you crack open your case, sit over there on that stump next to the hollow rock, and play your heart out."

I didn't think twice. Within seconds I was sitting on the stump tuning up. "Ready when you are, Gramps. You wanna take a seat?"

"No, I'll just lean over here again' the tree. I wanna see how well you're projecting. Now make all the little fellas out here stand up and take notice. Okay, I'm ready when you are."

I tapped lightly on my soundboard and launched into several upbeat jug tunes Gramps had assigned the week before. And when I finished singing and playing the last of them, I didn't immediately look up for his critique. I suspect the venue had a lot to do with it, but for the first time I felt I'd performed to my potential. Whatever Gramps could offer as "constructive criticism" would be purely academic.

As Gramps approached, he whispered, "Listen! You hear them? They're all singing along. You made them stand up and take notice."

I looked up. He was grinning proudly from ear to ear. Assuming the role of humble student, I responded lightheartedly, "It's not what the critters think, Gramps. It's what you think that's important."

"Well, I mean this when I say it. I've never heard anyone anywhere play 'You Shall' and 'Stealing Stealing' any better than you did just now. So come on, stow your guitar and let's head on up to the house. I've got something I need some help on."

I smiled proudly and responded, "Thank you, Gramps. That means a lot coming from you." I stood up, patted the hollow rock, and whispered, "My talisman."

As we began walking up the path, Gramps put his arm around my shoulder and asked, "When does school let out?"

"Still have a few weeks. Why you ask?"

"Just trying to get a gauge on when you'll be leaving for Memphis."

"Whatdaya mean?"

"It's what you've been saying all along. You were going to Memphis and playing the blues."

"Hadn't really set a time. Wanna make sure I'm ready."

"Let's see now. We've been at this going on a year and a half. You've done everything I've asked of you and then some." He stopped, turned, and smiled wistfully. "It's not saying I won't miss you, Todd. Believe me, I will. You're like a second grandson. And I wanna tell you here and now, once you finish your schooling, you'll be ready to hop a train and get steeped in the blues."

Fighting back the tears of hard-fought achievement, I just nodded and started walking toward the trailhead. And that was the last either of us spoke until we reached the tiny cemetery close to the house. As Grandpa veered off the path toward the markers, he said, "Have to say a few words for my wife and daughter." He then pointed toward a log lean-to some twenty yards up ahead on my side of the road. "I'll meet you there in a minute." He knelt down facing the headstones and whispered several muffled sentences in the cadence of the Lord's Prayer.

As Gramps approached the lean-to a few minutes later, he said, "Grab that end of the canvas there. I'll get the one down here. On 'three' we'll fling her up and over the roofline. You ready? . . . Okay now. One . . . two . . . three . . . let her rip!" With the tarp removed, I peered in. There were three large stacks of logs cut in two-foot lengths with either a "1," "2," or "3" painted on the end of each pile. "What do we have here?" I asked.

"Spruce cut to twenty-fours."

"And the numbers?"

"The years they've been air-drying."

"You need help hauling some of them over to the house?"

"Yes and no. Need some hauling but only one log today."

"Which pile?"

"The stack with the '3' painted on her."

"Okay, Gramps. This is getting to be like pulling teeth. Which log?"

He scratched his head teasingly. "I dunno. Why don't you choose one?"

"Whatdaya up to, Gramps?" I asked.

He stroked his beard and smiled. "Just trying to find one that's pleasing to you. You're probably gonna be looking at it for a long time."

"Didn't you tell me you made soundboards out of spruce that's been air-dried around three years?"

"Sure did."

I edged out on a limb but only halfway. I was hoping to avoid embarrassing him and me. "So you're making a new soundboard for my Gibson?"

Sensing I was just putting my big toe in the water, he laughed and continued playing along. "Is that what you want? A new soundboard?"

"Well, uh . . . uh . . ."

"Wouldn't you rather have a dreadnought like the one I showed you hanging on the wall?"

I ran over and embraced him. "It would mean more than anything, Gramps. More than anything." I skipped over to the pile of 3s, knelt down, and started sorting through them. But to my untrained eye one log looked pretty much the same as the next. One might be a little thicker in diameter or richer in color than another, but none of them truly spoke to me, saying, 'Pick me. I'm the one.' That is, until I got to the very last log at the bottom of the stack. I rolled it back and forth several times and inspected the cut ends. I looked up at Gramps and said, "I really like the looks of this one. But why is it so much different than the others? Silver on the ends and along the sides where the bark's been stripped away from the trunk. And look, there're black streaks running all through it. There's nothing else like it here among the 3s. Is it a different kind of wood?"

Gramps smiled and shook his head. "Amazing you'd hone in on that one. Took a liking to it myself. Never did anything with it. It'd take a rare bird to want something looking so, ah, unconventional. You'd never see a concertmaster playing a fiddle made of it."

"Why the silver and black tone, Gramps?" I repeated. "Is it a different kind of wood?"

"No, it's spruce like all the other 3s. But this log has a history all its own."

"What happened?"

"Remember that stump you were sitting on just now next to the hollow rock?"

"Sure."

"Well, that's where she stood for years and years. For as long as I've been walking these woods. And that started right after marrying Jesse's grandmother. She and I'd pack a lunch and picnic near that old spruce when I wasn't on the road making music. . . . Must be as old as Methuselah, but still small in girth. Must have matured real slow in the shade of the old-growth giants. Probably too small for harvesting when the woodsmen came through making their first cut. In fact, she was still standing strong when Jesse's mama and grandma died in the epidemic. Jesse and I then carried on the tradition to honor them, picnicking out here most Sundays, even in the dead of winter. We'd stop by the markers for a prayer and then head on out here to the hollow rock and that old spruce standing right next to it."

"But how'd she end up here, Gramps?"

"Well, that smallest spruce had finally become the tallest tree in the forest. And you know that's when things start trying to cut you down to size. First, there was the lightning, next the tornado, and just like that she was half her height. Didn't do anything the first year. Hoping she'd make a comeback. But that only happens in fairytales and bibles. I tell you, it made me sad watching her rot away in the snow and rain. So right after Jesse left for Jackson his first year, I sharpened my axe and did the merciful thing."

"Where's the rest of the tree, Gramps?"

"This here's the only piece I could salvage. It was right up against the lightning strike. Hauled the rest of her back and used her for firewood. More fitting than letting her rot away."

"You think the lightning changed the color?"

"Absolutely, and the tone as well. Explains the black streaks running through her. And ya know, ancient tribes swore there was magic in this thunderwood. So I was really curious how she'd turn out after quarter sawing her into billets and sawing boards off the flat sides. You're always looking for real tight grain running vertical to the surface. So this wood should look like a million and sound like one too! . . . Fessing up, I was gonna fashion a soundboard for myself but never got around to it. Got too busy with everybody else's commission work. So she just settled here to the bottom of the pile. And what do they say? Out of sight, out of mind."

I looked down at the log, disappointed. "Well, with all the personal history and such, I suspect you want to keep her for yourself."

Grandpa reached over and tousled my hair. "Nonsense, Todd. There's enough spruce here for at least two or three soundboards; and even if there weren't, I'd still want you to have that dreadnought I promised you. So why don't we roll her out of here, haul her over to the mill next door, and see what we've got. Whatdaya say?"

I jumped up and replied, "I'd say let's get started, Gramps. Let's get started."

9

WHILE WALKING OUT of the station onto the platform that early summer morning after my graduation, Mama
asked, "You think he's gonna get here? There's not much time
left before the ten o'clock."

"Never known him to break a promise. If he said he'd
be here, he'll be here and he'll be bringing my new dreadnought along."

Mama stopped suddenly. "What in the world? You hear
that, Todd? Listen."

"Sounds like the 'Ballad of Casey Jones,' Mama. Believe
it's coming from the far end of the platform there. See all
the people standing around the baggage cart? Let's go check
it out!"

As we approached the knot of passengers, the music ended and a familiar voice rang out from the center of the crowd:
"Thanks for dropping by. But I've got to put her away now
or I'll find myself in a whole lot of trouble." The onlookers
applauded and then slowly dispersed, exposing Gramps and
Jesse sitting together on a wrought-iron bench. They didn't
notice Mama and me closing in; they were too busy stowing
my six-string before I showed up.

"Caught red-handed!" I shouted jokingly.

Gramps looked up guiltily and replied, "Just checking the tuning."

Jesse stood up and smiled broadly, assuming his customary role as advocate-in-chief. "Good to see you, old man. I'm the culprit. Wanted to be here for the send-off so I got the late train in last night. Gramps showed me your guitar first thing when I walked in the door. But he said it wasn't ready to play yet. Said he'd made some final changes yesterday. He promised to tune it this morning while we were waiting for you to show up. But it seems every time Gramps starts tuning he draws a crowd. And the folks here started clamoring for a song or two, so Gramps obliged them." To deflect the heat from his grandfather even more, Jesse then turned toward my mother and asked in a flirtatious drawl, "And may I ask who this lovely young lady might be?"

I jumped right into the fray. "Mama, this here's my good friend Jesse." I winked and then added, "It's hard to tell sometimes, Mama, but he's the ministerial student at Lane I've been telling you about. And this here's Jesse's grandfather, Gramps, who's taught me everything I know about playing my Gibson. And now he's been nice enough to build me a custom dreadnought as a combination going-away and high school graduation present."

Showing her moxie, Mama played right along with our banter. She turned to me and then back toward Jesse. "It's always nice meeting such fine gentlemen and scholars, Todd. Seeing there're so few of them left these days. . . ."

Sensing he'd met his match, Jesse went into full retreat. He glanced toward the clock on the station cupola and then turned back to his grandfather. "You'd better get on with giving Todd his gift. Otherwise you're gonna run out of time."

I walked over and sat down next to Gramps, who slipped the guitar case over onto my lap and whispered, "I think there's magic in her, Todd, real magic. You'll see."

I gave him a big hug and replied, "Thanks for everything, Gramps. I'll never forget—"

He put his finger up to my lips and said, "Let's hear you make her sing right quick before you have to go."

I opened the latches and carefully lifted the striking six-string from its case. The lacquered soundboard was a brilliant silver with flecks of lightning strike throughout. The remainder of the instrument, including the neck, the bridge, the back, and the sides, framed the luminous soundboard in a gleaming black.

"My God, Gramps, she's beautiful!"

Deflecting the praise, he responded modestly, "The proof's in the playing, Todd. Let's hear how she sounds."

I must admit I was nervous. It was the first time I'd performed for anyone other than Gramps. Now it was my mother, my best friend, and anyone else on the platform who cared to listen. I calmed my nerves by sticking to the routine: check the tuning, clear the throat, pause for a deep breath, and then play.

As I picked each of the strings, I sang the tuning mnemonic in my head, "Eddy. Ate. Dynamite. Good. Bye. Eddy." I inhaled deeply. "What'll I play? Something . . . something real easy. Foster? 'Beautiful Dreamer'? No, why not a favorite? 'Hard Times.' That's it. 'Hard Times.'" I took a second deep

breath, played a brief instrumental introduction, and then began singing softly:

> Let us pause in life's pleasures and count its
> many tears,
> While we all sup sorrow with the poor;
> There's a song that will linger forever in our ears;
> Oh hard times come again no more.

Playing Foster's parlor song was surprisingly easy. The dreadnought practically played itself. And by the time I'd finished
the first stanza, I knew Gramps had crafted a visual and aural
masterpiece. While he had fashioned the oversized guitar to
"extract the boom from the thunderwood," he had managed
to strike a fine balance between that thunderous bass, the
mellow midrange, and the bell-like treble. And he was right
about the magic too. The ebony bridge added to the mystical
shimmer in the overtones. But suddenly the roar and rumble of the incoming express disrupted "life's pleasures." It was
now time to add to the many tears.

Once we'd reached cruising speed, my mind began swaying to
the rhythm of the southbound train—from the guilt of leaving
Mama behind to the comfort in knowing Jesse would be back
home now looking after her; from the pride of following in
my father's footsteps to the gripping fear of knowing I could
be letting everyone down; and from the hollow feeling of un-
tethered loneliness to the high expectations of meeting new
people and making friends. I opened the guitar case, peered

in at the dreadnought, and whispered, "Gramps says you're brimming with legends ready for mining, so I guess it's up to you and me, old man, to make all that happen."

We rolled into Memphis a little after two o'clock; and after gathering my luggage, I took a taxi over to the Peabody and checked in as I had promised Mama. But what I hadn't promised was staying there in its pampered luxury for an eternity. I was determined to get in and out of the Peabody within a week. So once I had finished supper, I returned to my room and began drawing up plans of prospecting for a job and a permanent place to live.

The next morning after a stick-to-your-ribs breakfast I headed over to the foot of Beale Street near the Mississippi River. I had divided the east-west thoroughfare into quarters—from the river to Main, from Main to Handy Park, from there to Church's Park, and from Church's on out to Lauderdale Street. I had allotted two days to cover every restaurant, theater, club, and saloon in each of these four sections.

I had especially targeted the Beale Street sites my father and I had visited to hear new music during that earlier political trip. These "high-potential" venues included honky-tonks like Pee Wee's Saloon, the Big Four, Jodie Farnlay's, and the Red Onion; theaters such as the Daisy and the Palace; and clubs like the Xanadu, the Shanghai, and the Vintage, where they'd have music during the week and prize fights most Friday and Saturday nights.

The first place I stopped was the last where I thought I'd ever have a real shot at finding work. While it seemed a bridge too far, I figured I'd use this first interview to hone my pitch without feeling the pressure of having potentially squandered a realistic opportunity. After all, this wasn't just any fly-by-night watering hole. This was the legendary Shanghai Gaming Club, arguably the finest pleasure palace between New Orleans and Chicago. In fact, the Shanghai was so well known that the company name had long ago been subsumed by its trademark, purportedly a rendition of the famous British clipper, the *Cutty Sark*, which the club owners proudly displayed on everything from the silverware to its public signage.

And the Beale Street entrance was no exception. The iconic crimson sailing ship graced the front door with a cursive tagline arced below promising, "You'll never be dying to leave our club." It was a reassuring message for sure in light of the long line of ambulances parked out front and extending westward for as far as the eye could see. The word had gotten out about these "vulture vans," as they were called in the Beale Street vernacular. Rumor had it, if you were alive when the attendants loaded you into a death cab, you'd certainly have met your maker by the time you arrived at your final destination, not the expected doctor's office or hospital, but an enterprising mortician's, with whom the driver had contracted earlier in the day. No, locals knew when you found yourself wounded in an altercation, you should stumble out of the establishment, shun the ambulances, and crawl to the nearest doctor or hospital for patching up.

I took a deep breath, opened the door, and entered an inviting foyer decorated tastefully with crystal chandeliers and floor-to-ceiling mirrors throughout. Despite the early hour, all the lights were on. I set my Gibson and dreadnought down, gave myself the once-over in the mirrors, and tried flattening an intractable cowlick with a generous glob of spit. I cracked a smile at the owners' ingenuity. I discovered the mirrors had their own subtle role to play in creating an initial make-believe atmosphere where patrons could begin feeling good about themselves and quickly shift into a more positive, albeit fanciful, state of mind. You see, the Shanghai mirrors had been placed at the entrance to flatter—to make you appear a little darker, taller, and slimmer than you were in the everyday here and now.

I pushed the heavy velvet curtains aside and passed through a doorway into a dimly lit lounge. As my eyes adjusted to the darkness, I noticed a reception desk on my left, a coat check on my right, and a dozen or so cocktail tables and stools scattered about straight ahead. As I weaved my way through the furniture toward a massive bar running the full length of the back wall, I called out, "Anybody here? Anybody?"

A baritone responded, "May I help you?"

I peered into the shadows trying to locate the questioner. The voice quickly added, "Back here, behind the counter."

"Oh, there . . . there you are," I replied as I continued walking toward the back wall. When I reached the bar, I set my guitar cases down and extended my hand. "Good morning, sir. My name's Taylor. Todd Taylor. I'm moving to town, so I'm out looking for work and a permanent place to stay. Just wondering if you might have an opening."

The stout, balding, middle-aged fellow threw a dishtowel over his shoulder and returned to washing the beer and shot glasses. "What kind of work ya lookin' for?"

"I'm open to anything."

"But why the Shanghai?" he probed.

"Been in your club before with my . . . with . . . with a friend. Saw some fellow playing the piano. Playing some ragtime."

The bartender glanced over the counter at my cases and asked, "So ya have an itch for playin'?"

"Yes and no. I can hold my own with ragtime, parlor, and the like. Not so much solo but wouldn't mind playing backup with a jug or minstrel act passing through. Being honest with you, though, that's why I dropped in. Looking for any kind of work that'll get me closer to folks who might be picking. I'll wash dishes, wait tables, do anything so long as I can talk to the musicians and maybe jam a little backstage. Hoping maybe some of it'll rub off on my playing."

"How old are ya, son?"

"Going on nineteen."

"Where's home?"

"The Peabody for now."

"No, no., before comin' here to Memphis?"

"Bounced around some, but the latest was Hollow Rock. Small place, halfway between here and Nashville. Not too far from Jackson."

"Ya say you're stayin' at the Peabody?"

"Not for long. Only 'til I find a decent place to live."

"Anybody here with ya?"

I smiled. "No. Traveling light, so to speak."

"Ya know anything about gamin'?"

"Gaming?"

"Yeah, like craps or 21?"

"Well, what I don't know I'll sure try learning. So I'm open to anything you have to offer."

A soft female voice interrupted. "That's some blank check you're writin' there, Todd."

Startled, I wheeled around and stared into the darkness at the far left end of the bar. "I'm sorry?"

"I said, 'That's some blank check you're writin' there.' You're willin' to take on anything?"

"Well, let's say almost anything, as long as I can stay close to the music."

The blurred figure rose and began walking toward the bartender and me. "Whatdaya think, Jacque?"

He shrugged his shoulders. "As proprietor, it's your call on this one Van. One way ya look, he fits in everywhere. The other way, he doesn't fit in at all."

Van stepped out of the shadows and eased up onto a bar stool next to where I was standing. She was wearing a full-length, red satin evening gown with a V-neck and sequined straps. Her vibrant black curls flowed down over her bare shoulders. She appeared to be in her early forties and quite attractive—full, red lips; small nose; blue, almond-shaped eyes, and large breasts suggestively overflowing her bold neckline. She looked over at Jacque and pointed to her empty coffee cup and then motioned for me to take a seat next to her up at the bar.

"Jacque, I come down on the side of his fittin' in everywhere. I realize he's rough right now, but followin' you around for six months or so should smooth out the edges some. Whatdaya think?"

He shrugged again. "If the missus says she's okay with it, I'm okay."

I jumped in, brimming with excitement. "So I'm hired?"

Van smiled warmly and replied, "Yes, handsome, you're hired!" She then turned to Jacque. "I want you to expose him to everything, ya hear? Don't hold anything back. Break him in for a short time with waitin' tables and washin' dishes but then get him into bartendin', cookin', and greetin'. And don't forget the prospectin' and bookin'. He'll like that part of it for sure, spendin' time with the musicians." She paused and glanced over. "Looks like you'll need a little fattenin' up to be takin' on all this work. Ya hungry?"

Lying to be hospitable, I replied, "Yeah, I could stand a bite to eat."

"Jacque, how about whippin' up some beignet for the three of us? And let's top it off with pralines and café au lait to celebrate!"

As the bartender turned away and got to work on my second large breakfast of the morning, Van began tracing the lip of her coffee cup with an index finger. "Well, that solves one of our problems."

"One of 'em?" Jacque asked with his back to us.

"Todd here says he needs a permanent place to stay."

"What about your brother's place. I know he's got a growin' family, but didn't he say he'd freed up some space on the second floor?"

"I don't know if Todd would be up for it. Not everyone's cup of tea, ya know."

"Whatdaya mean, 'Up for it'? Up for a room? At your brother's place?"

"Jacque, you know it's not just any place." She turned to me. "My brother's business is across the alley there right behind us. He runs a funeral home."

I interrupted, trying to assuage her fears. "If your brother and his family live there, I should be okay too!"

"Yeah, you'd be okay, if ya don't mind sleepin' with the deceased nearby."

"If your brother's family can stand it, I can too!" I asserted.

The bartender jumped in. "So that there's no misunderstandin', Van, ya better explain the layout."

"I was gettin' there, Jacque. Inchin' toward it." She paused to collect her thoughts before continuing. "Since my brother's added the crematory services, his embalming business has been way down. So he's converted one of his second-floor prep areas to a spare bedroom for family and professional guests already comfortable with the business. The new bedroom's on the alley side. The family's livin' quarters are up front on the street side. The dead kinda separate you from the livin', so to speak. But, Todd, if you think you're game, I'm sure I can talk my brother into helpin' his little sister out. And if ya take the room, I'll even pay half the rent as part of your pay. A dollar a day plus half your room and board. It'll be a win-win all around. It'll help my brother and help you too. So are you all in?"

Realizing I was so far down bravado road there wouldn't be any turning back, I just smiled awkwardly and replied, "Yeah, I'm all in. I've always loved the peace and quiet, and the temporary guests sure won't be having too much to say."

After polishing off the beignet, pralines, and coffee, I rushed back to the Peabody to retrieve my belongings. I sat on the side of the bed for a good half hour shaking my head and reliving what had just happened. I just couldn't believe it. I knew Mama would be proud, and I thought my papa would really be happy too. After all, I'd be working in one of the premier music venues in all the South and hobnobbing with the players he so admired.

I repeated the ringing phrase over and over in my head: "The premier music venue in all the South." And there I was that morning spending time with the folks who through trial and error somehow managed to pull off a miracle. And honestly, after meeting Jacque and Van, two unassuming and generous souls, I was even more convinced that *miracle* was the right word to describe their success.

I just couldn't imagine the two of them walking into an investment bank and procuring start-up funds for such an eclectic enterprise as they were running. I'm sure the financier would question the club's viability right off the bat; he'd immediately sense the marketing nightmare the multitude of services would present. "So you say you want to start an entertainment club. You want to give it a Chinese name, 'Shanghai,' hire 'Parisian' hostesses, serve Creole cuisine, and produce American music shows. Do I have that about right?" All the while the banker's reading the marketing plan, he's unconsciously shaking his head and thinking to himself, "No way! These rank amateurs would squander the funds in no time. What kind of customer would be drawn to this hodgepodge? This is a mess. A thousand-to-one odds of success."

And after living and working behind the curtain for a good six months, I'd have to raise the banker's odds from a thousand-to-one to at least half-a-million-to-one, the same odds as for getting struck by lightning. There were so many moving parts and so much that could have gone wrong. It was all theater to boot, all make-believe. When you dug below the surface, nothing was as it appeared on first blush. I should have known; it's what the lobby mirrors were trying to communicate from the start. Everything was upside down and inside out. It was truly a surprise in itself when a day passed without another revelation. Club life played out in a syncopated rhythm, in rag time.

For starters, the *Shanghai* Gaming Club was not a Chinese enterprise, but an incorporated American company founded by a French Creole. The iconic logo was not a depiction of the *Cutty Sark* but a picture of the three-masted Dutch schooner the *Oosterschelde*. Jacque was neither "Jacque" nor a New Orleans Creole, but allegedly "Jack" (from Jack of all trades?), the South Carolina descendant of a mulatto slave. Savannah—"Van" for short—was neither "Van" nor from Georgia, but the Creole daughter of the true proprietor of the Shanghai, Charles de Terrant, a wealthy Louisiana plantation owner and purveyor of indigo, cotton, and rice. "The missus" as Jacque liked to call Van, had purportedly never been married, but had a child and was the "madam" and mother to twelve "girls" working for her.

The club's entertainment was more of the same smoke

and mirrors. Van indeed took reservations, not for a hotel but for the third-floor stable of bedrooms rented by the hour and luxuriously appointed with embossed wallpaper and the finest furnishings. Her "Parisian ladies of the night" were neither French nor employees working only the graveyard shift, but attractive Tennessee belles sad to say on call twenty-four hours a day. The "genuine Tennessee shots" were neither whiskey nor from Tennessee, but corn lightning distilled somewhere in the hills of eastern Arkansas. The menu was neither Creole nor "haute cuisine," but more "faux cuisine," Jack's South Carolina mélange with a little of Van's Creole cooking thrown in for good measure. Not even the gaming was what it was billed. The professed Monte Carlo–style bank craps using "straight" dice on special layouts offering a "don't pass" betting option was in fact the old Mandeville–style of play, using loaded dice or "floaters" on plain tables without a choice of betting against the shooter.

Even something as seemingly solid as the three-story building itself had been designed with deception in mind. The third-floor bordello contained a false wall opening to a comfortable hiding space for the ladies, in case the police launched one of their infrequent raids. The second-floor billiard and gaming rooms had been constructed with notorious patrons in mind. If the police were closing in, folks like Machine Gun Kelley could disappear into the walls and safely exit the Shanghai via secret passageways. While the first-floor lounge and theater were similarly equipped with hidden exits, the ground floor also featured a secret tunnel running under the back alley and connecting the club to the funeral home the next street over.

So the owners had more than an exotic-sounding name in mind when they chose the "Shanghai Gaming Club." From its inception they knew how they'd deal with unruly patrons. Instead of resorting to deadly force in public view, they'd quietly escort the troublemakers to a back room, bind and gag them, and then "shanghai" them across the alleyway where Van's brother would ensure they'd never again see the light of day. It was a plan that would've done Machiavelli proud—bold, inventive, devious, and efficient. The owners had found a way to stay true to their promise that "you'll never be dying to leave our club." In addition, they would never have to rely on the unscrupulous ambulance drivers parked out front, who could sully the club's stellar reputation in the blink of an eye.

I know that if I had ever divulged any of this to my mother, father, Jesse, or Gramps, they'd have immediately asked, "Why do you stay on there knowing what you know now?" And I know I would've responded succinctly and honestly, "Because of the Delta blues." Years behind the curtain taught me that despite the artifice in everything else, Jacque did indeed have an uncanny knack for finding raw talent steeped in that authentic music of survival, which breaks your heart while lifting you up off your knees.

10

EVERY TIME JACQUE returned to the bar after introducing an act, he'd immediately try explaining away the giant beads of sweat erupting on his forehead. Favorite excuses in the repertoire included "Those damn thousand-watt lights" and "Just damn too little ventilation in that bandbox over there." But it didn't take us perceptive barflies long to discover Jacque, as so many strong-willed men before him, suffered inexplicably from a fear we mere mortals would deem trivial or commonplace. We'd all heard paradoxical tales of surgeons afraid of needles, aviators frightened of heights, submariners terrified of water, and actors uneasy around adoring fans. So we quickly realized our brave Jacque, who entertained patrons daily from behind his counter, trembled uncontrollably when he stepped out onto the Shanghai stage.

But his return this particular evening was different. While the heavy perspiration was still there glistening on his wide brow, his facial expressions were much more relaxed and his behavior more animated than usual. He significantly increased the number of off-color jokes in his standup routine and poured the white lightning like there'd be no tomorrow.

As his audience dwindled in the wee hours of a Saturday morning, Jacque drifted down to the end of the bar where I had taken up residence the past three months. "More seltzer before we hit the road?"

"Hit the road?"

"Yeah, you and me. I'm off at five, and then we're outta here! So pack a week's worth of clothes and grab some shut-eye. I'll meet ya out back at seven. I'll have Van's machine ready and rarin' to go."

"Where we headed?"

"South outta Memphis."

"Okay, but where we going south outta Memphis?"

"To Tutwiler and Moorhead, I suspect. That's before we really get down to doing business."

"And what'll we be doing, Jacque, when we 'really get down to doing business'?"

He smiled and answered, "Fishin'."

"Fishing?"

"Yeah. That's how I like to think of it. Fishin' for the next haul of musicians fillin' out the roster for this comin' fall and winter."

"You're taking me prospecting?" I asked. A jolt of electricity ran through my veins.

"Yep, gonna show ya some places where the trophies hang out."

The sun was just rising above a bank of coral cotton when we crossed over the line into Mississippi. We were headed southwest on Route 61 toward Clarksdale, where Jacque said we'd pick up Highway 49 twenty miles north of Tutwiler. He raised his right index finger off the steering wheel and pointed out through the windshield. "Think of 61 here as the backbone of Delta music. Ya can't go more than a mile without passin' a road headin' off to a hole-in-the-wall town or cotton plantation where the juke joints find ya—not the other way 'round."

"Juke joints?"

"Where we'll be doin' our fishin'. Better I explain when ya can see what I'm talkin' about."

"We going fishing in Tutwiler?"

"No, no fishin' there. Just some educatin'. Wanna show ya something there and in Moorhead. Things ya heard about. So when ya stand up in front of the crowd doin' the introductions, y'all know what you're talkin' about."

"Introductions?"

"Yeah, Van and I think you're ready to start helpin' out, puttin' your two cents in on the prospectin' and takin' over the theater introductions outright."

"So that explains it!" I blurted.

"Whatdaya mean?"

"Oh, nothing." I paused. "Well, okay then. It's just that you seemed to be in awfully good spirits last night."

He glanced over guiltily. "I have to admit it's a relief after all these years of introducin' the acts. Ya know ya get to a point when ya feel like it's time to move on."

I smiled knowingly while casting my sardonic reply in thick layers of empathy. "I know what ya mean, Jacque, but it's gotta be hard giving up something you've really enjoyed doing all these years."

"Yeah, but it's time to let ya spread your wings."

"You honestly think I'm ready?"

"Believe me, Todd, I wouldn't be bringin' ya down here fishin' and educatin' ya if Van and I didn't think ya could take it all on."

We were quiet then as I pondered my fate. What Jacque was suggesting had my stomach doing flips, and I was relieved he wasn't feeling talkative.

An hour later we rolled into Clarksdale, and Jacque began the "educating" in earnest. He glanced over and asked, "Remember our meeting with Mr. Handy backstage before he played the Shanghai?"

I nodded.

"He said he lived here in Clarksdale six or seven years directin' the Colored Knights of Pythias. Could be mistaken but I thought he said from '03 to—" Jacque stopped midsentence and thrust his arm in front of my face. "There it is! There!"

I looked through the windshield but didn't see anything remarkable. "What are you talking about? What is where?"

"Right there where I'm pointin'!" he exclaimed. "The shotgun house. That's gotta be it." We peered far to the left. "Sure enough, there's Issa . . . Issaquena Street," he said. "Yeah, that's it. That's where W. C. Handy lived while leadin' his band!"

"Such a small place for such a big man," I responded.

"Ya have to remember, Todd, he was not yet *the* 'Mr. Handy' the world came to know. He was just startin' out. Said he and the band would travel throughout the Delta and beyond, playin' concerts and dances for anyone would pay to listen. Mostly popular music, but he finally started addin' a few blues songs."

"Remember what caused him to do it?" I asked, recalling the story fondly.

Jacque nodded but motioned for me to carry on from there while he drove, repeating the tale Mr. Handy had spun for us backstage. I relished the opportunity. "Well, Mr. Handy said he and the Colored Knights were playing popular tunes for a white audience. And not long before taking a break, he called out for requests. A white fellow in the audience shouted, 'Play some of your own music!' But Mr. Handy and the Colored Knights picked up right where they'd left off, playing the popular tunes of the day. And when Mr. Handy announced a fifteen-minute intermission, the white audience began objecting loudly, calling out, 'Y'all ain't respectin' our request!'

"And then during the break, several in the audience encouraged some local Negroes working as stagehands to crack open their guitar cases and play them some of those Delta blues. When the guitarists started picking, the crowd erupted wildly, causing Mr. Handy to rethink the Colored Knights' repertoire."

"Ya tell it well, Todd. Ya got a gift for gab, that's for sure."

I smiled. "Thanks, Jacque. Appreciate it a lot coming from you."

"But that's not what really pushed Mr. Handy over the edge, so to speak, was it?" Jacque asked.

"No, but it wasn't long after that. . . ."

"Whew! Got so sidetracked with the story I almost missed our turn there onto Route 49."

"You want me to go on now?" I asked after we made our turn.

"Hold your thought there, Todd. We're gonna be stoppin' and gettin' out for a while."

Fifteen or twenty minutes later we passed a sign welcoming us to "Tutwiler, Population 1,391." We drove into the town center and parked at the depot. It had clouded over and begun raining. "Let's go," Jacque said.

"We gonna need an umbrella?" I asked.

"Nah. We're goin' in the station right there. We're not gonna melt in that little distance."

We jumped out, ran up the front steps, and entered the small waiting room, which was practically empty except for a young mother and son snickering at a disheveled octogenarian snoring to beat the band. I glanced over toward the counter. "We gonna need tickets?"

Jacque shook his head and pointed toward the rear exit. "No, we're just goin' outside for a few minutes and standin' under the overhang."

I didn't know what to make of it. I just followed him out the back door onto the wet platform glistening under the long row of goose-necked station lights. We huddled under the overhang and picked up the thread of our conversation, which had ended abruptly at the crossroads of Highway 61 and Route 49.

"So where were we?" Jacque asked.

"I was about to tell you what had really convinced Mr. Handy to take up playing the blues in public," I replied. "As I recall, it wasn't long after that memorable concert that Mr. Handy heard an old fella playing a guitar using a knife for a slide. Same kind of 'primitive' music he'd heard the stagehands playing just weeks earlier. But it was something about this lone fella's playing that moved Mr. Handy to act, to add a few of these Delta blues songs to the Colored Knights' concerts."

"Ya know where he heard the fella playin' the blues?" Jacque probed.

I thought hard trying to recall what Mr. Handy had said. I finally threw in the towel. "Sorry, Jacque. I just don't remember."

He laughed aloud. "I guess I should stop leadin' ya on. You weren't there when he finished tellin' the tale. Van had interrupted us and asked you to help her with somethin', I forget what."

I smiled, hiding my mild annoyance at having been led along. "Okay, so where'd Mr. Handy hear the old fella playing?"

He made a wide sweep with his arm and answered proudly, "Right here. Right here on this very platform while waitin' for an overdue train to Memphis." After staring silently at the empty memorial for several minutes, Jacque tapped me on the arm and said, "We gotta get goin'. We've got a lot more to see before it gets dark."

We raced back to the car through the rain and sped south now on State Road 3. There was nothing much to see in the winter. The highway was flat and lined on both sides with dormant cotton fields for as far as the eye could see. "Where we headed now?" I asked.

"Moorhead," he said.

"What are we gonna do when we get there?"

Playing his cards close to the vest, Jacque replied, "You'll see."

"Well, at least tell me how long it'll take us to get there."

"Little over an hour. So if you're tired, this would be a good time to catch a few winks."

I closed my eyes but continued speculating about our destination. Since I wasn't in the room for the tail end of Mr. Handy's story, I was truly flying blind. I wracked my brain but concluded I'd never heard of the place nor had a clue how Moorhead played into the Delta blues. I speculated it must have something to do with those juke joints Jacque was talking about earlier.

Jacque began whistling.

I did everything I could to keep from breaking into laughter. I knew he was offering up a clue and letting me know he knew I was playing possum. After several minutes of silence on my part, Jacque provided a second, more generous clue when he began singing some of the lyrics to the song:

> This is your Easy Rider struck this burg today
> On a southboun' rattler beside a Pullman car.
> Seen him here an' he was on the hog.

Without opening my eyes, I responded, "W. C. Handy, 1915, 'Yellow Dog Rag.'"

Jacque reverted to whistling without saying a word. It was as if I were learning a foreign language. I was parroting words without truly understanding their meaning. So I was now back to wracking my brain trying to connect the dots. What the hell does the "Yellow Dog Rag" have to do with Moorhead, Mississippi?

Well, I didn't have to wait too long to find out. Jacque

stopped the car and announced, "Moorhead, Mississippi. Everybody out!"

I sat up and rubbed my eyes, extending our silent cinema a little longer. I then looked around and discovered we were parked outside the Moorhead depot. The wind and rain had really picked up. "We're gonna need the umbrella this time?" I asked jokingly.

"Yeah, but it's because we're not goin' in the depot. We're headed up the tracks there a quarter of a mile."

The plot thickened. "We're walking the tracks there?"

He smiled and nodded. "I'll hop out and come around."

We squeezed under the umbrella; and as we trudged along, Jacque began whistling the "Yellow Dog Rag" again. Several minutes later he steered me over onto the ties between the rails and stopped. We were standing in the cold rain staring at the intersection between two railway lines.

I shook my head and smiled. "I don't know what I'm supposed to remember about this place, but I'll tell you now, I won't forget standing here with you in the middle of nowhere on this cold January Saturday afternoon. Now, since I wasn't in the room, what did Mr. Handy have to say about Moorhead in general and this spot in particular?"

"He just told me what the old fella was singin' on the platform up there in Tutwiler. Mr. Handy said he repeated a line three times while pickin' and slidin' up and down the guitar neck with his knife: 'Goin' where the Southern cross' the Dog.'"

"What does that have to do with this intersection here?" I asked.

"This rail here belonged to the Southern Railroad, and that one there belonged to the Yazoo & Mississippi Valley. Around here the Y&MV was called the Yazoo Delta or the Y.D., and those two letters were displayed prominently in yellow on the Yazoo locomotives and tenders. Some hobo then made the leap from Y.D. standin' for 'Yazoo Delta' to Y.D. meanin' the 'Yellow Dog.'"

"Ah, I get it now. The old fella was singing about going to Moorhead because that's where the Southern line crossed the Yazoo Delta or the Yellow Dog."

"Exactly!" Jacque exclaimed. "Mr. Handy said the music haunted him and convinced him to add some blues to the Colored Knights' playlist. And to honor the old fella's contribution to his later success, Mr. Handy wrote the 'Yellow Dog Rag.'"

Jacque now repeated the three lines he'd offered up earlier as a clue and then concluded the stanza:

> This is your Easy Rider struck this burg today
> On a southboun' rattler beside a Pullman car.
> Seen him here an' he was on the hog.
> All you Easy Riders got a stay away,
> So he had to vamp it but the hike ain't far.
> He's gone where the Southern cross' the
> Yellow Dog.

We stood silently in the rain staring at this second memorial until we heard the distant whistle of an inbound freight. We moved off the rails and started walking back down the rail bed toward the Moorhead depot. When the massive steamer rumbled into sight, we began waving heartily, and the engineer rewarded us with two forceful blasts as he passed by headed for the now legendary crossing just up the tracks.

After we were safely back in the car and warmed up a bit, I asked Jacque, "So where to now?"

"We're headed west through Holly Ridge back over to Route 61, and then we'll drive north to a place between Ruleville and Cleveland."

Jacque had done it again, giving me information without giving away the store. "What'll we be doing when we get to that place between . . . between . . ."

"Ruleville and Cleveland. Well, we're gonna finish your education and then get down to business. That's all I'm gonna say. So you've got a couple of hours now to catch some real sleep. And I mean it. You're probably gonna be up most of the night."

"Okay, okay, but you know the mysteries sure won't help me in getting to sleep."

11

DESPITE MY PROTESTATIONS I quickly succumbed to the rhythm of the road and began strolling along a cotton candy midway with Gramps, Jesse, and Mr. Handy. The bandleader was explaining how hearing the old man on the Tutwiler platform had inspired the "Yellow Dog," the "Memphis Blues," the "Beale Street Blues," and his most popular rag tune, the "St. Louis Blues." When he finished describing where he'd been in music, Mr. Handy said he was now going to let us in on where he was headed next. The three of us were enthralled. But the thrill didn't last long; every time Mr. Handy tried speaking, an annoying sideshow barker would drown him out shouting, "Time to go see Uncle Willy! . . . Time to go see Uncle Willy!"

I sat up and opened my eyes. The barker was staring at me and smiling the devil's grin. "Why were you doing that?" I exclaimed.

"Doin' what?" Jacque replied lightheartedly.

"Keeping Gramps, Jesse, and me from learning what Mr. Handy had up his sleeve?"

Jacque's grin dissolved into amused puzzlement. "What are ya talkin' about, boy? Mr. Handy? Up his sleeve? You awake, Todd?"

"Mr. Handy . . . ah . . . ah . . ." I rubbed my eyes for real this time and answered, "I . . . I must have been dreaming."

"Dreaming about Mr. Handy?"

"Yeah, and he was trying to tell us where he was going next with his music. But this sideshow barker kept breaking in screaming about seeing some Uncle Willy and— You know what, come to think of it, he looked a lot like you, Jacque!"

My friend muttered an aside, "Just like at the Shanghai: a sideshow barker."

I sensed it was time to move past the dream. I peered into the twilight at a small ramshackle building directly in front of me. It had a tin roof, boarded windows, and clapboard siding to the left of the front door and bat-and-board on the right. The elements had taken their toll over time. Most of the white paint had weathered away down to the bare wood. The frame had separated from its fieldstone foundation and shifted a good ten degrees to the right. The shack was no longer a solid rectangle but a parallelogram of instability.

"Where are we?" I asked.

"Uncle Willy's Juke Joint," Jacque replied with a sheepish grin. "I wanted ya to meet him and hear about our Hog Belly Circuit. Uncle Willy's been feedin' the Shanghai all kinds of musical acts for goin' on a decade now."

"Are all the juke joints like this one? Run-down and on the verge of collapsing on you?"

"Pretty much, yeah. What ya see here is about what ya get every place else: dilapidated barns, sheds, and shacks handed down to sharecroppers for blowin' off steam after escapin' the white-hot hell of the cotton fields. If these poor folk don't find heaven in a Sunday church, they look for it here in these gritty sanctuaries at the edge of plantations in the middle of nowhere. . . . And I'll tell ya straight up: this ain't the kind of place ya wanna haul your mother, sister, or wife to. Downright threatenin' at times. Hard drinkin', gamblin', womanizin', fisticuffs, and even a killin' now and then to spice things up. When these souls get lit up with the likes of Uncle Willy's downhome lightnin', it can go one of two ways—murder and mayhem or displays of some of the finest dancin', singin', and playin' this side of Beale Street. Solo, ring, and couples dancin' to ragtime, boogie-woogie, barrel house and the slow drag tunes. All of this, mind ya, for the lettin' off of steam. Like the choir shoutin' hosannas before the preacher man spins a yarn. So after the juke stompin's raised ya up to a fever pitch, the bluesman climbs the pulpit and sets ya straight with sermons of sufferin' and hope. Feelin's cut fresh in the fields and laid bare before ya now in these tiny makeshift chapels of the blues."

"You said you wanted me to know something about a 'Hog Belly Circuit.' What's that all about?"

"For most of the folks doin' the plowin', jukes are just brief refuges from the scorchin' fields; but for the talented few, these shacks hold the keys to the kingdom, offerin' these young musicians one-way tickets off the plantation and out of town. A bunch of proprietors, including Van, have formed a network supportin' these young fellas, with clubs runnin' up and down the Mississippi from New Orleans to Saint Louis. Here's how it works: Several of us scout the plantations and the jukes durin' the winter and arrange trips for the best of 'em to perform at our sites. After an engagement, the owner arranges for the young men to be driven to a rendezvous spot halfway between that club and the next stop on the circuit. Most of 'em travel south to north playin' one club after another. When they reach the place farthest north, they repeat the journey in reverse. So each club sees each act twice a year. And if these kids are really good, performin' well under pressure, well, it's not long 'til they take wing and fly off on their own to the four corners of the earth. And it feels real good when you see one of your own flyin' the coop. Real good, I wanna tell ya. Everybody's a winner there."

Jacque pulled out his pocket watch and checked the time. "It's gettin' late. Too bad we'll have to make this a quick visit today. The Dockery Farms shindig starts around eight o'clock, and all the new acts will be headin' up the program. Don't want to miss 'em. I'm sure we'll find a gem in there."

We climbed the rickety steps to the front entrance and entered a tight space with a low ceiling draped in blue fabric. The air was dusty and reeked of alcohol and cigarette smoke. The room was empty except for a half dozen small round tables and a dozen or so mismatched chairs lining the graffitied walls stained to chest height with sweat and body oils. Jacque walked to the back of the room, stepped up on the tiny stage, and opened a door leading to an anteroom. He shouted, "Uncle Willy! Uncle Willy! Ya around here anywhere?" Silence. Jacque shrugged. "Can't imagine him leavin' without lockin' up. Let's check around back."

As we moved toward the exit, Uncle Willy popped his head around the corner. "Is that you, Jacquie?"

Jacque rushed to the door and embraced the old man. "Good to see ya, Unc. I was about to send a party out lookin' for ya."

He winked and smiled from ear to ear. "I was just out back in the woods there samplin' the latest batch of refreshments. Customers demand the best, ya know. It's a lotta hard work, but somebody's gotta do it."

Jacque turned toward me. "Unc, this here's my new assistant, Todd. And, Todd, this here's Uncle Willy."

I extended my hand. "Nice to meet you, sir. Expecting a big crowd here tonight?"

"No, son, she'll be tighter than a tick. Everybody's headed over to the Dockery for the annual Gatherin'," Uncle Willy replied.

"The Gatherin'?"

"Yep. Half of Sunflower County will be showin' up to hear the music and see the stompin'." Uncle Willy looked over at Jacque. "I 'spect you're gonna be takin' this young man here over for the festivities. Lots of old-timers comin' back to play. I hear Henry Sloan, Charley Patton, Willie Brown, and Tommy Johnson are comin' back. Be one of the best shows ever."

Jacque nodded and said, "Absolutely. We're headed over there for sure. I guess it's about time to be closin' up shop, Unc. Would ya like a ride over with Todd and me?"

"Love to, but already caught a ride with the Neales. But I'll see ya over there. I wanna tell ya about some of the new acts been comin' through. Seems like these boys are gettin' stronger every year."

"We'll see ya over there then, Unc, and get all caught up."

"Nice meetin' ya, Todd."

"Same here, sir."

We exited the juke and raced down the steps to the car, doing our best to keep dry. As we drove over to the "Gatherin'," Jacque filled me in on the plantation. "Don't want ya to be surprised. You're gonna see something quite different than what ya just saw at Uncle Willy's place. Buildings and grounds at the Dockery are clean and kept up. We'll be spendin' the night in one of the boardinghouses there. You'll see. Will Dockery's always treated his workers well. Heard he got some schoolin'. University of Mississippi. Bought the land some thirty years ago for timber but soon discovered the soil was rich—perfect for growin' cotton. So he cleared the land, got into sharecroppin'. I hear there's now well over two thousand livin' on the land. Folks traveled to the Dockery from all over the South after hearin' of the fine treatment the plantation offered. Mr. Dockery built his own little town right here. Has its own currency for buyin' anything ya need. You'll see. There's a general store for furniture, dry goods, and food, a host of churches, an elementary school, a post office, telegraph office, blacksmith, drugstore, doctors, picnic grounds, decent livin' quarters, and even has its own depot and rail line connectin' to the Yellow Dog at Rosedale. They call the local train the Pea Vine because it runs all over the place before takin' root there at the Rosedale terminal. I hear Mr. Dockery's not much into music, but he provides the venue and some fine victuals for this annual Gatherin'." We wended our way over the rough roads of Moorhead until finally taking a right onto a dirt patch. "Ah, here we are now! Just in time. Ya see, it's only a stone's throw from Uncle Willy's. We'll park the car for the night, drop our bags off at the boardinghouse, and then get right on over to the big barn for some pulled pork barbecue and the show."

I looked down and didn't respond. A wave of nostalgia had rushed over me. Jacque's description of Will Dockery's compassion and his aim to provide his sharecroppers with decent living conditions reminded me of my father's intentions and the plantation community he'd built for his workers east of Warfield—the place I'd called home before we pulled up stakes and moved into the governor's mansion in Nashville.

"You okay, Todd?" Jacque asked. "You look mighty pale."

"Yeah, I'm okay."

"Somethin' troublin' you?"

"No, not really. But when you described Mr. Dockery and his plantation, I thought of a family back home that had treated their sharecroppers sympathetically just as Mr. Dockery had done here. That's all. Nothing more." I flashed a brief smile and said, "Come on now. Let's dump our bags, grab some barbecue, and settle in the barn for the opening acts."

Clutching plates piled high with succulent pork and steamed rice, we weaved our way through the throng seated on the sawdust floor and found space against the wall to the right of the stage. I had barely taken two bites when one of the local juke owners glided out onto the makeshift platform and announced that year's curtain raiser would be the popular Beale Street jug band, Cannon's Jug Stompers, featuring Noah Lewis on harmonica, Ashley Thompson on guitar, and Gus

Cannon playing everything else, including trombone, fiddle, piano, and, of course, the requisite jug.

Jacque leaned over and whispered, "Good thinkin' there. Startin' off with a damn good band before easin' into the whippersnappers." But contrary to all expectations, every one of the youngsters did themselves proud. The fiddler who followed the Stompers could easily make the cut for the next Hog Belly Circuit. And each successive amateur raised the ante even higher. The fiddler was outshone by the banjoist who was outdone by the guitarist who was topped by the harmonica wizard. Jacque was impressed. "Ya know, if I had the balls, we'd book that guitarist right now. What's his name?"

"Believe they said it was, ah, Son House."

"Yeah, and that kid harmonica player too. What's his name?"

"Believe they said it was, ah . . . ah . . . Spencer. Robert Spencer.'"

Jacque whipped out a notebook and wrote the names down. "We'll find 'em and sign 'em before leavin' the Dockery. By God, it's time now to risk it. Move some of these young Delta blues acts into the Shanghai."

After this respectable showing by all the young musicians, it was time for the main event, performances by established Delta bluesmen who'd lived and worked on the plantation and were now making a living playing clubs as far away as New York and Chicago. First up was the aging Henry Sloan, who performed "I'm Goin' Home" and "Screamin' and Hollerin' the Blues." All the while Sloan was playing, Jacque was elbowing me in the ribs and passing along jaw-dropping tidbits like, "You're lookin' at the real father of the blues there. He taught the blues to the next two headliners you'll see tonight, Charlie Patton and Tommy Johnson. Taught 'em at the Dockery"; and the most astounding assertion of all, "Ya know that old fellow that Handy heard pickin' on the Tutwiler platform? Well, there he is in the flesh and blood, playin' and singin' the blues for ya."

Tommy Johnson was the next man up. He sang his "Big Fat Mama Blues," "Alcohol and Jake Blues," and the "Canned Heat Blues." Throughout Johnson's performance, Jacque looked away stoically while tapping his hand to the music on his knee. This time he didn't elbow me or say a word until the hollering and applause began dying down and Johnson finally left the stage. Only then did Jacque lean over and whisper, "Rumor has it, sad to say, those songs there reflect his dangerous way of livin'—squeezin' the sterno and the women."

The closing act, the pièce de résistance, was the foremost bluesman of the day, Charley Patton, singing and picking with his friend Willie Brown, who was playing backup on guitar. They opened with what's become Patton's rousing signature song, "The Pony Blues":

> "Hello central, the matter with your line?"
> "Hello central, matter, Lord, with your line?"
> "Come a storm last night an' tore the wire down."

They followed "The Pony" with an early composition, "Down the Dirt Road Blues," and a favorite around the Dockery, the

"Pea Vine Blues," which set Jacque's elbow into action again.

> I cried last night an' I, I ain't gonna cry anymore
> 'Cause the good book tells
> Us you've got to reap just what you sow.
> I think I heard the Pea Vine when it blowed
> I think I heard the Pea Vine when it blowed
> She blowed just like she wasn't gonna blow
> no more.

And for their encore, Patton and Brown chose another local favorite, "The Green River Blues," which had Jacque beaming from ear to ear throughout the song.

> I see a river rollin' like a log
> I wade up Green River, rollin' like a log
> I wade up Green River, Lord, rollin' like a log
> Think I heard the Marion whistle blow
> I dreamed I heard the Marion whistle blow,
> And it blew just like my baby gettin' on board.
> I'm goin' where the Southern cross the Dog.

After bedding down at the Dockery for two nights, we headed north on Highway 61; and over the next few days, we paid visits to a number of juke owners during their quiet times from Monday morning through Friday afternoon. As we pulled up to the first stop, Jacque said, "We're crossin' the line now from educatin' to runnin' the business. Ya watch and listen carefully. There'll be a lot of bullshittin' and backslappin' goin' on.

Ya know, 'greasin' the skids.' But I'm lookin' for an honest assessment from 'em about new acts showin' up at their door-step. And after a few new names are dropped, we'll give 'em a hearty hug and move on to the next juke. Ya understand?"

"So far so good," I replied.

"So we'll be performin' the same act all week. Bullshit and collect names, bullshit and gather more names. Sometimes I might have twenty or so names by the end of the week."

"But how do you sort them all out?" I asked. "I mean, from top to bottom."

Jacque grinned teasingly and said, "Ah, a trade secret." He paused until he sensed he'd elicited a negative response from me and then carried on. "Just kiddin' ya, Todd. Ya have to know the tricks of the trade, and this one's pretty easy. Ya see, all ya have to do is list 'em by the number of times a young musician's name has been mentioned by the various juke owners. When ya hear a name repeated over and over, ya can make a pretty safe bet that you're lookin' at a successful candidate for the Hog Belly Circuit."

And so it went. After a solid week of prospecting, we rolled back into Clarksdale on Friday evening and whiled away the night doing some line dancing the locals called the Hully Gully. The next morning after breakfast, we drove back to the intersection of Highways 61 and 49 where a week be-fore we'd turned south heading for Tutwiler and Moorhead. Jacque parked the car, opened his door, and said, "Hop on out and follow me."

Despite knowing there was a snowball's chance in hell I'd get a straight answer, I played along anyway asking the obligatory question. "Where are we headed this time?"

The sphinx laughed aloud and responded, "Visitin' another shrine."

When we reached the junction, Jacque turned and said, "Delta folk say there are three ways to become a great blues musician: you're born with it or you practice day in and day out for years or ya go to the crossroads and sell your soul to the devil. Well, here ya are, standin' at the very spot they're talkin' about. The crossroads of Highways 61 and 49."

"You heard any tales of someone selling out?" I asked.

"Sure have, and rumors swirl about one fella in particular."

"Who's that?"

"Ya saw him playin' last weekend at the Dockery."

"Henry Sloan?"

"Nah. Another guess."

"Charley Patton?"

"No. It was Tommy Johnson. Story goes that folks heard him confessin' after a few shots of lightning, 'If ya wanna make songs for yourself, ya grab your guitar and go to them crossroads. Be certain of gettin' there a little 'fore midnight. Take a seat and start a'playin'. Won't be long, some tall fella will come up on ya from behind. Won't say a lick. Will just take your six-string, tune it, play a piece or two, and then give her back to ya. From then on, ya can play anything ya want.'"

"Makes you wonder after seeing him pulling off all those tricks, playing his guitar between his legs and behind his neck, twirling it in the air and not missing a beat."

"Yeah, it's hard arguin' with what your lyin' eyes are seein'. But ya can ask him for yourself when ya visit with him."

"Whatdaya mean, Jacque?"

"I finally bit the bullet. While you were off sparkin' those young ladies at the Dockery, I managed to get Johnson signed to play the Shanghai this April. Ya know, after most of the whippersnappers have gone back home for the plantin'."

"Ain't no way!"

"Sure did. And that's not all. I got Patton and Brown lined up to play the place too!"

"Okay, Jacque. How'd you manage to pull it off?"

"Explained to 'em that Beale Street so far really knows only one kind of blues, Handy's ragtime blues, or as some call it, the Memphis blues. Most folks there have never heard the Delta blues. Told 'em they'd be plowin' new ground. And they really warmed to the notion of playin' Memphis after hearin' that."

"Just imagine, the fellas we saw playing to thousands just last Saturday night will be playing our little place this spring! ...You did mighty good with the prospecting, Jacque."

"And that's not all. We've got that young guitarist and harmonica player lined up too. I keep forgettin' their names."

"Son House and Robert Spencer?"

"Yeah. Got both of 'em signed for the Hog Belly Circuit. Playin' the Shanghai together the middle of next month on their way up north."

"Van's gonna really be happy and proud of you."

Jacque smiled and put his arm around my shoulder. "And I'll be happy too, seein' ya up there on stage for a change, introducin' the finest bluesmen the Delta has to offer."

12

I'VE GOT TO give Jacque credit. He didn't immediately throw me to the wolves. Despite the obvious stage fright, he continued making the introductions until the first of the Delta blues acts was scheduled to play the Shanghai. Up until then he had had me "shadowing" him as he prepared his introductions—from interviewing the artists and outlining his notes to rehearsing before a large mirror and finally delivering his remarks.

After watching him prepare several of the introductions from start to finish, I privately concluded Jacque's difficulties lay not so much in his preparation but in the delivery itself. He allowed his fear of live audiences to erode his confidence and disrupt his train of thought. I quickly realized while I could adopt his rigorous method of preparation, I'd have to rely solely on my own instincts to deliver persuasive and entertaining presentations before the main event.

Six weeks to the day after returning from Clarksdale, I stood outside the Shanghai waiting for the guitarist Son House and his young protégé and harmonica wizard, Robert Spencer, to drive up to the front entrance. Since they'd be the first of the Delta blues acts performing, I was solely in charge of every aspect of their visit, from greeting them and escorting them to the green room to conducting interviews for their introductions and guiding them to the stage just before they'd be going on.

I didn't really have to worry about their showing up. The guitarist had telephoned earlier that morning to explain they'd arrived in town the night before and had slept over at the home of one of the harmonica player's Memphis relatives. And right on schedule a taxi I'd arranged for them turned onto Beale Street and rolled to a stop in front of the club. A tall, handsome fellow in his midtwenties stepped out of the cab carrying a suitcase in one hand and a guitar in the other. He had dark eyes and wavy black hair. He flashed a warm, engaging smile and extended his hand. "Todd Taylor?"

"Speaking." I glanced down at his guitar and said, "And if you're carrying a six-string, you must be Son House."

"In the flesh," he replied as he looked back toward the taxi. "And this here's Robert Spencer." A small, frail, stoop-shoul-dered boy perhaps sixteen stepped out from behind the gui-tarist and mumbled, "Nice to meet ya, Mr. Taylor." He was wearing the same straw fedora he'd worn while performing at the Dockery's Gatherin' six weeks earlier. He had the wide brim breaking down to the left over a lazy eye, which made it appear smaller than his right.

After ushering the young men to the green room and serving up two steaming plates of Jacque's South Carolina–style "New Orleans jambalaya," I got right down to business. "Y'all will be going on tonight a little past nine o'clock. I'll drop by the green room here, pick you up about quarter 'til the hour, and get you settled in backstage. I'll be making the introductions, but I wanna warn you now, they're gonna be a little longer than you're used to. You see, I have to do some educating about your style of the blues. Folk around here are used to popular tunes and rags written by our own Mr. Handy. And another thing. I wanna tell them a lot about y'all too. I want them to say to themselves, you know, these fellas' hopes and troubles are a lot like mine. It'll help them bond to you and to your style of playing." I smiled and continued half teasingly, "So if I get this just about right, we won't have folks walking out or throwing things up on the stage at you."

The musicians were game and agreed to answer my questions. Once I'd finished interviewing Son House, I showed him to an adjoining bedroom where he could relax while I was speaking with Robert. When I returned to the green room to conduct the second interview, I found the young musician sitting on the edge of the sofa strumming away on my Gibson six-string. A fleeting thought raced through my mind that he was far more accomplished on the harmonica than he was on the guitar.

As soon as he saw me, he stopped playing and looked down, embarrassed. "I'm sorry," he said. "I . . . I just couldn't help pickin' it up and playin'. I hope you're not mad."

I smiled to dispel any notion I was the least bit upset. "Why should I be angry with you for trying out my Gibson? When I see a nice six- or twelve-string lying around, I have the same urge to pick her up and see how she sounds."

"Well, you're not like Son House then."

"How's that?" I asked.

"He doesn't understand how much I wanna learn to play

like him. He gets cross with me when I try playin' his guitar whilst he's outside takin' a break."

"What's he say to you?"

"He comes a runnin' back into the hall grittin' his teeth and under his breath he says to me, 'Such a racket I never heard! Ya couldn't hold a tune in a bucket! Stop it now, ya hear? Stop that noisin' the people. You're gonna drive 'em crazy!' Then he'd come over and snatch his guitar away from me. He just doesn't know how much I wanna play like him. I know I could, if he'd just let me practice."

He lowered his head fighting back tears. I instinctively put my hand on his shoulder and reflected on the hurt and hopeful determination I'd felt in his words. I realized he and I shared a similar challenge and the same lofty dreams. I lifted his chin and gazed into his eyes. "Don't you ever give up on mastering the six-string, you hear? Don't you give up. And just so you know, whenever you're passing through here, you're free to play my Gibson anytime you like. You don't have to ask. Just pick her up and play. Now take a few deep breaths and settle down. I need to ask you a few questions so I can let the folks this evening know the kind of fine young fella they've got playing for them." Talking to young Robert that day, I never would have guessed how far he would go with his guitar.

The time had finally come for my stage debut. I dropped by the green room to pick up my young bluesmen and found Son House hard at work adding another layer of tape to the back of his guitar. He looked up and explained, "I've had her from the beginnin'. Bought her for a buck and a half from Frank Hopkins. She only had five strings and a big hole in the back. I guess ya get what ya pay for."

"She has served you well. How'd you get her into playing condition?"

"Oh, that's a story in itself. I took her with me when I went to see Willie Wilson. Told him I wanted to learn to play the way he did. Well, he took one look at my guitar, shook his head, and said, 'Boy, yer missin' a string and she's got a real big hole to boot. I'll see what I can do about patchin' her up, but no promises now.' So he took her into the next room, added a string, and sealed the hole up with a lot of tape as best he could. I've been playin' her like that ever since. I think she sounds fair to middlin' but every now and then, ya see, my sweat causes the tape to curl up. So I just get to work addin' a few more layers to hold the rest of the old tape down."

I smiled but didn't let on what I was thinking. If I hadn't heard these two playing at the Dockery, I'd be scared to death right about then. There I was walking out on the stage and introducing two "whippersnappers," as Jacque called them, a shy, fragile harmonica player who'd rather be strumming a guitar and a preacher turned musician playing a guitar with a hole in the back of it almost the size of my head.

But I had to muster my confidence. I was about to make my own first solo appearance. After getting my charges settled backstage, I took my position at the left edge of the proscenium holding my six-string thunderwood in one hand and a tall bar stool in the other. I took several deep breaths, glanced back at the stage manager, and signaled I was all set.

As the curtains swung open, I moved toward center stage and positioned the bar stool over the chalk marks I'd drawn earlier in the day. There was a polite smattering of applause as I hopped up on the stool and began tuning my guitar. Unlike poor Jacque, my apprehension quickly faded. I felt at home there, thriving in the warmth of the lone spotlight piercing the darkness. I knew then what I had suspected all along: that was where I was born to be.

I quietly began picking a Memphis favorite, Handy's "Yellow Dog Rag." When the cheering died down, I eased into the introductions.

"Good evening, ladies and gentlemen. Welcome to the Shanghai. Well, it's been almost twenty-five years to the day now since our beloved Mr. Handy dozed on the railway platform in Tutwiler, Mississippi, while waiting for a delayed train to Memphis. Hearing him describe it, he said, 'A lean, loose-jointed Negro had commenced plunking a guitar beside me while I slept. His clothes were rags; his feet peeped out of his shoes. His face had on it some of the sadness of the ages. As he played, he pressed a knife on the strings of a guitar in a manner popularized by Hawaiian guitarists who used steel bars. The effect was unforgettable. His song, too, struck me instantly. "Goin' where the Southern cross' the Dog." The singer repeated the line three times, accompanying himself on the guitar with the weirdest music I ever heard. And the tune stayed in my mind.'

"Now, ladies and gentlemen, I wanna tell you it took a little bit of deciphering, but y'all are gonna be the first to know that the lean-jointed fella Mr. Handy heard playing on the platform that day was none other than Henry Sloan, the father of what folk south of here call the 'Delta blues.' And you can bet your firstborn, Mr. Sloan was headed for Moorhead, Mississippi, where the Southern cross' the Dog. Y'all say, 'Beg yer pardon. Where the Southern cross' the Dog?' And I reply, 'Yeah, there's a junction there near this Moorhead where the Southern rails cross the Yazoo Delta tracks.' Then y'all ask, 'But how does this "Dog" come into play?' And I answer, 'When you consider the letters "Y" and "D" at the front end of Yazoo Delta, your mind can make the easy jump from there to the letters "Y" and "D" on the front end of Yellow Dog.'"

When the audience grasped the play on words from Yazoo Delta to Yellow Dog, they began laughing and murmuring among themselves. And I remember thinking how easy this public speaking was compared to mastering the Delta blues.

As I continued softly picking the "Yellow Dog Rag," I explained the importance of the composer's chance encounter with Mr. Sloan that evening way back in '03. "Mr. Handy said, 'The tune stayed in my mind.' And we know that's true because it kept on percolating there for some nine years before he blessed us with his new sounds and tempos. First, penning the 'Memphis Blues,' next the 'Saint Louis Blues,' then the 'Yellow Dog,' and finally the 'Beale Street Blues.' And these twelve-bar hits one after another inspired further innovation—changes to our way of dancing with the introduction of the one-step, the fox trot, and the tango.

"Now I collectively refer to these popular tunes with which we are all familiar. I like to call 'em the Memphis-style blues, or simply the Memphis blues. But what we'll be frying here this evening is a second kettle of fish, another style of playing quite different from the first. I like to call this style the Delta-style Blues, or simply the Delta blues."

At this point in my introductions, I transitioned from Mr. Handy's "Yellow Dog Rag" in the Memphis style to Sylvester Weaver's "Guitar Blues" in the Delta style. I began picking with my right hand and sliding my knife up and down the fret with the other just as Mr. Sloan had done that day on the Tutwiler platform.

"Ya hear the difference there? . . .Ya see, by flattening my E string, I get those 'blue' or 'worried' notes pitched just a tad lower than normal. Gives ya something of a feeling of agitation or disquiet. You're hearing about the fella's troubles, which are giving him the blues. Did his wife or lover leave him? Did a friend up and die? Did the boss man beat him? Not too hard putting yourselves in the fella's shoes, is it? No, because we've all been down that road. Been down on our luck. Felt betrayed and suffered the wrath of others. Now you say, 'Whoa! Did I come here to listen to all this suffering and then leave here as sad as can be?'"

Some members of the audience laughed uneasily and began whispering among themselves. I joined their laughter and shook my head in an exaggerated fashion. "But hold on there. I'm here to tell you right now the opposite's gonna happen. You can take it to the bank. Y'all are going to be stepping out of here feeling mighty good about yourselves because these Delta blues are all about overcoming your hard luck and then having the strength to carry on. Now what can be any more uplifting than that?"

After the applause died down, I carried on to the conclusion. "And come to think of it, I don't believe there are two better examples of folks overcoming their circumstances and finding their way than these two young men we have playing for you tonight. Our guitarist this evening, Mr. Son House, tells me he's seen his share of rambling about and says he's tried every job imaginable—working on a Mississippi tugboat, a Kentucky railroad, a trolley line right here in Memphis, a horse ranch in Louisiana, and even a steel mill in East Saint Louis. And when none of it worked out, he fell back on the hard life of a sharecropper.

"Mr. House says while working an alfalfa field in his early twenties, something came over him and caused him to fall to his knees and begin praying. He says it wasn't long after getting religion 'til he was standing up in the pulpit and doing the preaching. And everything was all right for a spell. But he says it was mighty hard staying on the straight and narrow."

Identifying with his plight the audience burst into laughter. I nodded and looked heavenward wistfully. "Yes, I think we can all agree with Mr. House on that one! Now he tells me later on he got in with some bad company, and they encouraged him to take a little nip. He refused at first but finally gave in. And y'all know how that works. A little nip leads to quite a few big ones!"

The audience cheered. I stopped strumming and raised my hands to quiet the crowd. When order was restored, I resumed picking the "Guitar Blues" and finished his story, "And Mr. House says he knew then he had a real dilemma. The hard labor had helped push him into preaching, and now the corn liquor was pushing him right back out of the cloth again. How could he continue telling folk to change their ways while he was running off and doing the same thing he was condemning them for each and every Sunday?

"But lucky for him and for all of us, he didn't have to wait long for an answer. He tells me while out strolling one night, he passed a house party where a host of folk were collected around an old fella picking his guitar and sliding a small medicine bottle up and down the fret. And it was this wail of glass on steel that stopped him in his tracks. Shook him to his core. He says he knew immediately he had found his way. Yes, sir, the devil's music had gripped him! So you can kind of think of Mr. House as doing Saint Paul one better because Mr. House took a round-trip to and fro on his road to Damascus!"

When the applause and laughter died down, I transitioned to another Delta blues tune, Charlie Patton's "I'm Goin' Home." I quietly cleared my throat and launched into the second introduction. "And, ladies and gentlemen, that brings us to our last but certainly not our least performer this evening, the young harmonica wizard Robert Spencer, who'll be accompanying Mr. House on all the tunes. Unlike Mr. House, the preacher man, young Robert is short on words and long on questions when it comes to his past. He says he was born in Hazlehurst, Mississippi, a stone's throw south of Jackson, on May 8, 1911. Or was it 1912? Or perhaps even 1910? . . . Says his mama's name is Dobbs. Julia Dobbs. And his papa's name is Noah Johnson. He tells me his mama's husband, a Charles Dobbs, escaped a lynching and relocated to Memphis several years before Robert was born. He says a couple years after his birth, his mama sent him and some of his ten brothers and sisters up here to Memphis to live with her husband, Mr. Dobbs, who had changed his name to Spencer to avoid being tracked by the Hazlehurst lynchers."

I paused and took a deep breath to lightheartedly convey the difficulty in relating the murky tale Robert had passed along during our earlier interview in the green room. When the laughter faded, I continued, "Let's see now. Robert tells me when he was either seven, eight, or nine, he rejoined his mama in the Mississippi Delta around Robinsonville, where he started playing his first instruments, the harmonica and a handmade diddley bow, consisting of wires strung between nails he'd driven into the side of a barn. But sad to say, Robert tells me his mama's new husband, a Mr. Willis, didn't take too kindly to him, so when Robert got a bit older, he just packed up and left. And from then on until now, home has been wherever he's laid his head and rested in the blues." I picked up the bar stool and left the stage knowing the audience was well primed. Confident that many a Delta blues fan would be made that night.

13

AT AN EARLY age we learn when someone says, "I'm doing this for your own good," the "this" is going to inflict some pain. And it wasn't any different this time, when Jacque moved down toward my customary end of the bar after closing up shop for the night. He looked down while tapping his fingers nervously on the counter. "Would ya like a little bit of Jack we've got squirreled away?"

"I'm sure it couldn't hurt," I replied. "Might even help me with my writing. . . . I don't know what it's gonna take to pen a winner. First I thought it'd be the 'Pineapple Special' in '25; then I was sure it'd be the 'Roller Mill Rag' the next year; and finally, I'd have bet the farm on the 'Hollow Rock Blues' this past September. But nothing much ever came of any of them. It just doesn't make any sense."

Jacque fetched the whiskey and poured a generous amount in two tumblers. We raised and clinked our glasses. "To the future," Jacque toasted.

"To the future," I echoed and then sampled the prized stash. I savored the smooth fire flowing down through my chest. "Why you think nothing's happening, Jacque? No one's playing my songs, and there aren't any invitations to solo anywhere even after playing my fingers day in and day out down to the bone. Just getting the courtesy offers to join the jug bands here playing backup. It's frustrating and downright discouraging having to get up there on stage and introduce fellas so many years younger."

Jacque took several sips of his whiskey and then downed the rest. "I really don't know how to say this. I guess there's no good way to say it. You told me your first day here your dream was to write and play the blues. Well, I'm gonna tell ya this for your own good. Please understand I don't mean any harm. As for your writing, you've got the form, the words, and the ideas for the blues. And as for your playing, you've got the picking and the sliding down just right too."

I jumped in impatiently, "So what the hell's wrong then? I don't understand how I'm doing everything right and still nothing's happening!"

Jacque paused to collect his thoughts. "Maybe I can explain it by usin' one of Van's old stories. She says a lot of folk in Louisiana favor gumbo. She says there's well nigh a thousand recipes with different combinations of the standard ingredients, includin' the shrimp, chicken, sausage, tomatoes, okra, bell pepper, and the like. She says you can put all this together but ya still ain't got gumbo 'til ya add the roux."

"The roux?"

"Yeah, the thickener. A mixture of flour and bacon drippin's."

"What are you driving at?"

"It's one of Van's old Creole expressions. She uses it in describing the girls she hires. Ya see, they might have all the 'wares,' so to speak, but they might still be missin' the roux.

Or as Van sometimes says, the '*Je ne sais quoi.*'"

"Roux? *Je ne sais quoi?* For God's sakes, Jacque, speak English!"

"In other words, you've mastered the technique, but it overwhelms the feelings. Should be the other way around. Ya see, the bluesmen who'll be playin' here have perfect technique, but it doesn't get in the way of the feelin's. The outstandin' precision in their singin' and fingerin' is buried in the heartbreak and sufferin' they're expressin'. And I honestly don't know where that knack comes from either. Is it from the swelterin' fields they've worked in? Or is it from somethin' they were born with? Somethin' coursin' through their veins with which you and I are unfamiliar."

I downed the rest of my whiskey. "So in a roundabout way you're saying this roux I'm missing will keep me from ever playing and writing on their level?"

"Yeah, I guess that's what I'm tryin' to say. I'm sorry. I . . . I didn't mean for our conversation to get off the tracks like this. My intention was to compliment ya and . . . make a suggestion."

"A suggestion on how to improve my playing and writing?"

"No, no. Nothin' like that."

"A suggestion to do what then?" I blurted.

"Ya may not like this, but . . . but hear me out. Please. I wanted to make a suggestion to use your skills in . . . in another line of work."

"Give up the blues for something else?" I was incredulous.

"Please, Todd. Hear me out. You've got a talent the likes of which I've never seen. When you walk out on the stage

135

and start tellin' your stories, ya have 'em all eatin' out of your hand from the very beginnin'. Ya see? You've got the roux, but it's for speakin'. I told ya long ago, you've got a gift for gab. And my only wish is to see ya use your talent to your own good. Ya could make a fortune."

I laughed. "A fortune doing what? I'm all ears."

"Sellin'."

"Selling? Selling what?"

"Securities."

"Stocks and bonds?"

"Yes! Fortunes are bein' made every hour. The market's on fire! Ya see how the fellas are throwin' their money around in here on the booze, the gamblin', and the babes. And where do ya think all that money's comin' from? Their day jobs? Hell no! It's comin' from the market! And whose gettin' richest of all? The brokers. They're makin' fortunes hand over fist. Doesn't matter whether you're buyin' or sellin'. They're gettin' paid either way! And with your gift for gab, you'd be a natural. You've got the roux!"

"Hold on, Jacque. You've gotta be kidding me. I don't know the first thing about securities, let alone anything about selling them."

"But T.J. does."

"T.J.?"

"Yeah. T. J. Cavanaugh. You'd know him if ya saw him. He drops in once or twice a week prospectin' for clients. Always wearin' a plaid vest with a thick keychain, gold tooth top front, laughs real loud, big round red face. Ya can see he's never missed a meal."

"But, Jacque, I'm telling ya I don't know the first thing about his business. And besides, maybe I wouldn't like it. I don't think it could ever be as exciting as being up there on the stage performing for a lot of people. T.J.'s doing one-on-one selling. What kinda fun is that?"

"Look, I'm just tryin' to help. I'd hate to see ya stuck doin' what I'm doin' for the rest of your life. Ya could be doin' so much more. And as far as not knowin' anything about brokerage, T.J.'s told me a number of times to be on the lookout for natural salesmen. He says he'd rather have a natural than a financial wizard who can't sell his way out of a paper bag. Says he can teach stocks and bonds, but he can't teach sellin'. Ya either have it or ya don't."

"I don't know, Jacque. I need to think about it. It's a big step giving up what I've dreamed of doing to sell securities to one person at a time. And what if it doesn't work out? Like T.J. and I don't hit it off or I can't get the hang of it."

"No skin off your nose in that case, Todd. The way I see this workin', ya meet with T.J. and talk it over. If ya decide to get on board, ya can still keep doin' the introductions here on weekends and any other night we have a blues act in town. And ya can even go recruitin' with me, if ya can find the time off from sellin'. But if worst comes to worst and it doesn't work out, just know you'll always have a job here. Van's already said as much."

"She knows what you're up to?"

"Yeah, she agrees. And you have her blessin' to speak with T.J. She thinks it's best all 'round."

"Well, that means a lot. But I still need to think about it."

"Makes sense. I'd do the same, if I were in your shoes. You won't get any more pressure from me."

And Jacque was good to his word. A week passed without any further discussion of stocks, bonds, or T.J. In fact, most of our conversations focused on firming up travel plans for acts scheduled for the following month. But during the second week of my deliberations, I was sure Jacque was about to break his pledge. After he had completed filling all the "last call" requests, he eased down to my end of the counter and whispered, "Would ya like another sample of the reserve?" I nodded, and he returned with two tumblers half full of Jack's amber gold.

As before, we raised our glasses and clinked them, but this time Jacque's toast was different. He smiled broadly and said, "Happy Birthday, Todd."

I laughed self-consciously and took a sip of the whiskey, buying time to conjure up a response. "You, you remembered. I wasn't expecting that."

"How could I forget. When we were at the Dockery, you told me about sharing a birthday with Henry Sloan. That's a helluva coincidence, sharin' a birthday with the fella who inspired Mr. Handy to spread the blues! So drink up now! Celebrate your day! And before I forget it, when you've downed your Jack, take the back stairs there, hang a right, and knock on the last door at the end of the hallway."

"Who's there?"

"Van."

"Be honest with me now. She gonna try putting the squeeze on about Mr. Cavanaugh?"

"No, nothin' like it. She just wants to wish ya a happy birthday."

"How'd she find out?"

"It came up when we were first talkin' about Mr. Cavanaugh and your future. She's got a memory like a trap. There's nothin' to it. Believe me. No pressure. I mean it. She likes ya and just wants to be nice. Show ya she cares."

I finished off the tumbler and said, "Well, wish me luck."

"I'm tellin' ya now, no pressure. Oh, by the way, don't let on like ya know anything. Act surprised that she knows it's your birthday, ya hear?"

"Okay, okay. Well, here goes nothing."

I climbed the stairs and moved to the end of the hallway. I paused to catch my breath before knocking.

"Who is it?"

"It's me. Todd."

"Come in. It's unlocked."

I slowly opened the door. Van was seated at the far end of the room. She was propped up against the scrolled arm of an elegant Empire sofa with striped upholstery. Her long legs were drawn up under her scarlet floor-length "hostess" dress. She was holding a book in one hand and stroking the head of a black and tan Yorkie curled beside her with the other. A crackling fire blazed in the carved marble fireplace just to her left, and French impressionist landscapes lined the walls. She patted the cushion next to her and said, "Push the button on the wall there next to the baby grand, and then come on over here."

I rang the bell and then took a seat at the opposite end of the sofa. "I hear birthday wishes are in order," Van said. "So happy birthday, Todd!"

Feigning surprise, I responded, "But how'd you know it was my birthday?"

Before she could answer, a short, balding Negro appeared in the doorway. He looked vaguely familiar. I had seen him downstairs occasionally but had never spoken with him. He was wearing the standard maroon uniform with a white bow-tie. He moved to where Van was seated and inquired, "Yes, ma'am?"

"Raymond, would ya please take Beau here, and then bring us a drink. We have to celebrate Todd's birthday, so don't skimp."

"Yes, ma'am."

She looked over and asked, "What's your pleasure?"

"Well, I was drinking whiskey downstairs, so I'll stick with it."

She turned back to Raymond and said, "A tumbler of Jack for our birthday boy, and I'll have a Brandy Alexander to warm me up."

As she placed the book on the end table, I asked abruptly, "Anything you'd recommend?"

"You mean my book here?"

I nodded and smiled, embarrassed by the clumsy intrusiveness of my question. "I'm sorry. I wasn't trying to pry or anything. Just curious. I like reading in my spare time. Always looking for something new, special in some way, perhaps another angle of vision. Something that can teach me something about living."

She responded teasingly, "I have to say, young man, you've

got the brains to go along with those good looks there. I'm impressed. But seriously, no need to apologize. I respect folk with healthy curiosities. . . ." She paused and looked over at the book. "It's by the English writer Woolf. Virginia Woolf. It's her latest novel, *To the Lighthouse*. I'd read a couple of her earlier works, *Jacob's Room* and *Mrs. Dalloway*. Hard to explain, but her thoughts flow on to the page spontaneously like poetry. Blank verse with insight fused to the phrases . . . especially in the brief second part, 'Time Passes,' which I was just now rereading after finishin' the novel last night. I think ya have a better perspective once ya know how things are goin' to turn out. You can concentrate on the themes because you're no longer distracted by the plot."

I nodded and asked, "What's it about?"

"It's in three parts. All of it takes place in the Hebrides at the summer home of an English family, the Ramsays. The first act covers an afternoon and evening; the second act, the interlude, spans ten years; and the third act describes a morning at the end of the ten years. But that middle part is brilliant. Woolf uses the imagery of a house lying dormant, unoccupied for ten years, visited only occasionally by caretakers and flashes of light from the lighthouse beacon across the bay. Uses these static images to depict the passage of time. A decade of consequence, mind you. . . . It's genius!" she added with relish.

"The first and third parts?"

"Ah, usin' a musical analogy, the openin' is full of hope, expectation, promise. Woolf's writin' in a major key. But the last part, it's all about pickin' up the pieces of what might have been and then bravely movin' on."

"In a minor key, huh?"

"Exactly. A minor key. In the first part the Ramsays forgo sailin' across the bay to the lighthouse because of bad weather, and then in the third part ten years later, after the deaths of key family members over the decade, Mr. Ramsay and a couple of his eight children finally make that bittersweet voyage to the island, thus symbolically roundin' out the unfulfilled promises of the past."

"Excuse me, ma'am. Drinks are served."

"Thanks, Raymond. That'll be all for the night. You've worked hard this week. Take the rest of the evenin' off and spend it with your family."

"Thank ya, ma'am."

As he moved toward the door, Van turned and said, "Raymond, pull the door to on your way out. It'll cut down on the draft in here."

"Yes, ma'am. I'll make sure it's shut tight."

After the latch clicked, Van smiled and motioned for me to slide over next to her. "We can't let the day end without a toast for your birthday." She raised her glass and offered, "To the Lighthouse!"

I smiled knowingly. "To the Lighthouse!"

We clinked our glasses and took long sips of our drinks.

She gazed into my eyes and whispered, "Ya know, Todd, I don't want to see that happen to you."

"Follow my dream?"

"And perhaps forfeit your future? Eventually dreams curdle like cream. If what you're doin' isn't workin' out, ya have to keep tryin' new things." Van smiled. "Hell, I thought

I wanted to be a New York actress, but look at me now. Last time I checked this wasn't Broadway." She paused to reflect and then caught herself. "I'm sorry, Todd. I promised Jacque I wouldn't talk business, and now look at me."

"It's okay, Van. It's okay coming from you. You have a way of rounding the edges, the way my mama does."

She swung her legs around to the floor and stood up. I instinctively followed suit, sensing it was her way of signaling the party was over. She placed her hands on my shoulders and said, "In that case I'll make one last pitch. Meet with Mr. Cavanaugh. It won't hurt. And trust me, ten years from now you won't be regrettin' you at least listened to his proposal."

I winked and replied lightheartedly, "Okay, Van. But I want you to know now I wouldn't do this for just anybody."

Van slid her hands down off my shoulders and slipped her fingers in between mine. She squeezed lightly, raised my arm, and stroked the side of her face gently with the back of my hand. She pulled me close, crossing the nebulous boundary separating mother and lover. She closed her eyes and whispered, "Kiss me, Todd. Again. Softly . . . softly."

She took my hand and led me into her bedroom. "Pour yourself a whiskey and make yourself comfortable. I'll be right back."

As I nervously scanned the elegantly appointed room, I noticed a thin volume resting on the nightstand next to the telephone. I distractedly moved over to the side of the bed and picked up the book trying to calm my jitters. I read the title. *Harmonium: Poems by Wallace Stevens.* The book fell open to a dog-eared, penciled page containing the opening lines of an extended poem, "Sunday Morning."

I had just finished scanning the lyric and placing the book back on the table when the door swung open. Between the acts there had been a wardrobe change. Van glided back into the room wearing a silky lavender gown with a sheer lace bodice and plunging neckline in a scallop lace trim. The matching silk robe hung open, flowing down off the shoulders over her firm breasts. She smiled invitingly and extended her arms. I moved toward her and leaned in. "Slowly . . . gently . . . ," she murmured, as I lowered my hand from the side of her face to her shoulder and then to her breast. "Slowly. Softly. That's it," she sighed.

I eased my hands up under her robe as she unbuttoned my trousers. She then lifted her shoulders allowing the peignoir to cascade into a lilac pool on an emerald landscape of art deco cockatoos. I embraced her. She clutched my buttocks. "Softly now," she said. "The touch of angels. Yes. Yes." We slowly settled back onto the bed. I held her close and responded to her rhythmic waves. Her breathing quickened as I caressed her breasts and then her inner thighs. She stiffened, shuddered, and pulled me up over her. "My God! . . . Yes! Yes. Yes."

I lay quietly among the silk sheets staring at the thin break of sunlight angling in between the velvet drapes. Van was still sleeping, her head resting on my chest. It was remarkable. I was holding my lover in the crook of my arm, and yet it was I who basked in the warm afterglow feeling safe and secure. There was no need to honor the distant church bells summoning us to worship this brilliant Sunday morning. We'd found deliverance here beneath the crucifix in the holy darkness of this sanctuary.

As the soothing rhythm of Van's breathing slowly coaxed me back to sleep, Raymond knocked loudly and shouted, "Rise and shine, ma'am. Rise and shine. Breakfast is served!"

Van groaned and replied, "Oh, all right then. Come in," and within seconds, he had entered the bedroom and was in the process of drawing the drapes. While Van lay there completely exposed, I immediately dove for the covers. She laughed aloud. "No need to hide, Todd. Raymond sees very little and says even less. Right, Raymond?"

"Yes, ma'am. My lips are sealed."

I loosened my grip on the sheets and sat up next to Van. "Ya hungry?" she asked.

"Starving. Thanks to you I could eat a bear," I teased.

She winked, acknowledging the compliment. "Let's see what's on the menu." She called out to Raymond, who had stepped outside the room, "What have ya whipped up for us this mornin'? We're famished."

He returned pushing a cart with two domed sterling plate covers and a crystal pitcher filled with tomato juice. "Scrambled eggs and ham, with sliced oranges for dessert." He parked the wagon, moved over to my side of the bed, and held open a plush terrycloth robe. "Mr. Taylor, sir."

"Thank ya, Raymond."

He then motioned for us to follow him over to the small dining table positioned near the large bay window overlooking Beale Street. After seating us, he poured the tomato juice, removed the gleaming plate covers with a proud flourish, and then asked, "Café au lait, ma'am?"

"Absolutely, and double espresso in both."

While pouring the coffee, he asked, "Anything else, ma'am?"

"That'll be all for now. Thanks, Raymond. I'll ring when we've finished."

After he had exited, Van looked up from her plate and said, "Jacque tells me ya have a special concert tonight."

I nodded and smiled broadly. "Yes. Sundays are usually slow, but the theater will be packed tonight."

"Who's playin'?"

"W. C. Handy, the father of the Memphis blues. Took some doing but we got her done. Folks will be all excited and start showing up for tickets early this afternoon. Should be a good day for us all the way around—food, drinks, gambling and . . . and the like. Yes, this'll be a day to remember."

"For sure," she replied as she toyed teasingly with the edge of her robe. "Landin' Mr. Handy's indeed a big deal."

"You know what I meant, Van. Mr. Handy makes the day memorable, but you've made it unforgettable."

She leaned over and fed me one of the succulent orange slices. "You're sweet, Todd, and a good young lover to boot. Another?"

I nodded. "God, they're heavenly."

As she leaned over with another slice, she playfully asked, "The orange or my breast?"

I laughed guiltily. "There's only one right answer. Both."

She extended the repartee. "The orange and my breast or

both my breasts?"

"Touché! So let the record show an amended response: all three!"

She smiled and leaned over again. "Here, the last one's for you."

A sudden noise made me jump. "What the hell was that?"

Van didn't react.

"Didn't ya hear that?" I asked. "First the scream, then the laugh, and now the talking. Are you deaf? Sounds like the nut house."

Van laughed aloud. "It's only Jake in the other room."

"Jake?"

She pointed to the ivory birds woven into the emerald carpet. "Jake's my cockatoo. Or perhaps I should say Raymond's cockatoo."

"I don't remember seeing him last night."

"Ya didn't. Raymond takes him out back under the pretense of cleanin' his cage. They've pretty much adopted each other, and all the better. Jake demands a lot of attention, which I can't afford to give him. And when ya ignore him, he starts screamin' and chewin' up everything in sight. Jake and Raymond keep each other company."

I settled back in my chair. "What was he saying?"

"I didn't hear it. I've gotten used to ignorin' the chatter. Could have been anything—something mundane or a lot more colorful. Raymond takes great joy in teachin' Jake bawdy phrases, tryin' to shock all of us. Only danger's when Jake gets loose in the girls' rooms and calls a patron an asshole or something worse."

"Tell ya the truth, I was wondering what it was with the birds. First I see the carpet and then the small drawings on the wall there."

"Oh, they're pigeons."

"Pigeons? You like pigeons?"

"Not as much as Matisse does."

"Matisse?"

"French painter. Lives in the south of France. My father became a collector; visited him several years ago in Cimiez on the French Riviera, not far from Nice. My father said Matisse had a passion for birds—cages scattered throughout his apartment and studio. Said the painter gave him the drawin's and the still life of oranges next to 'em for his birthday, which happened to coincide with my father's pilgrimage to the artist's home." She laughed, shrugged her shoulders, and said jokingly, "And knowing my love of animals and my *passion* for oranges, my father loaned 'em to me for my apartment here."

I smiled. "Yeah, I was beginning to wonder about the oranges too. I'd seen the canvas there, and then the next thing, we're having oranges for breakfast."

Van pushed back from the table and stood up. "I hate to say it, but I'm gonna have to get dressed and get downstairs to start welcomin' the crowd you're expectin' to show up early today. And ya have no idea how long it takes us old, ah, takes us *mature* ladies to make ourselves presentable."

I stood up and murmured, "Forget that, Van. You're one of the most beautiful women I've ever met."

She smiled and pinched my cheek. "Get yourself dressed. You've got a lot of work ahead of you today too!"

"I know, I know," I replied reluctantly. "I just don't want it to end."

After I had finished dressing, Van escorted me to the door. She held my face in her hands and gazed into my eyes. "I don't know what the future holds. I'm not a strong believer in God's will. I struggle with my faith. I think we fashion our own futures, create our destinies. You're at a crossroads, Todd. I pray you'll make the right choice."

"I promise ya I'll speak with Mr. Cavanaugh the next time he pays a visit. If it makes sense, I'll be moving on."

"To the next dream."

"To the lighthouse."

"Yes, to the lighthouse."

I leaned in. She tilted my head down and kissed my forehead. And as I walked back to my apartment, I sensed my lover had now become my mother.

14

THE FOLLOWING TUESDAY afternoon, Jacque introduced me to my future. He had arranged a private meeting with Mr. Cavanaugh at the Shanghai. When we entered Jacque's office, Mr. Cavanaugh was sitting behind the desk smoking a substantial cigar and poring over a thick ledger. He was just as Jacque had described: wearing a plaid vest, sporting a gold chain that matched his front tooth, portly, and ruddy-faced. "Excuse me, T.J., I'd like to introduce ya to Todd Taylor, the young fella I've been tellin' ya about."

I approached the desk and extended my hand. "Good to see you, Mr. Cavanaugh."

Uncharacteristic of multimillionaires, Mr. Cavanaugh stood up, shook my hand, and replied, "I've heard a lot of good things about ya, son. I think it'll be beneficial for us to have a nice long chat."

Jacque interrupted. "Excuse me, gentlemen. I'll leave it to you fellas to hash things out. I have to get back to tendin' bar."

Mr. Cavanaugh extended his hand. "Thanks for hookin' us up, old man, and for lettin' us borrow your office. I'll put ya in the will."

As he turned to leave, Jacque laughed aloud and replied, "Ya heard that, Todd. It'll be up to ya to hold him to it. You're my witness."

I joined the banter. "Well, don't plan on spending it anytime soon, Jacque. Mr. Cavanaugh here appears to be the paragon of fitness and good health."

Jacque chuckled, shook his head, and shut the door behind him.

"Fine fella, that Jacque. He's been tryin' to play matchmaker for some time now. Here, come on up, take a seat, and let's talk this out."

"Sounds good to me. I'm all ears."

"Ya know what I do, Todd?"

"In a general way," I said. "Jacque says you're in the brokerage business selling securities. I believe it's retail. One-on-one."

"That's right. I spend a lot of time poundin' the pavement to drum up business. Ya ever done any sellin'?"

"No products per se, just selling myself, building credibility."

"That's a solid response, boy. Most folks twice your age don't get that. They think they're sellin' somethin', but you're spot on. You're sellin' yourself, and if ya do a good job of that, the product sells itself. Ya understand?"

I nodded.

"And do ya know the best way of sellin' yourself? Ya know what to say?"

"This may not be what you're looking for, sir, but what I've found most helpful is just listening and saying nothing."

Mr. Cavanaugh just sat there shaking his head and smiling broadly.

"I suspect that wasn't the answer you were looking for?"

"Au contraire, young man. Ya know, Todd, you're somethin' else. I've been at this for decades, and no one's ever gotten that one right. You're wise beyond your years." He paused to collect his thoughts and then continued, "Ya know, this is kinda fun tryin' to find a question that stumps ya. Wanna play on?"

"Your call, sir."

He rubbed his hands together gleefully. "Okay then. Here are a couple of tricky ones. Ready?"

"Ready."

"When do ya stop sellin' the customer?"

"I suspect you'd stop when you sensed they were gonna say yes."

"When do ya start sellin' the customer."

"Probably the opposite, after you've made your pitch and you sense they're gonna say no."

He shook his head slowly and murmured, "That's amazin'. Listen here, as far as I'm concerned, if ya want the job, son, you've got it! But first, ya probably have some questions for me. So fire away!"

"Well, Jacque probably told ya I don't know the first thing about buying and selling securities. So how am I gonna sell what I don't know the first thing about?"

"You'll pick it up like swimmin' or bicyclin'. You'll watch me for a spell, then I'll set ya up with some prospects. You'll do the sellin' with me in the room. I'll give you advice after each of the meetin's. Eventually you'll be out there doin' it all on your own. But I wouldn't get too hung up on the sellin'. To be honest with ya, this stuff pretty much sells itself. Here, I'll show ya what I mean."

He opened the ledger and thumbed through the pages until he found what he was looking for. "Okay, come on around here and I'll show ya what I'm talkin' about. . . . Ya see, I've been keepin' track of selected securities, especially technology stocks, for a number of years. People say, 'Buy low, sell high.' Hell, that sounds simple enough, but it's not that easy to do even in normal times. And how do ya know when to jump in when stock prices keep goin' up and up?"

I shook my head.

"Well, ya look for extended flat spots with little price movement one way or the other. And when the stock breaks out above its previous high, ya jump on it real quick!" He pointed to the ledger and continued. "Here's a good example. Ya ever heard of Radio Corporation of America, or RCA?"

"Company sells radios and radio equipment, right?"

"That's it."

Mr. Cavanaugh pointed to a specific line. "I started followin' the stock back around 1920. Ya see here, it was sellin' for a dollar fifty per share in 1921. And what was its high in 1923?"

"Ah, looks like four seventy-five a share."

"Okay, this symbol means there was a one-for-five split. The company issued one new share for every five old ones turned in. So what happened to the share price then?"

"Ah, in 1924 . . . looks like the high was fourteen twenty-five."

"That's right. And from there it kept climbin' to what?"

"Looks like it got to about sixty-seven dollars a share."

"Then what happened?"

"Ah, it looks like it stopped going straight up."

"That's right. It traded in a narrow range, as we say. So, is it time to bail out?"

"I think ya said to keep your powder dry and wait for the stock to start climbing again. So ya don't bail out. Ya do the opposite. Ya start buying more."

"Very good. And if ya had followed that strategy in late 1926, you'd have been nicely rewarded. Ya see, RCA created the National Broadcasting Company, or NBC, which started its network broadcastin' in late 1926. And where did the stock price end up in 1927?"

"Looks like a hundred and one a share."

"And look where we are now."

"Close to three hundred dollars a share. Wow!"

"Ya see? That's two hundred times the price you'd have paid in 1921! And ya can take it to the bank, it'll be up well over four hundred dollars per share sometime next year! As I said, this stuff pretty much sells itself."

"But, Mr. Cavanaugh, that's one example. Surely they're not all going straight up like that."

"For sure. But that's where I come in. I'll help ya choose the stocks you'll be pitchin'. So whatdaya say? Sounds excitin', huh?"

I nodded. "But . . . ah, let's talk turkey. How do I get paid?"

"Commission. We'll work out the percentages, but the concept is the more ya sell, the more ya make. So now whatdaya say?"

I extended my hand and replied, "I'll give it everything I've got."

"Believe me, Todd, ya won't be sorry."

"So when do we get started?" I asked, my voice trembling with excitement.

"I have a meetin' with a potential client downtown tomorrow mornin'. Be at my office at the address on the card here at half past nine. We'll walk over together. It'll give me time to tell ya a little bit about the fella."

"I'll be there, and dressed to kill."

Unfortunately out of the limelight now I trudged along shadowing Mr. Cavanaugh during his one-on-one interviews. But the more of them I observed, the more convinced I became there had be a more effective way to market securities. Granted, the man had made millions, but his approach was incredibly inefficient. Since the prospects controlled the timing of our visits, we'd have the first meeting of the morning on one side of town and then the next one ten miles away at the opposite end of Memphis. So if we were lucky, we'd make four calls a day and close sales on two of them.

At the end of that first month of training, I nervously approached Mr. Cavanaugh with a plan to improve efficiencies. "Excuse me, sir. I know it's Friday evening, the weekend and everything, but I . . . I have something I'd like to discuss with you."

Mr. Cavanaugh smiled broadly and said, "You'll learn pretty quickly, young man, there aren't any weekends in this business. Ya can make a lot of money, but ya have to work long hours to earn it. And ya don't have any days free. That's the trade-off. Ya don't get somethin' for nothin'. You'll see, startin' next week."

"How's that?" I asked. A lump was quickly rising in my throat.

"Because you're gonna start doin' the sellin' come next Monday mornin'. Don't worry now, I'll be right there beside ya helpin' out if ya get into hot water. But believe me, you'll do just fine. And it won't be long until you're out there sellin' on your own." He paused, looked down at the notes I had placed on the desk, and asked, "You've got somethin' ya want to discuss?"

"Yes, sir." I slid the notes across the desk. "I have an idea to make us more money."

Mr. Cavanaugh smiled as he picked up the papers. "Well, as you like to say, Todd, 'I'm all ears.'"

"If you don't mind, sir, I'd prefer you scanning my outline there before we start discussing it. Will take you only a few minutes. It'll get us both on the same page."

"Okay then," he replied and then added teasingly, "Why don't ya take a look at my bookshelves there, see if there's anything you'd like to take along to read over your last free weekend."

I laughed. "Thank you, sir. My friends will tell you I'm always on the lookout for new books."

But to be honest I don't remember a single title on his shelves. My heart was racing. I didn't know how he'd react to my proposal. While pretending to survey the volumes, I was continuously monitoring his demeanor trying to determine whether it was thumbs up or thumbs down. After about ten agonizing minutes, he placed his reading glasses on the desk, cleared his throat, and said, "Okay, Todd, I've finished readin' the outline. Come on over, take a seat, and let's discuss your plan." He rested his elbows on the desk and steepled his fingers. I sensed he was searching for the right words to express his concerns. "I'm gonna be honest with ya. I wasn't expectin' anything like this. It's so far out there. Ya really think this would work?"

To release some of the tension in the air, I tried responding lightheartedly while remaining respectful. "As my mama says, 'We'll never know unless we try. . . .'"

"But surely you know this is serious business. We're dealin' here with other folks' money."

"Yes, sir. But I think we'd be dealing with it to their benefit."

"Well, let's see if I've got this straight. Ya don't want to sell prospects on individual stocks but sell 'em on me and my ability to make 'em a good rate of return? Have I got it right so far?"

"Yes, sir, you've got it right. That's the linchpin of the concept."

"And ya don't want to target the wealthy but the middle class—the office workers and folks makin' a livin' with their hands?"

"Yes, sir, we'd be fishing the ocean rather than angling the small lakes stocked with the wealthy."

"And ya wanna start this ball rollin' by gettin' several men of the cloth involved?"

"Yes, sir. Probably won't take more than a couple of them ministering to sizable congregations. We get the first members on board, and they'll influence the next group, who'll persuade the next. Pretty soon the congregants will be telling their friends outside the church, and those folks will be looking for *us* rather than our looking for them. And they won't be seeking us out one at a time but by the carload!"

"And ya want these reverends to invite their congregants to attend a gatherin' at the Shanghai on a Saturday afternoon for a presentation and a free meal?"

"Yes, sir."

"And ya don't think the ministers will balk at havin' their members gracin' a gamin' house?"

"No, sir, not after I remind them the Lord spent most of his time mingling with sinners."

"And speakin' of the free meal—you expect us to pay the freight on that along with forkin' over the rent for the room?"

"Yes, sir. Ya have to think of the expenditures as investments, not as costs."

"And ya don't wanna sell 'em individual stocks in companies. Ya want 'em buyin' a basket of securities, buyin' shares of the basket, so to speak?"

"Yes, sir, buying the basket you're gonna weave. And while I'm thinking of it, sir, I believe your name should be displayed prominently on any marketing materials. Something like 'the Cavanaugh Fund.' Whatdaya think?"

He smiled noncommittally. "I'm still listenin'. I haven't signed on to anything yet. . . . So let's talk turkey, talk about how we're gonna make money. But before we get started, though, a clarification. Ya say there's no limit to the number of shares of the basket we can sell?"

"That's right, sir, it's not like those new closed-end funds you've told me about."

"Okay. Now the money. Ya say we'll earn commissions on both the buy side and the sell side just as I do today, correct?"

"Yes, sir."

"And ya say we earn a monthly 'management fee' calculated as a percentage of the net value of the overall basket?"

"Yes, sir. Ya see, that's the icing on the cake. The bigger the basket grows, the more money we can assess monthly. Think of it like clockwork. Every month, revenue just flying in here. It'll be a lifetime annuity for us."

Mr. Cavanaugh trimmed the end off a cigar, lit it, leaned back in his chair, and took several puffs. "Well, Todd, you've kinda put me on the spot. You can ask anyone in Memphis what's the one thing they most admire about me, and ten to one they'll say they admire my darin', my willingness to take a risk. Since I have a reputation to protect, I don't see any way out." He smiled mischievously and extended his hand. "We'll have a slight change of plan for this comin' Monday mornin'. Instead of your goin' with me on that sales call, you'll be knockin' on Pastor Conrad's door at nine o'clock sharp. Second Street between Beale and Gayoso. Ya can't miss it. His house sits right next to the church, the one with the steeple towerin' over everything else in the city."

Despite my overwhelming excitement, I kept my composure. "So you're really willing to try it?"

"We'll give it a whirl. But please note I'm goin' about my business Monday mornin' just as if we'd never had this conversation. As they say, the proof will be in the puddin'."

That following Monday morning I was up long before day-break rehearsing my lines. The strategy for my unsolicited sales call was, first, to provide the pastor with an overview of the plan; next, to briefly describe the benefits accruing to his parishioners; and finally, and most importantly, to empha-size the advantages for his church and its charitable work in the community.

At nine o'clock sharp I climbed the front steps of the rectory and knocked. The door swung open, and a tall, bearded man wearing a clerical collar stepped out into the sunlight.

"Pastor Conrad?" I asked.

He nodded and said, "May I help you, young man?"

"Todd Taylor, sir," I said, extending my hand. "Actually, I've come hoping I could help you and your members."

The priest reluctantly took my hand and said, "And how do you propose to do that?"

"By showing you how to increase the money in your pa-rishioners' pockets and add to the charitable funds in your church's coffers."

At that, Pastor Conrad's demeanor warmed and he responded cheerfully, "When an angel of the Lord comes a-callin', you invite him in for tea . . ." He then stepped inside and motioned for me to follow him. "Come this way. We'll brew some oolong and head to the study." As he guided me down the darkened hallway toward the kitchen, he asked, "You working with anyone on your project?"

"Yes, sir. Mr. Cavanaugh, the securities broker over on—"

Pastor Conrad stopped and turned. "You're working with Mr. Cavanaugh on this?"

I nodded. "Yes, sir. He suggested I stop in . . ."

"Well, now I'm really interested. If he thinks something's a good idea, I want to know more about it. He's not a member here, mind you, but he's been very generous over the years. Helped us with our building fund and donated the money for three of our stained-glass windows. I'll have to give you a tour of the sanctuary when we're finished."

"I'd be delighted, sir," I replied, as I thought, "This is way too easy."

After brewing the tea, we moved to the study where I outlined Mr. Cavanaugh's plan for the Cavanaugh Fund. In fact, during my fifteen-minute presentation, I dropped Mr. Cavanaugh's name more than a dozen times. As Mama says, "When you strike a gusher, you keep going back to the well." And this was indeed a highly productive one. Every time I'd mention my esteemed associate, the pastor would nod his head and smile. I suspect I could have stopped after the fifteen minutes, suggested he pitch the fund to his flock, and then returned to the office to prepare for my next meeting with the Memphis clergy, but I wanted to give him the ammunition he needed to motivate that first group to stop by the Shanghai for an informative seminar and a free meal.

"So you've pretty much got the gist of Mr. Cavanaugh's proposal?" I asked.

Pastor Conrad nodded. "Yes, but can you give me some pointers on how to convince members to attend the workshop at the—" He stopped midsentence, turned his head from side to side pretending to see if anyone was listening, and then said in a stage whisper, "attend the workshop at the Shanghai?"

I laughed at his mock conspiratorial drama and replied, "You read my mind, Pastor. That's exactly where I was headed. You have to get the flock excited enough to get up out of their easy chairs and trudge down to Beale Street on a weekend."

He laughed aloud. "I don't think I'd go as far as that. You might think of the flock as trudging down to the club for a seminar, but I think you've gone way too far to suggest they'd trudge down to Beale Street. I'd be more inclined to use words like 'run,' 'race,' 'bolt,' or even 'fly' down to that broad thoroughfare of iniquity."

And after that brief, lighthearted exchange, I sensed Pastor Conrad was a man after my own heart. There was no doubt he took his religion seriously; but at the same time, he demonstrated a degree of flexibility, understanding, and forgiveness of human frailties that would have surely pleased the Lord. The pastor had heard the promise made on the Mount, "Blessed are the merciful, for they shall obtain mercy."

"So as I was saying, Pastor, here are some benefits of buying shares in Mr. Cavanaugh . . . ah . . . in Mr. Cavanaugh's *fund*. First of all, we plan to keep the share price low so regular folk can participate in the market and prosper just as the wealthy do now. Secondly, we plan to reduce the risk by diversifying into a number of quality stocks in a variety of sectors. Thirdly, we plan to allow shareholders to buy and sell their shares daily at the net asset value of the fund. And lastly, we want to maximize shareholder profits by ensuring no one other than Mr. Cavanaugh makes investment decisions for the fund.

"Oh, and one thing more. When I introduce Mr. Cavanaugh to the attendees at the presentations, I plan on looking them straight in the eye and telling them that I'm putting almost all of my own life savings in Mr. Cavanaugh's hands. If I'd trust him with my life, I would surely trust him with my money! And if you wanna quote me on that during your meetings with your members, please feel free to do so."

"Believe me, I'll do just that!" he replied. "That's a pretty powerful one-two punch: first, that the inestimable Mr. Cavanaugh will be guidin' the fund and, second, that his top assistant is gonna trust his life savings to his senior associate for safe keepin'!"

I nodded and rode the wave. "So let me tell you now how Mr. Cavanaugh's plan will benefit you . . . ah . . . benefit the *church* overall. Ya see, the more profit your parishioners earn, the more money they'll tithe. And the more they tithe, the more funds you'll have available for your charitable causes." I winked and lowered my voice into the pastor's conspiratorial tone. "And I'm sure I can convince Mr. Cavanaugh to supplement the tithing with a small percentage of the buy and sell commissions on your members' transactions. All, of course, in the name of the Lord."

Pastor Conrad smiled. "Yes, of course, all in the name of the Lord."

"Think of it, sir. The more money you have to invest in the community, the more your . . . ah . . . the more the *church's* reputation grows. And the greater the church's reputation, the larger the congregation grows. You . . . ah . . . your church becomes 'the light of the world. A city set on a hill that cannot be hid.'"

Pastor Conrad lifted his eyes to the heavens and said hopefully, "Yes, a shining city on a hill."

15

IT SEEMED THE more things changed the more they stayed the same. During the first ten months of fund operations, the number of presentations doubled; the audience size tripled; and Mr. Cavanaugh gave up his one-on-one interviews to focus exclusively on investment decisions and becoming the public face of the Cavanaugh Fund. But on my side of the ledger, I continued living with the departed in the funeral home; I stayed on as concert host for the shows at the Shanghai; and I rarely walked about town with more than a few dollars in my pocket. Despite earning hefty commissions and profits, I stuck to the promise I'd made to initial investors and reinvested almost everything in Mr. Cavanaugh and his fund.

In fact, I literally hadn't moved an inch. I would stand at the left side of the proscenium weekend mornings and afternoons waiting for the cue to introduce Mr. Cavanaugh, and then I would return to the same stage in the evenings, stand in the same spot, and wait for the cue to kick off the latest concert. Notwithstanding all the financial hurly-burly and market success, I'd ironically still not crossed the boundary from support team to solo artist. I had remained the rarely observed manipulator tugging at the marionette's strings.

But as Christmas approached, I felt it was time to change things up a bit. Instead of reinvesting the upcoming special dividend, I decided this time to take a lump sum payment in cash. I climbed the stairs and knocked on Mr. Cavanaugh's door.

"Come in. It's open," he said.

"Sorry, didn't want to take you away from your research, but I needed to speak with you before you processed the latest dividend."

"So what's up?"

"Well, instead of reinvesting the dividend this time, I thought I'd take it as a lump sum payment in cash."

"Whoa, Todd. That's quite a departure from the past."

"I know, but it's for a good cause."

"Ya found a charity we're not already supportin'?"

"Oh, no, it's nothing like that, sir. It's about my mother. I wanna invite her here for the holidays. Do it up right. Put her up in the presidential suite at the Peabody. Buy her a nice gift. Show her a good time."

"I know your heart's in the right place, boy, but ya sure ya wanna do that? Cash in the dividend?"

"Well . . . ah . . . if I don't . . . ah . . . The thing is, Mr. Cavanaugh, I know I have a friend, Jesse, who watches out for Mama—like a son, she writes—but Mama never gets away from Hollow Rock. It must really be lonely for her much of the time. Jesse can't be there with her around the clock."

"What if I were to tell ya it's too late to change the method of payment this time?"

"I'd be disappointed, sir."

"What if I were to tell ya there's no need to do it?"

"I'd tell you I don't understand."

Mr. Cavanaugh smiled and said, "There's no need to do it, son."

"Why's that, sir?"

"Because your accrued commissions will cover much more than what you've planned on spendin' on your mother."

"My commissions? I . . . I've been plowing most of the twenty percent back into the fund."

He continued smiling as he responded, "I know, but you're not countin' the difference between the current twenty percent and the new thirty-five percent commission that the fund will be payin' ya from the beginnin' of this past year."

"Am I . . . am I hearing you right, sir?" I asked. My pulse was beginning to race. "Fifteen percent more from the beginning of this past year and a rate of thirty-five percent from here on out?"

"Ya heard me right. After all, this was your crazy idea, Todd. And look at it now. Everybody's winnin'. Even the poorest among us are bein' clothed and fed because of the fund's success. For me, goin' forward at sixty-five percent commission rather than the current eighty percent, it's academic in the big scheme of things. I've accumulated so much stock I'll never need to worry about money again. And besides, if I leave it behind for my son and daughter, they'll burn through it in no time. So bein' honest with ya, I'd rather see ya have it. I know you'll put it to good use. And one thing I know you can do with some of it for sure."

"What's that, sir?"

He laughed. "You can invite your mama to Memphis, put

her up in that presidential suite, buy her a nice Christmas gift, and show her a good time."

I extended my hand. "Thank you, sir. I'll never forget—"

He put his finger up to his lips, signaling I should stop right there.

"Okay, okay," I said. "But I've gotta tell ya. You had me worried there for a minute."

He laughed aloud and then replied lightheartedly but with a tinge of truth, "I'm shocked you'd ever be concerned. Have I ever let ya down?"

"No, sir. And I don't think you ever will either."

So two days before Christmas, I hired a taxi and drove over to the Union Station to collect my mother, who had gratefully accepted my invitation to spend Christmas week with me in Memphis. Once her train had rolled to a stop, I moved up the platform to where first-class customers would be exiting their private car. I watched and waited as the genial conductor assisted one passenger after another in climbing down the steep stairs. After a brief break in the steady stream of businessmen and their wives, Mama finally appeared at the top of the steps loaded down with suitcases, boxes, and bags, which would have arguably supplied Hannibal's entourage in their remarkable march across the Alps.

Since it was impossible to embrace her, I leaned in over the packages and gave her a light kiss on the cheek. "Welcome back to Memphis, Mama. It's really good to see ya."

"Good to see ya too, son."

"Here, let me help you with the bags. I've got a taxi waiting out front to get you over to the Peabody."

"Not so fast, Todd. You'll have to wait for the porter to fetch the bags I've got stowed underneath the car."

"You have more luggage underneath?"

"Well, ya never know what's gonna happen. Ya have to come prepared for all contingencies."

So after snagging a trainman, rustling up a wagon, and retrieving the checked baggage, we finally piled into the taxi and drove the short distance over to the Peabody. As we entered the cavernous two-story lobby, Mama stopped suddenly and pointed toward the black marble fountain at the center of the room. "Ya remember standing over there with your father and me and tossing coins into the basin and making a wish?"

"Sure do, Mama. That's the first thing that crossed my mind, too, when I checked in here to start looking for a job."

She laughed and muttered wistfully, "And to think, even after investing all those coins, my wishes never came true."

I laughed aloud and responded, "Same for me too, Mama. None of mine ever came true either."

We moved over to the front desk and checked Mama into the presidential suite. As we turned to leave, the clerk called out, "Pardon me, sir. Excuse me, ma'am. I forgot to mention y'all are invited to join the holiday staff and the other guests over by the tree there on Christmas mornin' for breakfast and presents."

"Did I hear that right?" I asked playfully. "Breakfast *and* presents?"

"You heard it right, sir. Gifts for all. The manager says everyone deserves to celebrate who has to be away from loved ones on Christmas Day—those of us who have to work and all of you folk who are separated from loved ones for God knows why. So don't forget, ten o'clock Christmas mornin' over by the tree."

Mama turned to me and asked, "Ya have anything planned?"

Without explaining the double entendre, I replied, "No, it'll be pretty quiet over at my place."

She looked back at the clerk and said, "You can mark us down as attending."

"Yes, ma'am. That'll be two for breakfast and gifts. Oh, by the way, the bellhop will be in with your luggage in just a minute. If you'd like, you can wait over by the elevator and check out the mystery presents and the tree. It's a beauty. Took us all of a week to get all the decorations and lights on her. . . . Anyhow, we'll see y'all day after tomorrow. Merry Christmas!"

Mama responded cheerfully, "Until Thursday then. Merry Christmas to you too, young man."

As we walked over to the elevator, we were naturally drawn to the "Christmas Corner" featuring a twenty-foot spruce surrounded by a multitude of presents of every shape, color, and size. Mama put her arm around my shoulder and pulled me in close to her side. "Reminds me of the decorations and piles of gifts we used to have at the farm when you were a little boy, long before your father got into state politics and before we moved to the governor's mansion in Nashville."

"Yeah, I remember several of those Christmases. Don't know the years. I just remember them by the gifts Santa left me: the rocking horse, the wagon, the train . . . But honestly, even with everything that was going on at the mansion our last days there, I think the Gibson six-string was my best gift ever."

Mama looked away and pulled me even closer. She didn't speak at first. The memories of that last Christmas together with my father were still too painful. I sensed the hurt in her voice as she awkwardly changed the subject. "It's funny how children recall the presents and the parents remember the decorations on the trees. Like this tree here, we always had dangling tinsel, red, yellow, and blue bubble lights, and handmade ornaments from the old country. Oh, the ornaments! I remember each of 'em as old friends: the funny cook, the harlequin with a pipe, the snow maiden, the magic rooster and the brave fireman. We all had our favorites. Yours was a rotund pink fellow. You called him Mr. Bubble."

The porter appeared with the luggage cart, breaking Mama's reverie. "Excuse me, ma'am, I have your things here. Are ya ready to inspect the suite?"

"Yes, yes, that'll be fine."

The suite, of course, needed no inspection, and after Mama had settled in, we left the hotel and walked a few doors down to Arturo's for some of the finest cappaletti served this side of ancient Parma. I slipped a five spot to the maitre d'. He escorted us to a back room behind the curtain reserved for family members and "valued guests" who appreciated fine wines during those highly restrictive times. As we raised our glasses of Chianti Classico, I offered a simple toast, "To your health, Mama, and Merry Christmas!" We clinked our glasses, swirled the velvety Chianti, and then savored the cherry flavors with hints of earthy spiciness.

"So tell me, Mama, how's old Gramps doing?"

"Every time Jesse takes me out to the house, we find him hard at work on two or three instruments at a time. The orders just keep pourin' in from orchestras all over the country. He grouses about all the work, but you can tell he revels in all the attention he's getting from professionals who respect his craftsmanship. I'm convinced he'd be doin' the work even if he weren't getting paid."

"Sounds like the Gramps I know. And he hasn't lost a step?"

"Oh, no. He's sharper than a tack. Doesn't miss a beat. The work keeps him young."

"You mentioned Jesse. How's he doing? And what's he doing now that he's out of college?"

"Oh, he's doing just fine. He's assistant pastor at Mount Nebo now. All the ladies just love him. His looks and his having taken up the ministry—strong attraction there. Gramps and I attend occasionally to hear him speak. You know I'm not really the church type, but I've never felt closer to heaven than when I'm there. The singing, the praying, the teaching. Those folk have the Holy Spirit coursing through them. When Gramps and I first started attending, we, being white and everything, we'd sit in the back. Didn't want to offend. But wouldn't ya know it, wasn't long until the brethren had taken us by the hand and marched us right down into the middle of the celebratin'. Gramps and I agree. If the afterlife is anything approaching Mount Nebo's services, then count us both in." My mother's laughter sparkled like fine wine.

"Speaking of the afterlife, how's Father holding up after his defeat in the primary?"

Mama came back to earth then. "You know, I never speak with him. Every now and then when he sends the support money he'll enclose a brief note asking how you and I are doing. I think its more a gesture than anything else. Never says a word about himself. All I know about your father is what I read in the newspapers."

"I never thought it would happen. Father losing an election. Whatdaya think cost him the nomination?"

"Circumstances overwhelmed him. He's still human, you know. The administration had to absorb one shock after another in a relatively short period of time. First, the announcement I was taking a 'leave of absence' as first lady, then our divorce, followed by his engagement and marriage to Mrs. Burrows. And after all that, the spurned young lover divulging he was in charge of organizing late-night parties . . ." Mama stopped to reflect and then said, "I suspect if the revelations had stopped there, your father would've survived. He'd married Mrs. Burrows for just that contingency. She'd provide the plausible deniability for the young man's charges. But it was his Uncle Aaron's testimony from the grave that sealed your father's fate."

"His Uncle Aaron? Speaking from the grave?"

"For reasons obvious now, your father never talked with me about his situation. So what I know I've learned from the reporting in the *Commercial Appeal*."

"I'm so busy I never have time to keep up with politics

or scandals. What'd the reporters have to say about this, ah, Uncle Aaron that caused Father to lose the primary?"

"They reported a demolition team had found a safe hidden behind a false wall in Aaron's old publishing offices."

"Publishing books?"

"No, a newspaper designed for Negroes. Had a lot of hard-hitting editorials on Negro issues."

"Whoa! A white man publishing a newspaper and writing serious editorials for Negroes? . . . I'm sorry. Go on. . . . So a demolition team found this safe. . . ."

"Yes. They were demolishing the building and surrounding structures to build a trolley barn. Apparently no one had been in the offices since the lynchings."

"Lynchings? Who was lynched?"

"Uncle Aaron and two of his workers. It happened the night before your father's victory in the gubernatorial primary. A mob lynched the three of them right there at the publishing office. They proceeded then to the poor fellows' homes, torched the houses one by one, and fired a lot of shots into the flames. Apparently many of the family members died too."

"What could Uncle Aaron have done to rile up the mob enough so they'd want to lynch him and kill his family?"

"Turned out the lynchers were supposedly your father's supporters. They became enraged after Uncle Aaron published an article containing certain allegations."

"But where does the safe come in? And how'd it play a part in Father's defeat this year?"

"There was a journal inside—Uncle Aaron's—giving a

complete account of a secret meeting your father had had with him not too long before the article and his lynching."

"Keep going. What'd it say?"

"It described your father's request for Uncle Aaron's help. Your father explained he'd just about caught his primary opponent and needed a final push to get him over the top. Had to do something to get his folks excited enough to get them out to the polls and vote."

"What did Father want Uncle Aaron to do?"

"Tell the truth."

"Tell the truth about what? I don't understand."

"Tell the truth about him. Write an article for Negro readers explaining there'd be hope for them in the future, if your father became governor, since . . . since he had Negro blood coursing through his veins."

"Negro blood?"

Mama nodded. "That's right. It wasn't the divorce, the remarrying, or the young men that did your father in. It was the diary and . . . and his hidden past."

"Father then is . . . is a man of color?"

"No reason now to believe it's not true."

"And me?"

Mama paused, took several sips of wine, and nodded. "I suspect ya have the curse of Ham coursing through you too."

I turned away, ran my fingers back through my hair, and whispered, "Yeah, blood thick enough for shunning but not nearly enough for mastering the blues."

16

I'VE HEARD MEMPHIS described as a "city of a thousand churches." I have no reason to doubt the assertion. There seems to be at least one house of worship on every street; and if the avenue is long enough, there are usually four or five stretched along the blocks. And now I have to stop and laugh when I consider that by the beginning of '29 this areligious fellow straddling the theological fence had become a friend and business associate of most of the pastors, reverends, and rabbis ministering to all these congregations. In fact, by year-end '28 these men of the cloth comprised our primary sales team and, along with Mr. Cavanaugh, had become the public face of the Cavanaugh Fund.

And the more involved the clergy became, the less time I had to spend pounding the pavement to drum up business. I now had so much time on my hands that I was becoming bored. One day while visiting the office, I picked up several of Mr. Cavanaugh's financial newspapers and examined them. Admittedly, I didn't understand the details, but I did grasp the overall gist of what I was reading. One financial piece led to another; and before long I was ensconced daily in a small anteroom adjoining Mr. Cavanaugh's office reading every financial report that flew in over the transom.

But that's where I drew the line. Despite his proximity, I never stepped into his office to ask general financial questions or discuss any of the workings of the fund after that first time shortly after I began. That is, I didn't cross that threshold until I had experienced the nightmare a second time. I rarely ever remembered dreams, but these I couldn't forget. I was walking down the avenue toward the office. It was a crisp autumn day. As I approached the building, I noticed a small crowd was standing out front staring up at the second-floor window. Someone was hanging outside suspended from a rope—someone with a round face, wearing a plaid vest and sporting a thick gold chain. And then the realization that Mr. Cavanaugh was dead.

I tried dismissing the nightmares as the ridiculous conflation of Uncle Aaron's lynching and Mr. Cavanaugh's business success. But it was hard to ignore the sweat-soaked pillowcases, the violent shivers, and the understanding that the only thing separating my and our investors' fortunes from complete financial ruin was Mr. Cavanaugh's beating heart. And it was that alarming insight that induced me to interrupt Mr. Cavanaugh and address my growing concerns.

When at last I broached the subject, Mr. Cavanaugh shrugged it off with a smile, saying he hadn't been sick in years and didn't plan on becoming sick anytime soon.

"You may laugh, sir. I know the doctors say your health is excellent and you'll outlive Methuselah, but what if you were hit by a trolley or a truck? It'd be the end of the fund and everything we've worked for."

Mr. Cavanaugh stopped smiling and spoke sincerely. "No

doubt ya have a point, Todd. It's been in the back of my mind for some time now. Things just keep gettin' in the way. Tell ya what. We'll start tomorrow mornin'. Now mind you, this ain't something that'll happen overnight. Even with your smarts it'll take a year or two to become entirely proficient. So from now on out, I want ya to feel free to ask questions about anything. I mean it. Ya hear?"

I nodded. "Yes, sir. It'll take some gettin' use to, but I'll try."

It was no more than two weeks later I made my first foray into Mr. Cavanaugh's office to test his resolve. "Excuse me, sir. Ya have a minute?"

Mr. Cavanaugh lowered his paper and peered at me over his horn-rimmed glasses. "Ah, sure. What is it, Todd?"

"Ya seen the article in this past week's issue of *Collier's*?"

"No, I've been way too busy preparin' the latest fund report. What's it about?"

"It's by a fellow named Babson. . . ."

"I suspect you're talkin' about Roger Babson, the economist. He heads up *Babson's Statistical Organization*. I can probably guess, but tell me, what does he have to say?"

"Says there's almost a general belief that it's easier to make money in the stock market now than in your own occupation. Says the market can't continue going up indefinitely, that there's gotta be a break in the popular stock leaders, which have been manipulated to foolish heights."

Mr. Cavanaugh smiled. "Yeah, he's questioned the rally for some time now. Some have accused him of bein' unpatriotic and sellin' the country short. Now I don't go as far as that, but there's a good lesson here. Ya have to know where people are comin' from. It's okay to read him, but ya have to read him with your eyes wide open. For instance, I could have probably told ya what the article was about, if I'd known Babson penned it. He's been a perennial bear. Nothin' bullish about his beliefs."

"A bear?"

"Wall Street lingo. A bear thinks the market's gonna go down. A bull believes it's goin' up."

"Where'd that come from?"

"Bears attack ya standin' on their hind legs and droppin' their front claws down on ya. Bulls, on the other hand, attack ya by drivin' their horns up into ya. Bears attack down, bulls attack up."

"So ya don't put much credence in his analysis?"

"Let's put it this way: for every Babson out there, ya have ten to twenty other economists, bankers, and entrepreneurs sayin' there's no end in sight to this bull run. There's Tom Lamont at J.P. Morgan, Charlie Mitchell at National City Bank, and Will Durant, the industrial titan who founded General Motors. They're all bullish on the year. So I'd put my money with them, not because they're famous and have made fortunes but because my own research points in that direction too."

"Despite what Babson's saying, you're certain?"

"Almost as certain as death and taxes." He paused and gazed into my eyes. "Believe me, boy, I wouldn't do anything to hurt you, me, or the thousands of shareholders who've put their faith in us."

Two months later, at the end of March, my curiosity—no, let's be honest here—my doubt and fear got the best of me and I stepped into Mr. Cavanaugh's office again. He was leaning against a bookshelf, thumbing through the pages of a thick volume, and half humming, half singing Irving Berlin's popular tune "Blue Skies."

"Excuse me, sir. Can you spare a minute?"

"Absolutely, Todd. Come on in. Take a seat. I'll be right over there with ya."

Several minutes later he walked over, placed the book on his desk, and sat down. As he settled in, I quickly stole a glance at the spine of the book, which read *Economic Almanac 1907*.

"So ya have a question?"

"Yes, sir. Maybe it's more of a general concern again. But hearing you singing there just now about the blue skies almost embarrasses me enough to just wanna get up and walk out, not trouble you with my doubts, since you pretty much have already addressed them through the lyrics."

Mr. Cavanaugh smiled. "Oh no, I still wanna know what's on your mind. If you're havin' questions that means I'll be hearin' the same things from the clergy and their members. Gotta be prepared, ya know. So tell me, what's troublin' you?"

"Well, I've just finished reading a summary of recent business activity. Sure doesn't look all that promising; construction's lagging, steel production's down, and car sales are declining. So when the market started going through its gyrations again last Friday, I got the jitters. I'm wondering if you'd explain how you're feeling about the market and our investments these days."

"Now don't ya ever be embarrassed about comin' in here, you hear? Ya know a helluva lot more about the business already than I did at your age. But it takes time to gain perspective, to learn, as they say in poker, to learn when to fold and when to hold 'em. Experience helps ya take the gamblin' out of gamblin', if ya know what I mean."

"Yeah, you're not leaving anything to chance."

"That's right. You're bettin' on sure things."

Trying to hide my lingering anxiety, I asked humorously, "So given what's been going on in the market the past week, how can you be so sure those skies are gonna remain blue from now on?"

"Well, it all boils down to an adequate supply of money to keep primin' the pump. Worry about that's been eatin' away at business and stock market confidence. Ya see, everybody's afraid the Federal Reserve's gonna stop printin' money and cause credit to dry up and interest rates to go through the roof. In fact, some of the governors on the board have been makin' speeches questionin' the boom, sayin' it's all been based on cheap money, loose credit, and wild speculation. And folks have been takin' all this noise in and have gotten the shakes. They reason if the Federal Reserve stops printin' money, then entrepreneurs won't have capital to invest in their businesses and ordinary folk won't have the money to continue buyin' stocks."

"The Federal Reserve?"

"That's right. It's an independent board in Washington charged with keepin' our economy on track. The board of governors is the only governin' body in the US authorized to print money. They can crank up the presses from time to time to stimulate economic growth. But once they feel the economy and the stock market are heatin' up too much, feel everybody's havin' too good a time at the party, they can vote to take the old punch bowl away. And when they signal the party's over, the economy begins contractin' and the stock market takes a dive."

"So this board's been making noise about cutting back on the printing?"

"No, not officially. Ya see, that's the problem. The board's been meetin' for days now, and there hasn't been a peep out of 'em about anything. And I'll tell ya, that's what's been spookin' the stock market."

"Well, what are you doing with all the money pouring into our fund?"

He smiled and whistled the first few bars of "Blue Skies."

"Okay, but what about the downturn in construction, in steel and autos? Aren't those sure signs something's afoot and the stock market could be heading south?"

"In the past, I'd have said you were spot on, Todd. But I believe things have changed. The stock market's gotten separated from both the economy and the actions of the Federal Reserve. In the past, when the economy slowed or the Federal Reserve reduced the money supply, you could bet the farm that the stock market was indeed headin' south." He paused, smiled knowingly, and added, "But ya better not be makin' that bet anymore."

"Why's that?"

"Because some of the bankers and capitalists are so awash

in cash, they'll continue lendin' large sums of money to Wall Street. It's in their interest to keep rates low enough for individual investors to borrow money to invest in the stock market. Despite what the economy or the Federal Reserve's doin', the market keeps risin' because the demand for stocks and the supply of cheap money never dry up. It's old school versus new school. Old school's worried about economic indicators and the Federal Reserve. New school's concerned about which stocks to buy when prices get depressed."

"Did I hear you right? You just said people are borrowing money to buy stocks? They're not just using their own money?"

"Yeah, that's right. Been going on forever. Nothin' wrong with it. It's called buyin' on margin. Like with most anything these days ya can buy shares at ten percent down plus interest on the loan. Instead of gettin' a hundred dollars' worth of stock for your hundred dollars, you're gettin' a thousand dollars' worth! . . . Look what it does for you and for the price of stocks with the increased demand for shares. I'm tellin' ya, Todd, the sky's the limit!"

"So all the ups and downs in the stock market can be traced to a fear the Federal Reserve might act?"

"That's right."

"Okay, I can buy fear driving the stock market down, but what caused it to finally stabilize after several days and then start rising again?"

"Well, one of those wealthy bankers I was tellin' ya about, Charlie Mitchell, announced his company, National City Bank, was gonna make $25 million available for new investor loans. And within the blink of an eye the interest rate on investment credit fell from twenty percent down to just eight! So despite the worries about the economy and the Federal Reserve, Mitchell had supplied a fresh punch bowl to keep the party rollin' on."

Despite the wide swings in the market over the next six or seven months, I managed to keep my anxiety in check. I kept reminding myself of what Mr. Cavanaugh had said: "Believe me, boy. I wouldn't do anything to hurt you, me, or the thousands of shareholders who've put their faith in us." So if Mr. Cavanaugh wasn't running around with his hair on fire, I reasoned, I shouldn't be either. I should remain calm and roll with the proverbial punches.

But "Black Thursday" was just too much of a downdraft to ignore. I knocked lightly on the open door and said, "Excuse me, Mr. Cavanaugh." He didn't hear me. He had the radio turned up and was singing along with the latest song sweeping the country.

I approached the desk and repeated, "Excuse me, Mr. Cavanaugh. Excuse me . . ."

He finally looked up from his work and said, "Oh, sorry, Todd. I didn't see ya come in. What's up?"

"You been watching the ticker today? It's in free fall, down eleven percent in heavy trading. People can't even get bids for their shares."

"Yeah, it caught my attention. I made a few calls around to be sure nothin' big was gonna happen. Just between you and me now, the word is several leadin' bankers have been meetin' all mornin' to address the issue: Lamont at J.P. Morgan, Wiggin from Chase, and Mitchell from National City. I hear there'll be some kind of an announcement any minute now."

And just as if this whole scene were staged, an announcer broke into the music:

> We have a late-breaking bulletin from the wire services. Dateline: New York. A consortium of bankers from Chase, National City, J.P. Morgan, and Bankers Trust has just announced it would make millions of dollars available to ease the credit crunch and lend support to the stock market. Our sources tell us Mr. Richard Whitney, vice president of the New York Stock Exchange, will have more to say at 1:30 this afternoon on behalf of the consortium. . . . We now return you to our regular programming.

Mr. Cavanaugh pulled out his pocket watch, checked the time, and said, "Ya might as well sit tight for a few minutes. . . . I'll make a call or two to the exchange to find out what Whitney has to say."

At a little past two, Mr. Cavanaugh made the call and spoke with a stock specialist with whom he had dealt for a number of years. After placing the receiver back on the hook, he leaned back in his chair, locked his hands behind his head, and laughed. "My friend Jack says Whitney strode across the floor of the exchange stoppin' at one tradin' post after another and puttin' in massive orders for blue chips like Standard

Oil and US Steel at prices well above their current levels. Go over and check the ticker there. Let's see what's happenin' to 'em now."

I walked over to the corner, scanned the tape, and announced, "The bankers' plan seems to be working. Trading's becoming fairly routine, prices leveling out, some even rising."

"Had a feelin' this is what the bankers were up to. You'll learn, Todd, there's nothin' ever really new under the sun. The tactic here's similar to what the bankers did in the Panic of '07. It worked then, and I'll lay money on it, it'll work again this time."

I stood up to leave and responded, "I hope so, sir, because I think we've already placed the bet."

At the end of the day Mr. Cavanaugh poked his head in my office and said, "I'm gonna be leavin' early today. Meetin' with several of our ministers for dinner. Will have to relay the good news."

"What's that?" I asked.

"The market made a real comeback. Closed down only six points on the day, just like '07."

So things were looking up; and I was looking forward to the weekend, when I would have a respite from Wall Street. Ma Rainey was coming to town, and I would have the privilege of introducing the "Mother of the Blues" to a packed house at the Shanghai. Looking back on it now, I recall the actual concert was far more exciting than anything I had ever dreamed. She sang all my favorites that night, the "Moonshine

Blues," "See See Rider," "Black Bottom," and the "Boweevil Blues." But most of all I remember her strong voice, lively disposition, and command of the stage. As soon as she stepped out into the limelight and sang the first bars of "Soon This Morning," everyone in the audience knew they were in the presence of genius.

17

CITIZENS STUMBLING UPON the scene that Monday morning might have been reminded of the Messiah's ascension or the installation of a new pope. But where they might have seen celebration, I saw fear. I was reminded of a sea captain standing on the bridge of his crippled ship calling out to the frightened passengers that everything would be all right. I stopped several doors down and listened to Mr. Cavanaugh as he hung out of the second-floor window and addressed the black-robed throng that had gathered outside the fund's office with lists of parishioners desperately seeking to redeem their shares.

Instead of trying to run the gauntlet out front, I circled the block and entered the property through a locked gate in the back alley. As I entered Mr. Cavanaugh's office, he was still hanging out the window trying to allay the clerics' fears. He was calmly suggesting the ministers deposit their members' sell orders in the mailbox below and then promising to execute their instructions by the close of business that day. My heart sank as I recalled his old adage that there was nothing ever really new under the sun. I realized Mr. Cavanaugh was using the same worn tactic he'd employed successfully in the past—delay immediate action with the hope that someone or something would intervene to miraculously save the day.

While Mr. Cavanaugh addressed the holy mob, I turned on the radio and checked the stock ticker. I quickly discovered the panic was not limited to the congregants in Memphis. The stampede to the exits was widespread. It was as if somehow every investor in the country had communicated over the weekend and decided to unload everything at once. Despite the bankers' bold investment moves on Black Thursday, we now found ourselves dealing with a much more critical Black Monday. I became sick to my stomach as I scanned the tape, watching the horrific tale unfold: AT&T plummeting more than fifty percent and RCA floundering at twenty-six dollars after trading near five hundred.

Our communications that trading day were limited primarily to shouts and glances. We were both working feverishly to bail out the boat. As Mr. Cavanaugh manned the telephones selling stocks to fund investor redemptions, I was calling out the latest results crossing the tape: "Dow down ten! . . . Dow down fifteen! . . . Dow down twenty! . . . Twenty-five! . . . Thirty! . . . Forty!" And finally, sometime after seven o'clock that evening, I announced, "The Dow's settled out down thirty!"

We collapsed into the chairs near Mr. Cavanaugh's desk and stared silently at the pile of ticker tape that had accumulated in the corner. Mr. Cavanaugh sighed and whispered, "Dow down thirty-eight points. Let's see. . . . That's about thirteen percent. We got battered today, Todd, but ya watch, the bankers and industrialists will be in the market tomorrow buyin' stocks and offerin' up cheap credit. We'll rally and be just fine."

I had enough energy left to respond numbly, "I hope so, sir. We've got a lot riding on it. . . ."

And as if he were trying to convince himself of his hopeful assertion, he repeated his prediction, "Yes, sir, we'll rally and be just fine."

By the time I reached the office the following morning, Mr. Cavanaugh was already addressing a second ecumenical crowd that had gathered outside the office demanding their members' shares be redeemed at once. With discretion being the better part of valor, I took the circuitous route again and entered the property through the secured gate in the back alley. I immediately manned my post near the radio and the stock ticker and read the morning papers until the market opened.

I shuddered when the first key clicked against the tape. Would we be up or down at the start of the day? I rushed over to the ticker and began reading the financial EKG aloud. Since Mr. Cavanaugh was still at the window interacting with the crowd, I suspect he didn't hear the grim results I was reporting: "Down, dammit! . . . Down big time! Dow off twelve! . . . Eighteen! . . . Twenty-four!"

But sometime in the early afternoon the radio came to the ticker's rescue. The announcer interrupted the music:

> We have a breaking bulletin from the Associated Press. Dateline: New York. Sources tell the Associated Press that Mr. William Durant and the Rockefellers intend to invest millions in

severely depressed stocks. The industrialists are quoted as saying they see tremendous overall value in equities at current levels. Stay tuned. We'll report further details as we get them. . . . We now return you to our regular programming.

I rushed over to Mr. Cavanaugh, who was now at his desk busily working the phones. "Did you hear that?" I whispered.

He smiled for the first time in days and nodded as he listened to a client railing on the other end of the line. He picked up his pencil and scribbled on a notepad, "Watch the ticker." And within minutes the tape began spinning the tale—the Durant-Rockefeller announcement had stemmed the tide. But as the day wore on, the precipitous decline resumed; and by the time all was said and done around eight o'clock that night, the Dow had settled out down an additional thirty-one!

We collapsed into our chairs and stared blankly at each other for several minutes. I finally gathered enough energy to offer several worrying observations and a key question. "If my back-of-the-envelope calculation's correct, the Dow index lost twenty-five percent, which extrapolates to a market loss of thirty billion over the last two days."

Mr. Cavanaugh wearily nodded his agreement.

"So do you think the market will come back?"

He nodded again.

"Well, what do ya think will drive the market up?"

You could tell the juices were beginning to flow again.

He sat up straight in his chair and replied, "The Rockefeller-Durant purchases."

"I don't know, sir. Looks like they may have already shot their wad today."

"We'll see. But if I were a bettin' man, I'd give ya odds the market will bounce back tomorrow."

"Because of the Rockefellers and Durant?"

"Believe so."

"Well, why didn't the announcement have much effect today?"

"Too late for it to really bite. But ya watch tomorrow. I suspect you'll see the real impact."

Just as the clairvoyant Mr. Cavanaugh had predicted, the Dow opened on the upswing the next morning and continued climbing steadily throughout the day. And because of the heavy volume of shares traded, the market didn't settle out again until around eight o'clock for the third straight day. Once the phone stopped ringing Mr. Cavanaugh and I moved over to our customary chairs to assess the current health of the market, the economy, and most importantly, the Cavanaugh Fund.

Given what had transpired over the past two trading sessions, I wanted to open our conversation on a positive note and see the old fellow smile for a change. "I don't know how you do it, sir, but you called it right again today. The Dow shot up twenty-eight! . . . So we've already cut the overall decline in half, and I suspect the trend will continue into the trading tomorrow. The ticker was telling me there was panic *buying* going on at the end of the day."

But I could never have been prepared for his response or

the fear that surged through my body as he replied resignedly, "It's over, son. It's over."

I refused to accept what I'd just heard. "It's over? What's over? The current rally?"

"It's all over. The economy, the market, and . . . and the fund."

"The fund? But stocks are recovering. How could it be over for the fund? That's crazy. How could it be over?"

"The goddamn margin, that's how!"

"What's that have to do with us?"

"How'd ya think I was parlayin' the members' weekly pittance into sizable fortunes? Through luck? Magic?"

"To be honest, sir, we never gave it any thought, the clergy and I. We trusted you to make the right calls."

As if carrying on simultaneous conversations, he reverted to a prior thread muttering, "Goddamn margin, the goddamn margin."

"Okay. The margin. But what's so bad about this buying on margin you talked about? You said it was like anything else these days, putting ten percent down plus interest on the loan. Instead of getting a hundred dollars' worth of stock for your hundred dollars, you were getting a thousand dollars' worth. What's so wrong with that? When you explained it to me the first time, you seemed to think it was a good idea."

"Truth be told, it's a two-edged sword. Ya have incredible leverage when the market's goin' up, but when it peaks and starts tumblin', margin becomes a quick race to zero."

"Zero?"

"The value of your holdings."

"Ya can lose everything?"

"Everything. And when everybody loses—you, the merchant, the fireman, the tailor, the widow—the market collapses too."

I sat there in stunned silence for a good five minutes before taking a deep breath and asking about the elephant in the room. "And the fund, sir? You said it's all over. But how bad off are we really with the fund?"

Mr. Cavanaugh squirmed in his chair, put his finger to his lips, and whispered, "Come now, let's sit upon the ground and talk about the death of kings."

"Beg your pardon, sir?"

He pointed toward the front window and snarled, "The sea's a-changin' from black to blue, from frocks to denim, from calm to angry waves, from preachin' to lynchin', from kings to knaves. Strike the bell, Jack. Mama says our time's up. 'It's over. . . . It's over.'"

He dropped his chin on his chest and within minutes began snoring. I was sure that with rest he would be in a better place the next day. I eased out of my chair, turned off the lights, locked the door behind me, and wandered home numbly through alleyways and half-deserted streets.

The following morning loyalty trumped fear. I crawled out of my nightmare, dressed, and headed back over to the office. As Mr. Cavanaugh had pointed out in his mad rant the day before, there had indeed been a change in the mood and makeup of the mob roiling below our second-floor window. The belligerent laborers who had gradually replaced the passive priests were now thrusting ominous nooses into the air and shouting, "Death to Cavanaugh! Death to Cavanaugh!"

As on previous mornings that week, I avoided the crowd by entering the property through the secured back entrance. I fumbled around in the dark hallway for the right key and finally managed to open the door. The lights were off and the curtains still drawn. I groped for the switch near the threshold. The flash of first light blinded me. I called, "Mr. Cavanaugh! Mr. Cavanaugh! You here?" I peered into the shadowy front office and discovered an indistinct figure lying on the floor next to our chairs. As I moved through the doorway, I asked, "Is that you, Mr. Cavanaugh?" I knelt down next to him. "Mr. Cavanaugh! Wake up! . . .Wake up, sir!"

When he didn't respond, I jumped up, crossed the room, and flipped on the rest of the lights. I was relieved. He appeared to be sleeping soundly. But wait. What's this? That's odd. A piece of paper pinned to his plaid vest. I knelt down, and as I leaned in to unpin the note, I discovered a pool of blood oozing from the back of his head and puddling on the floor beside him. I instinctively jumped up and moved over to his left side. But I immediately recoiled. I could see large pieces of his skull and brain were missing and had splattered against the far wall. I became weak and nauseated and quickly turned away. I returned to his right side, removed the folded paper, opened it, and read what Mr. Cavanaugh had penned while teetering on the cusp of sanity:

Y
O
U
MY OWN REDEMPTION
V
E
N
G
E
A
N
C
E

ALL SAINTS' EVE

1929

T. J. CAVANAUGH

18

As **OUR DREAMS** thickened and dried on Mr. Cavanaugh's wall, I boarded the two o'clock headed for Hollow Rock. After contacting the police, I had slipped out the back entrance, returned to my apartment, and emptied my armoire of everything except a favorite shirt and pair of slacks I'd worn while introducing the blues acts at the Shanghai. Psychologically, I was signaling I was resolved to return someday and that my departure was not a rout but only a strategic retreat.

After tipping the cabbie, I climbed the front steps and rang the doorbell. Mama opened the door and screamed, "Todd, is that you, boy?" She rushed out onto the porch, gave me a big hug, and said, "It's so good to see you, son. . . . Here, let me help you with your things. Looks like you don't travel light, do ya?"

I deflected the unintentional cutting remark and made light of it for now. "It's your fault, Mama. You always taught me to be prepared for anything coming my way. And I distinctly remember a young lady visiting Memphis last Christmas stepping down out of that coach juggling suitcases, hat boxes, and presents. And to top it all off she had checked luggage stowed beneath the car. And when folks acted surprised, what did she say? She put her hand on her hip and explained, 'Well, ya never know what's gonna happen. Ya have to be ready for all contingencies.'"

She laughed aloud at my good-natured teasing and then quickly moved on to mothering me. She gave me a quick once-over and said, "They aren't feeding ya right down there. I can tell. You're getting to be as thin as a rail. Now let's get you inside and get you a thick ham sandwich on rye and some rib-sticking bacon and potato soup."

With all that had transpired over the past few months, I welcomed the warmth and comfort of my mother's love. I slipped my arm around her shoulder, pulled her close to my side, and said, "Sounds real good, Mama. I've really missed your home cooking."

Once we'd finished our hearty lunch and got caught up on all the local news, Mama suggested we move up to the front parlor. We curled up on either end of the sofa, and she turned and said, "You've had a lot of questions about this, that, and the other, Todd. But I've been doing all the talking, and I haven't heard a peep out of you about how you're doing. I swear it was the same thing last Christmas, too. So tell me now, what've you been up to?"

"Nothing really noteworthy, Mama."

Sensing I had a lot to say but didn't know where or how to begin, she gazed into my eyes and said knowingly, "Why don't you just start talking, and let's see where the conversation takes us. I'm your mama. You know you can confide in me."

"I know, Mama. That's not the issue. I'm just ashamed."

"Ashamed? Ashamed of what?"

"My failings, Mama."

She smiled and responded, "Well, there's nothing really new there. . . . God knows, we've all had our failings."

"Maybe 'debacle' or 'fiasco' would be a better choice of words."

"Hey, now that sounds a lot like you're being too hard on yourself, like you're blowing up a temporary setback into a disaster."

"No, I mean a real debacle, Mama," I said impatiently. "And I'm not talking about just one of them either. I'm talking about two."

"Well, start at the beginning, or wherever ya feel comfortable, and then we'll see whether you're describing a failure or a fiasco, a debacle or a setback."

"Just between you and me then?"

She nodded. "Absolutely. Just between you and me."

"Okay, here goes." I then spent the better part of an hour describing everything that had transpired at the Shanghai—well, everything except for that memorable birthday I'd celebrated with Van in her apartment. And after divulging the painful denouement—that is, when Jacque explained I could never be a solo blues artist—I segued from Beale Street to Wall Street and spent the better part of a second hour detailing everything that had occurred at the Cavanaugh Fund, except for my mentor's suicide, which had happened only that morning.

When I had concluded the second part of my narrative, Mama shook her head and said, "Well, I've gotta hand it to you, Todd. You've done more living in the past few years than most people experience in a lifetime. And despite the outcomes, I want ya to know I'm proud of you. You took risks. It's gonna be up to you now to glean the lessons from your setbacks. And yes, that's what they really are. Setbacks. Believe me, you'll learn from them and move on, just like everybody else. Once you get to spending time with Jesse and Gramps, you'll begin to heal and Memphis will recede into the past."

"I'm not so sure, Mama. I know it sounds awful saying this, but I don't think I could spend time with either of them right now."

"Why's that?"

"I feel so guilty. I'd be thinking the whole time how they're happy doing what they love, and I tried but . . ."

"Don't ya say it."

"Okay, so I tried but . . . but had a setback."

Mama smiled. "Now that's better."

"But I'm serious. I really don't want to spend time with them until . . . until I know how the next chapter's gonna begin."

"Ya know ya can stay here as long as it takes for ya to figure that one out."

I slid over on the sofa, gave her a big hug, and rested my head on her shoulder. "I know, Mama, but what am I gonna do for an encore now that performing's gone along with a fortune that until this past week rivaled the value of Father's empire? What will I do to top that?"

"Maybe that shouldn't be your goal for now. Maybe it should be as simple as getting back up on the horse and beginning to ride again. Exceeding and topping the past—that can come later."

"How do you think I can get back up on the horse, as you say?"

"Now I know this'll sound strange coming from me, but if I were you, I'd be making a beeline to see your father."

"Are you sure about that? After all he's been through, he's probably sitting over there on the farm licking his wounds the way I am here."

Mama shook her head and laughed. "Knowing your father, Todd, I wouldn't be so sure of that. I suspect he's already got another nine irons in the fire. Go visit him. I'm sure he'd like to see you. If ya don't go, ya might be missing out on an opportunity. But if you're right and there's nothing really going on, perhaps he could at least offer ya some free fatherly advice. Go see him."

"Okay, Mama, I'll pack a few things and leave first thing in the morning. But I'm sure not gonna get my hopes up. With the economy acting the way it is, Father's probably got a lot on his mind right now too."

After the short haul from Hollow Rock to the Warfield depot, I hired a taxi to drive me the five miles east out to our old farm. As we drove up Anderson Road to the house, I catalogued the property and was reassured that at least some things in life don't change. "Stop here under the persimmon tree. I'll jump out and walk the rest of the way up to the house. How much do I owe ya?"

"A dollar and a quarter."

"Here's two, and keep the change."

"Thank ya, sir. But at least let me help ya up the hill with your suitcase."

Before I could respond, a deep voice behind me interjected. "That won't be necessary. I'll help my son with his bag."

I wheeled around. "Father!"

He opened his arms and smiled. "Welcome home, son."

I rushed over and embraced him. "Good to see ya, Father. It's been a long time. It's really good to see ya."

He grabbed my suitcase and put his arm around my shoulder. "I was just headed into the house to finish off the ham and biscuits we had for breakfast. Plenty there. And it looks like you need some fattening up."

I laughed. "Now you're sounding a lot like Mama. She claims they haven't been feeding me since I moved to Memphis."

"Well, while we're working on the leftovers, I wanna hear all you've been up to."

"And I wanna hear what you've been up to the last couple of years, since you"—I caught myself—"since . . . since you came back home to the farm."

"It's okay to call it the way it is, son. It's okay to ask what I've been doing the last couple of years since I took a whuppin' in my bid for reelection. . . . Best way to get along is to just shoot straight with one another. And you wouldn't believe how long it's taken me to get that through this thick skull of mine. So simple. Just shoot straight. It'll iron out most of the wrinkles."

As we polished off the leftover country ham, Father initiated the conversation. "So you say you moved down to

Memphis. How'd that all come about? Margaret throw you out on your ear?"

I laughed. "No. Got the idea of moving to Memphis when you, Mama, and I spent a week there during one of your political meetings. You remember?"

"Ah, shooting straight, been there dozens of times. Jog my memory."

"You and I, we went down to Beale Street to take in the music. Remember now?"

"Ah, keep going. . . ."

"It was the first time we'd heard a guitarist playing the blues. Remember?"

"You mean, ah, Handy?"

"No, no. The Delta blues, not the Memphis blues."

"Ah, shooting straight?"

"Yeah, shooting straight."

"Can't say as I do. I'm sure it must have been a fine day. You and me, spending time together on Beale Street, one of my favorite places in all the world. But sorry, son, there's been a whole lot of water flowing under this bridge."

Hiding my disappointment, I smiled and said, "No matter. I'm sure you had a lot on your mind being governor and everything."

"I'm truly sorry." He paused and picked up the initial thread of our conversation. "So you say you decided to move to Memphis after we heard the blues on Beale Street. What did you have in mind?"

"You remember the Gibson six-string Santa brought me the last Christmas we spent together in the governor's mansion?"

Father looked relieved and smiled. "Now I can say I remember that. And I also remember offering to pay for lessons. But that's the last I ever heard of it. Did you get lessons and learn to play?"

"Yeah. A fella that makes instruments offered to teach me the basics. And after I got proficient, I moved to Memphis to follow my dream."

"Your dream?"

"Becoming a bluesman. Like the one we heard on Beale Street that day."

"So how'd you make out? Did you find work?"

"Yeah. In a gentleman's club. The Shanghai. But I wasn't playing much, only backup now and then. Mostly I was doing administrative work—prospecting, hiring, and introducing acts. Lots of new artists. Bringing them up out of the juke joints in Mississippi; mostly the Delta blues."

"You still picking and strumming?"

"No, ashamed to say it wasn't working out and finally gave it up after a friend explained I had the technique but not the feeling. The blues are like something you're born with. You have them or you don't."

"I'm gonna shoot straight with you now, boy. Don't ever be embarrassed about trying something and failing at it. Believe me, we've all gone chasing down a lot of rabbit holes. You'll learn that these folks, the risk takers, they're the ones to admire. That's right, even when they fail, they get up, dust themselves off, and try something else. And you know what? They may fail two, three, four, even five times, but they have the will to survive and try again. And believe me, there comes a day when it all comes together. Something clicks, and all the pain and failure's forgotten."

He paused to reflect before continuing. "You see, life's a lot like war. It dawned on me while reading General Prescott's book on military tactics. The general emphasized the enemy has a brain and uses it to find new, unexpected ways to exploit our weaknesses. And I thought, yeah, that's a lot like life, too. Something's always rearing up, getting in the way, turning sure success into demoralizing failure."

"The general have any recommendations for avoiding defeat?"

Father nodded and smiled. "You read my mind, son. He says there are four steps to his strategy. He makes them easy to remember. Each step begins with the letter *A*. Sounds so embarrassingly simple, but I've tried them and, by God, they work!"

By now I had really become engaged. "So tell me then, what are the steps?"

"Absorb. Adjust. Attack. Anticipate."

"But how does that work? What's the strategy?"

"Okay, let's start with 'absorb.' The enemy, or for that matter, life attacks you, knocks you down. So you absorb the blows. Next you adjust. You get up. You regroup and plan your counterattack. How am I going to react to this invasion? What am I gonna do to win outright? After you adjust, you attack aggressively with overwhelming force, trying to defeat the enemy or staring down the life forces with everything you've got. And finally, you anticipate—and that's the key to everything, the key to outright victory on the battlefield or success in any of your ventures."

"Anticipate? Anticipate what?"

"Anticipate the enemy's next move. Fortify your positions so that when the inevitable attack occurs, you'll withstand the onslaught and end up in a stronger position than you were in during the previous attack. You get stronger as the enemy weakens. And after two or three of these thwarted attacks, a discouraged, weakened enemy furls its flags and absconds in the night. Same in life, son. Folks forget this critical step. They never look beyond their noses, never anticipate what's lurking just beyond the horizon."

Understandably, a perverse thought occurred to me then. Had the physician followed his own prescription after taking a drubbing in the last election? Had he anticipated his defeat; absorbed it; adjusted to the new reality; and then attacked with a vengeance? I looked away, too embarrassed to meet his gaze, and asked innocently, "I'm curious, Father, not being disrespectful, just trying to learn . . ."

"Go ahead," he urged. "Remember, we're shooting straight. So ask me what's on your mind."

"Did . . . did you anticipate your primary defeat? Did you see it coming?"

Father smiled broadly, rose from the table, and said, "Come along. I'll let you be the judge of that."

19

WE JUMPED INTO father's Desoto Six roadster and headed south on a paved extension of the old Anderson Road. I observed, "Now this is all new. The road and everything. You buy the land here?"

"Yeah, got wind that the large Gorman Hollow tract abutting us was gonna be listed for sale, so I snapped her up before she ever hit the market."

"Looks like there's a lot of good timber in there. You got plans?"

Father smiled. "Hold on there. You'll see."

We must have gone another good half mile when we approached a guardhouse with a gate extending across the road. As we rolled to a stop, a uniformed guard stepped over to the driver's side of the car and peered in. "Governor, sir. And you have a guest?"

"Yes, Corporal Jackson. My son."

"Very well then, sir. Proceed."

As we cleared the gate, I whispered, "Is that a Thompson submachine gun he's carrying?"

"Sure is, with a fifty-round drum. State of the art. For the price of two of those you can buy a car. I wanted to send a clear message I wasn't playing around, so I armed all my security men with Thompsons."

"Security men. You've never had them on the farm be-fore. You got them now because you were governor?"

Father smiled again. "Now hold on there. You'll see."

We must have driven another quarter mile when we en-countered still another guardhouse, a gate, and an officer armed with a Thompson. The guard moved over to Father's side of the car and asked, "Governor, sir. You have a guest?"

"Yes, Sergeant Martin. My son," Father responded.

The guard saluted. "Very well then, sir. Proceed."

While passing through the open gate, I said, "Sorry, Father, but you've really piqued my curiosity now. How many of these fellas do you have working for you? Ten? Fifteen? Twenty?"

He turned and said teasingly, "Oh, nothing like that."

"Well at least five then?"

He laughed and then delivered the punch line: "How about closer to sixty all told."

"Sixty! What do you have going on back here requiring an army to secure it?"

"Now I told you to hold on, son. You'll see."

As we rounded a wide curve, I gasped. "My God, what's this? You've built a whole city back here! Houses, barns, buildings, and will you look at all the cars and trucks parked over there!"

"It's a family compound for Mrs. B and her sons. Too bad you picked a time when they're all away. Mrs. B's in Nashville visiting her brother, Workman, who was my spokesman, and her boys are traveling on business."

"What are all the vehicles doing parked over by that large building there?"

"Belong to the trucking company."

"Trucking company?"

"Hurricane Express. Started her up just after buying the Gorman Hollow tract here."

"What do you haul?"

"Anything and everything, and all across the country too. But most of the business right now's between the distilleries and the drug wholesale company."

"Distilleries? Thought they were all shut down by the Volstead Act."

"For the most part you're right, but you'll learn they're always exceptions wedged in between the lines of every law. And two exceptions in particular jumped out at me in the Volstead Act, which stated, one, 'Except that a person may purchase and use liquor for medicinal purposes when prescribed by a physician as herein provided,' and two, 'That nothing in this act shall prohibit the purchase and sale of warehouse receipts covering distilled spirits on deposit in government-bonded warehouses.'

"And this is where that all-important word 'anticipate' came into play in my case. With all the scandals swirling about my administration, I concluded firstly, there was a better than even chance I'd have a strong challenger in the primary, one who'd most likely win, and secondly, that my defeat under these adverse circumstances would translate into lost business when I returned to private life running the enterprise.

"So, given this negative outlook, I asked myself a series

of questions: What if I could replace this projected loss in my agricultural and manufacturing operations with new businesses somehow exploiting the loopholes in the Volstead Act? What if I owned a drug wholesaler, which could supply whiskey to retailers dispensing prescribed liquor to patients? What if I could obtain government withdrawal permits allowing me to tap into the millions of gallons of liquor produced before Prohibition started and which are now stored in bonded distillery warehouses? What if I controlled an adequate number of trucks to move the whiskey first from the distillery to the drug company and then from the wholesaler to the retail druggists? And what if I had a reliable security force protecting the shipments from the distilleries to the drug company and then from the wholesaler to the retail outlets dispensing to patients? You with me so far?"

I nodded. "Yes, so far so good."

"Okay. But before moving on, I've got to ask you a few questions."

"What's that?"

"Shooting straight now, father and son talking, how do you and the folks down in Memphis feel about Prohibition in general?"

"Many who first thought it was a good idea soured on the law. Honestly, there isn't a dry establishment on Beale Street or anyplace else in the city for that matter."

"But shooting straight, how do you feel about it?"

I smiled and announced proudly man-to-man, "I've been known to sip my share of Jack."

"So you have nothing against folks fulfilling customer

needs while making a little profit on the side?"

I laughed and shook my head. "I tend to agree with one of the ministers frequenting the Shanghai Club there in Memphis. He likes to quote Saint Paul when ordering up a shot or two. He raises his voice so everyone at the bar can hear: 'Drink no longer water, but use a little wine for thy stomach's sake and thine infirmities.' Sometimes he'll add, 'How dare man's laws try overridin' the divine teachin' of the scriptures. It's sacrilege, I tell ya. Sacrilege.'"

"Okay then, so back to that word 'anticipate.' And shooting straight with you now, just between father and son, I continued asking myself questions and then began supplying answers. What if I could make more money fudging the law than following it? What if I bought four or five distilleries outright, started my own drug wholesaler, controlled a transportation company to deliver the goods from here to yonder, and founded a first-rate security firm to protect my operations. What if I invested money in officials at the highest levels of the federal government to ensure I'd have an unlimited number of government withdrawal permits for my distilleries? Now let's say I bought a sizable tract of land for all these 'off the book operations.' And say the distilleries and the drug company lost shipments along the way and the financial records of the distilleries and the wholesaler failed to reflect any of these losses. What if I were to then build bottling and distribution facilities on a secluded property to accommodate the lost shipments and, further, hired thousands of loyal, like-minded employees and paid them extremely well? Now let's say I ran the bottling operations twenty-four hours a day, seven days a week, and offered customers either pickup or delivery of the finest whiskey money could buy. What would happen if I then invested thousands of dollars in state and local officials to ensure the feds never got wind of Gorman Hollow? What would happen?" He paused and added, "Anticipate, absorb, adjust, attack! And then start anticipating all over again."

I sat there momentarily speechless staring out the windshield at his unprecedented covert operations. I finally turned toward him, smiled embarrassedly, and said, "I've gotta confess I never expected anything like this. Now I understand what you really mean by 'anticipating the next move.' But you've got my curiosity going again."

"About what?"

"What you're anticipating now."

Father smiled and replied, "It's not so much what I'm anticipating but what I'm hoping."

"Hoping for what?"

"That you'll get on board and become a part of the team. You see, I set all these operations up under the umbrella of a holding company. One of Mrs. B's boys oversees the distilleries; the other heads up the drug wholesaler. I'm in charge of security, and I have a placeholder running distribution and the trucking company. So I was hoping someday you might come home and take on those responsibilities. Maybe even get married and have a couple boys to ensure the future."

I ignored his hints at succession and replied, "I don't know the first thing about distribution and trucking."

"Believe me, the folks currently in charge would be rewarded handsomely for ensuring you have the knowledge and resources to succeed."

"Where would I start?"

"Well, Capone's got eastern Tennessee and we've already got everything sewn up between here and Nashville. I'd suggest you start with familiar territory—say, for example, with Memphis. And then you could work your way back east toward Warfield."

"I hear you. It makes sense. But how do I shoehorn my way into Memphis, where, as I told you, they've been selling lightning from the very first day of Prohibition. So back to the basic question again, where would I start?"

"If I were you, I'd first try the club where you've been working."

"What'll I say?"

"Nothing."

"Nothing?"

Father smiled. "That's right, nothing. You see, the sale will be in the doing, not in the saying."

"How's that?"

"You let the whiskey do the selling, son. You just set some jiggers up in front of the owners, fill the glasses first with the bootlegged swill they're now serving customers, suggest they down the moonshine, then fill their jiggers with our smooth, barrel-aged whiskey. Suggest they sip the finest liquor money can buy. When you ask them to compare the two samples, I guarantee you they'll say our whiskey is far superior to what they're serving customers today.

"Now here's where it'll get tricky. They'll probably push

the jigger back and say, 'No doubt your whiskey's so much better, and I'd buy some for my own use. But it'd be too expensive to serve to our customers every day.' That's when you smile and casually ask them, 'Would you say the same if I told you you'll have an unlimited supply at a cost per case less than what you're paying the bootleggers today?' You then pour them a second round, and this time you add a jigger for yourself. You raise your glass for a toast and ask them if they're ready to do you the honor of signing up."

"Sounds so easy."

Father nodded. "It is when you have a bona fide product beating everything else out there hands down. And once you get a toehold in there, you can start pounding the pavement repeating the same show with generous samples for every bartender and owner all up and down Beale Street."

"I wouldn't go that far, but maybe halfway."

"Whatdaya mean, halfway?"

"While you were talking, something hit me, something the club owner's daughter said one day, kind of an aside. She said her father down in Louisiana had his hooks into half the watering holes on Beale Street. And if that's the case and we get our whiskey sold into the Shanghai, then the rest of the dominoes should fall pretty quickly."

Father extended his hand. "Now you're talking like a leader and a true partner! You'll do me proud, if you come on board. Whatdaya say?"

I extended my hand and said, "Okay, Father, I'm all in."

He paused, smiled, and slowly shook his head reflecting on what he had just accomplished.

"You happy?" I asked.

"Extraordinarily so. . . . It's not every day you can say you own a holding company where you have your three sons heading up the operating units."

"Three?"

"Yes, three. No one told you? You didn't read it in the newspapers?"

"Read what?" I asked.

"I've legally adopted Mrs. B's boys?"

"But they're grown men, and one of them has children."

"That's right, but when Mrs. B and I worked out the arrange—our wedding plans, I insisted they take the Taylor name, that is, if they ever wanted to get involved in any of the Taylor ventures. It just looks and sounds so much better when everyone at the top's sporting the same name. So, Todd, the reality is you have stepbrothers by name and by law who are now also your partners in the holding company, J. Taylor & Sons, Inc.

I turned away, disappointed. I realized Father had indeed been doing some "anticipating" earlier on. And I suspect he figured if I never came back and joined the business, he'd at least have two adopted Taylors to continue on when it was time to relinquish the mantle. But if I did return home and accepted a leadership position as I had then, he could have a rigorous competition among the three of us to assess and then decide who should be the rightful heir controlling the enterprise, that is, until his grandchildren were then ready to take the reins. Hell, Father had already hinted at my getting married and having children not once, but twice that day.

As we slowly circled the compound, I continued staring out the side window pretending to show interest in the sights. Father reached over and slapped me heartily on the shoulder and said, "Whatdaya say we go back to the house and down a couple of those fine whiskies we've been talking about? Down them to celebrate the prodigal's return."

I smiled ironically and muttered, "And commemorate the fulfillment of a father's dream." I knew I was trapped. If only I'd known minutes before what I knew then. But despite the anger and resentment, I knew I'd throw myself into the work and do everything I could to succeed. Once again I found myself in the unenviable position of trying to prove myself to my father.

20

THE FIRST THING I did upon arriving back in Memphis was return to my apartment, open the bottom drawer of my armoire, and ritualistically touch the shirt and pants I'd left behind for good luck. I honestly thought I'd be away a lot longer than a month. But here I was back on Beale Street preparing to make a pitch that could resurrect me from the ashes of Black Tuesday.

I changed into my "good luck" clothes, grabbed the suitcase full of Gorman Hollow spirits, and headed over to the club. As I approached the bar, I called out to Jacque, "Boy, do I have a deal for you!"

He rushed out from behind the bar and gave me a big hug. "Good to see ya, Todd. We were really worried about ya. You just disappeared. We figured ya got swallowed up by the crash and Mr. Cavanaugh's sui— Death. Awful, just awful. Understandable, though, when ya consider he lost everything and everyone was out lookin' for him. His passin' and the market have cast a pall over everything, especially with the holidays comin' up."

I didn't respond. I just nodded in agreement.

"So ya said somethin' about havin' a deal for me?"

"Yeah, but before getting into it, we need to get Van down

here too."

"Okay, I'll give her a call."

Several minutes later the beautiful madam of the Shanghai glided into the room, extended her arms, and embraced me warmly. She then held me out at arm's length and admonished me. "Shame on you disappearin' without tellin' anybody. We were all worried sick about ya. Now don't ya ever do that again, ya hear?"

I lowered my head, nodded, and responded defensively, "But it was a nightmare. The crash. Mr. Cavanaugh. And then the mobs. I had to get away, clear my mind."

Van embraced me again, signaling all was forgiven, and then said, "Jacque tells me ya have something ya want to discuss."

I laughed nervously as I swung my suitcase up on the bar. "As I told Jacque, I have a real deal for you." I snapped the latches, slowly opened the lid, and held up a bottle of Gorman Hollow. "Solid reinforcements here. I'm sure your stash of Jack must be getting low, and this is the next best thing to it. Aged in the barrel, eight year old."

"Where'd ya come by this?" Jacque asked.

I smiled and replied, "That's for later on, after y'all have done a little sipping. Ya got a couple tumblers handy?"

Jacque placed two glasses up on the counter and said, "Here, fill 'em up."

I poured the whiskey into the tumblers. The professionals held their samples up to the light. "Old oak color," Jacque said. "Dark enough to have been in the barrel eight years."

Van nodded and swirled her glass several times. "Thick

enough for eight years too. Ya see how slow the legs are?"

"Yeah." Jacque then swirled his whiskey, placed his nose at the top of the glass, and took a small, brief smell. "Earthy. Pickin' up the mash—the corn, barley, and rye."

Van nodded. "Agreed. And now for the real test."

They swirled their glasses, took small sips, swished the whiskey around for a few seconds, and then swallowed. "I'm pickin' up the barrel," Jacque said.

"Yeah, woody with slight hints of charcoal."

"And how about that finish!" Jacque exclaimed. "Long and lingerin'."

"And smooth as silk," Van added. Her face was alive with excitement.

"It ain't Jack, but it's damn close," Jacque said.

Van turned to me and asked, "So ya say you can order up enough of this to replenish our stash?"

I nodded. "And enough to treat the customers too."

Jacque glanced over at Van. "That's all well and good," he said, "but think how much that would set us back."

Van then turned to me. "He's right, Todd. It's a nice thought, but it'd cost a fortune."

"How would you feel if I said I could get you an unlimited supply and charge you the same amount per case as the lightning you're serving now?"

Van glanced over at Jacque, looked back at me, and smiled. "I'd say we're interested."

I continued probing. "Did I hear you right some time ago? Did you say your father has partial ownership in a lot of the establishments on Beale Street?"

"Ah, yeah. That's right. But it's not meant to be broadcast around here, ya understand?"

"Fair enough. So what would you say if I told you I could get your father an unlimited supply of this Gorman Hollow at a lower price per case than he's paying now?"

Van looked over at Jacque once again and then back toward me. "I'd say I have to go make a call, and I'll be right back."

After she disappeared around the corner, Jacque whispered, "That's a good sign. She's telephoning her father, Mr. de Terrant, down in Louisiana to get his okay."

Several minutes later Van returned and extended her hand. "Of course we'll have to put all this to paper; but as far as Daddy and I are concerned, you have a deal, Todd. You have a deal. And Daddy wants to explore making shipments down to the Bayou too."

As I refilled their glasses, I asked Jacque, "May I have one more tumbler please?"

"By all means," he replied.

Van offered a toast. "To a happy and prosperous venture!"

We clinked our glasses. Jacque and I chimed in, "Here! Here!" And we sipped the velvety Gorman Hollow until the crowd began rolling into the lounge a little past five o'clock.

Several weeks later I was sitting in my customary seat at the end of the bar quietly celebrating the first successful delivery of spirits to Mr. de Terrant's establishments on the west end of Beale Street. Jacque moved over to where I was sitting, smiled, and whispered, "Van just called. She said she'd like to see ya up in the private quarters in fifteen minutes or so. Ya remember the way? Back stairs, hang a right, last door at the end of the hallway."

I nodded and thought, "Yeah, I remember, even though I've only been up there once. A one-night wonder and nothing since." It was back to business as usual then. Never a hint of what we shared that night. I never understood why nothing developed afterwards. Something I said? Something I did? The age differential, which would have never been an issue for me? I really had feelings for her and still hadn't given up hope that one day. somehow. some way. it would still work out. A charge of electricity surged through my body as I speculated perhaps this *was* that day, when someway, somehow, it would all finally begin to work out. I downed my whiskey in a hurry, gave Jacque the high sign, and headed up the stairs.

I took several deep breaths and knocked on the door.

"Yes?"

"It's me. Todd."

"Come on in. The door's unlocked."

I slowly opened the door and discovered perhaps you can go home again. As on my birthday, Van was seated on the sofa near the roaring fireplace, surrounded by French impressionism with her legs drawn up under her floor-length dress. She placed the book she was reading on the end table, tapped the cushion next to her, and said, "Hit the button there, and then come on over and take a seat."

Before I even reached the sofa, the butler appeared and said, "Yes, ma'am?"

"We're goin' to need drinks, Raymond." She then looked

over at me and confirmed, "Gorman Hollow?"

I smiled and responded proudly, "Absolutely!"

"What else, ma'am?" the butler asked.

"We'll need a brandy and a gin and tonic over ice with lime."

"Very well, ma'am."

I glanced over toward the end table. "Curious. Anything you'd recommend?"

Van smiled knowingly and began reciting lines from the last section of Stevens's poem, "Sunday Morning":

> We live in an old chaos of the sun,
> Or old dependency of day and night,
> Or island solitude, unsponsored, free,
> Of that wide water, inescapable.

I then joined her, and together from memory we finished the final lines of the extended work:

> Deer walk upon our mountains, and the quail
> Whistle about us their spontaneous cries;
> Sweet berries ripen in the wilderness;
> And, in the isolation of the sky,
> At evening, casual flocks of pigeons make
> Ambiguous undulations as they sink,
> Downward to darkness, on extended wings.

After a long, reflective silence, I whispered, "What do you make of these last lines?"

She gazed into my eyes and replied wistfully, "I hear acceptance."

"Acceptance? Acceptance of what?"

"That her dream will never be fulfilled as imagined. . . . And what do you hear in the stanza?" she asked.

"I think you nailed it. But to capture the thrust of the last lines, perhaps I'd add the words 'courageous' and 'willful' to your reading."

"So how would you read it then?" she asked softly.

"A courageous and willful acceptance that her dream will never be fulfilled as imagined."

She turned away as tears welled up in her eyes. I quietly rose from the sofa, moved over to the fireplace, and stared into the flames.

By the time the butler returned we had both regained our composure. "Your drinks, ma'am," he announced as he crossed the room.

"Just put them over here on the table, Raymond."

"Is there anything else, ma'am?"

"Yes. Please fetch Catarina. She should be in her apartment."

"Yes, ma'am."

As the butler exited, I returned to the sofa and sat down close to Van. "You okay?" I asked caringly.

She nodded and laughed. "Yeah. Stevens and that poem in particular just get to me sometimes."

Just then a young woman entered the room and approached the sofa. She was wearing a shimmering turquoise dress with spaghetti straps. Her glimmering brunette curls eased down over her bare shoulders. She appeared to be in her early twenties and stunningly beautiful—blue, almond-shaped eyes; small nose; full, red lips; and large breasts hidden beneath a modest neckline.

As our guest extended her hand, Van announced, "Todd, this is my daughter, Catarina. And Catarina, this is Todd, the young man I was tellin' ya about."

Catarina gazed into my eyes, smiled, and said, "Pleased to meet ya."

"Same here," I mumbled as I absorbed her beauty.

Van then added a bit of biography. "Catarina just finished her liberal arts degree at St. Mary's Dominican in New Orleans. During the summers, she's been stayin' with Daddy and soakin' up as much of the plantation business as possible: the farmin', factorin', accountin', lawyerin', and"—Van paused, glanced over at her daughter, smiled, and emphasized—"and independent thinkin' too. Now that she's older and earned her degree, Daddy, Catarina, and I think it's time for her to learn somethin' about the entertainment business too."

As I picked up the mahogany tray and served mother and daughter their drinks, I smiled and responded self-effacingly, "And if y'all'd like, I'll be very happy to share the little I know as well."

Van turned to Catarina and warned her teasingly, "Now I'm tellin' ya, dear, you have to watch out for this fellow. He's really smooth. He could sell ice to Eskimos."

After about ten more minutes of banter, Van finished her brandy and announced, "Well, I'm gonna make an early night of it. I'll leave it to the two of you to welcome in the dawn." She picked up her copy of Stevens's *Harmonium* and added, "A little light readin' before puttin' out the light." As she neared the doorway, she turned and said, "It's really good havin' the two of ya back home here tonight."

"Good bein' home with ya, Mother," Catarina said.

"Same here, Van," I added.

Once the door clicked shut, Catarina moved over to the sofa and sat down where Van had been sitting. She took a long sip of her gin and tonic, laughed nervously, and admitted, "I want to have this conversation, but I don't know if there's really a good way to start it. . . ."

Dying with curiosity I encouraged her to begin. "No worries. Just get the ball rolling and we'll keep her on track."

"Okay then, here goes." Catarina took a deep breath and said, "All that talk about independent thinking you were hearing just now?" Her cheeks flushed.

"Yeah. what about it?"

"You can forget it. Well, at least when it comes to my case. Ya see, Mother and Grandpa do all the independent thinking in our family. And they've concluded since I've finished my education, it's time for me to settle down. So, Todd, tell me, how does it feel to be the chosen one?"

"The chosen one? I don't understand. Chosen to do what?"

"To be my suitor and join me and my uncle as heirs apparent in our line of succession."

"My God, Catarina, you make it sound like royalty."

"You've got it! In my grandfather's and mother's minds, we are royalty. Oh, not in any kind of a haughty way, but in a feeling we have a bloodline and unique lifestyle to protect."

I laughed skeptically and questioned her premise. "If you

knew my background, you wouldn't be making that assertion."

"You mean your missteps into music and the market?"

I gasped and muttered, "Van told you?"

Catarina patted me on the shoulder and responded empathetically, "Yeah, she told me everything. But as Mother says, 'With youth you rely more on potential than record. Early mistakes make you wise and strong. And failure's the real highway to success.'" She paused and then asked, "You understand what I'm saying about royalty?"

I nodded, took a sip of my Gorman Hollow, and replied reflectively, "All too well, Catarina. Believe me, all too well. . . . You see, my father controls a multimillion-dollar enterprise some hundred and fifty miles or so east of here. I won't bore you with all the sordid details, but there are stepbrothers, competition, and increasing interest in making sure we're all married with lots of children straggling along behind us. So, yeah, I know something about that kind of royalty and its trappings."

"Mother says you're getting into the liquor trade."

"Yeah, my father's taking advantage of some of the loopholes in the Volstead Act. I'm doing the marketing and distributing this fine—" I stopped midsentence, smiled, and said, "But you probably already know all about it and you're probably also aware your mother and grandfather have contracted to be my first customers. And if I can build off that substantial base, I should recoup much if not all of what I just lost in the market." I paused and then drove the ball back into Catarina's court. "So given your education and summers working with your grandfather on the plantation, you have plans to start working full time?"

She laughed and replied coyly, "Of course, as long as I can avoid marriage and children."

"But, God forbid, you get tangled up in nuptials. What would you do then?"

She reflected and answered honestly, "Oh, I suspect my husband and . . . and any children would be my top priorities. But knowing me, I'd have to stay connected to something outside the house and the family. Maybe something to do with the symphony or the opera."

I leaned in excitedly and asked, "You take an interest in music?"

Catarina nodded. "I've been playing piano since I was five. Mostly classical: Chopin, Liszt, Beethoven, Brahms. Some concerts but mostly house and church recitals."

"You ever hear of Jimmy Yancey?" I asked.

She shook her head. "But let me guess, a local musician."

"Pianist. Blues player. The boogie-woogie."

"The boogie . . . ah . . . ?"

"The boogie-woogie. Come on over to the piano and I'll try showing you a few licks. I can sort of tease it out. Used piano sometimes to scratch out a song." I led her over to the piano and instructed her to take a seat next to me. "Now your left hand is the regular bass line," I explained, "and you're playing in common time with repetition—like this." I tapped out a few bars. "And the right hand does the decorating. like so." A few more notes graced the air. "Then you put it all together, and it sounds something like this"—I gave it my all—"but a lot faster than I can manage. You're the pianist. Why don't you try it?"

"I don't know."

"Try it! There's no one here."

"Okay. How's this?" Her fingers flew over the piano keys light as a butterfly.

"Yeah, maybe a little heavier on the bass line." She tried again, this time with a little more oomph. "Good!" I said. "Now pick up the pace a bit. That's it. See, you're playing the boogie-woogie."

She missed several keys, broke out laughing, and stopped. "Whew! You know, that's tougher than Beethoven or Bach. What is it?"

"One of my all-time favorites, 'Pine Top's Boogie-Woogie.' Clarence 'Pine Top' Smith wrote it. I'm gonna ask Mr. Yancey to play it in Pine Top's memory."

"He died?"

"Yeah, less than a year ago. Chicago. Random gunshot while playing in a dance hall. Hit him in the chest. Died in four hours. Just twenty-five and on the verge of making it big."

"Sad."

"By the way, would you like to hear Mr. Yancey play? He'll be coming through this Friday night."

Catarina smiled. "I'd like that."

"Great! It may be the only time we'll ever get a chance to see him. Lives in Chicago, rarely travels. He played in the Negro League, and of all things, signed on as groundskeeper for the Chicago White Sox."

"White Sox?"

"Sorry. A professional baseball team. You see, the only time he has to travel is in the dead of winter after the baseball

227

season's over. And wait 'til you hear him play. Ends every song in E flat no matter what key she's been written in."

At first Catarina didn't respond. She sat staring at our hands positioned on the keyboard. She slid her hand over on to mine and said, "Thank you, Todd."

"Thanks for what?"

"For talking this out."

"Believe me, I've enjoyed it."

"Yeah, me too. And we're now starting on an honest footing. And if anything ever comes of us, we'll know it wasn't because of the family and their sense of royalty."

"That's right. And we won't let on that you and I'll be sailing this ship from now on. Agreed?"

She turned to me and smiled. "Agreed."

"Until Friday night then?"

"Yeah. Friday night."

I returned to my apartment, undressed, and crawled in under the heavy blankets. I stared out the casement far beyond the late-November stars. What was Van really up to? Was it just about solidifying the future ownership of her father's enterprise? Or was this matchmaking much more personal than business? Did she mistakenly believe her dream could "never be fulfilled as imagined" because she was too old for me? Did she sacrifice her own happiness—substituting this striking, youthful lookalike for herself? And then, what about our birthday rendezvous? Was this when she concluded she'd be more mother than lover? Or did she envision the tryst as an opportunity to school a future son-in-law in how to please her daughter?

21

ONCE VAN AND my mother had informed the grand- and great-grandparents, Catarina's and my newborn, Raphael, was welcomed into our families and at both weddings. Since neither patriarch would relinquish his privilege, Catarina and I double tied the knot, exchanging vows first at Gorman Hollow and then at Saint Louis Cathedral in the heart of the Big Easy.

After the ceremonies, life could not have been any sweeter. Everyone on both sides of the aisle settled into a comfortable routine, drifting along somewhere between tolerable boredom and excruciating happiness. As my book of business and responsibilities grew, I regretfully spent more time away from home. And just as Catarina had predicted, she fought her loneliness with outside activities—not supporting the arts as she'd imagined, but founding her own benevolent organization, the Mary Magdalene Charities.

I especially recall returning home one Friday evening after an extended period on the road selling liquor. As I drove up the entryway to our manor house on the bluffs of Memphis, I spotted Catarina standing beneath the portico, waving and resting our three-year-old son on her hip. I rolled to a stop on the circular driveway, rushed up the steps, and gave both of them a big hug. "I missed you guys. Y'all doing okay?"

Catarina smiled broadly. "We're doing just fine. Your mother's been here the last few days helping out while I've been tending to the food drive. Grab your things out of the car and hurry on in. The three of us have something to show you."

"I'll be right there. Believe me, I've been gone way too long this time."

After greeting Mother and checking up on Jesse and Gramps, I turned to Catarina and asked, "What was it you wanted to show me?"

Catarina looked over at my mother and beamed. "Margaret, would ya watch Raphael for a few minutes while I . . ."

Mother laughed and interjected, "Sure will! Let me know when you're ready for us."

Catarina grabbed my hand and tugged. "Come along. Wait 'til ya see this." We climbed the stairs, walked the length of the hallway, and entered Raphael's room. "Here. Let me open the curtains so ya have light. Now look around. Ya see anything unusual?"

I briefly scanned the furniture, the bed, and the walls. I looked over at Catarina, shrugged my shoulders, and said, "I give up. I don't see anything. What is it?"

"Take a better look at the dresser."

I stepped closer and discovered some elastic bands stretched between the knobs on the bottom four drawers. "That's clever. Raphael do that?"

Catarina nodded and laughed aloud.

"You think we have an architect or maybe a bridge build-er on our hands?"

She shook her head and replied, "Perhaps a little more exciting than that!" She patted me on the arm and turned toward the door. "Stay here. I'll fetch Margaret and Raphael."

Several minutes later the three of them crowded into the room. Raphael broke loose from my mother, hopped up on his bed, and began jumping up and down. I looked over at Catarina and shrugged. "This is the other thing you wanted to show me? Maybe a gymnast in the circus and not an engineer?"

Mama and Catarina both laughed conspiratorially. "Stay here with Margaret and Raphael. I need to run downstairs for a minute," Catarina said.

After she disappeared around the corner, I turned to my mother and asked lightheartedly, "Okay, so what's going on here?"

She shrugged her shoulders innocently and answered, "Hold on. You'll see."

Silence and then music began flowing upward from the music room below. Catarina was at the keyboard playing the exquisite andante from Beethoven's "Appassionato" sonata. Mother looked at me and then over at Raphael, who had stopped jumping and was standing at the center of the bed transfixed by the melody.

I looked over at my mother and shrugged.

She put her finger to her lips and then whispered, "Just keep watching."

And as if on cue, Raphael climbed down off the bed, moved over to the dresser, and began plucking the elastic bands attempting to replicate the sonata Catarina was playing a floor below. "He did all this himself?" I asked incredulously.

Mama nodded with vigor. "Yes. I was mystified. I watched him out of the corner of my eye as he stretched the bands over the knobs this morning. I didn't have a clue what he was up to. But then Catarina began playing and voilà! . . . Not just the Beethoven either. This morning it was a Brahms intermezzo."

"You think there's something to this?"

"If I were you, I wouldn't ignore it."

"Whatdaya think we ought to do?"

"I'd introduce him to several instruments—the piano, the fiddle, the . . . the . . . you name it! You could see if he's drawn to any of 'em in particular."

"I had an idea just now, Mama."

"What's that?"

"Maybe Gramps would like to get involved. Offer to pick him up and just keep him here overnight. I think he'd be curious enough to do it if we explained what was going on and promised to get him back to Hollow Rock the next morning. Whatdaya think?"

"If Catarina's okay with it, I think he'd be a good place to start."

Two weeks later Gramps made his first foray into Memphis in years; and within minutes, he'd made a friend for life. The ever-cautious Raphael was sitting on Gramps's knee bouncing up and down and singing. "I think he's got a good ear and a sense of timing." Gramps said and added, "So let's check it out. Where's your piano?"

"In the music room down the hall," Catarina replied.

"Where are my bags?"

"Upstairs in a guest room near us," I said. "You need something out of them?"

"Yeah. Could ya get my violin and the canvas bag?"

"No problem," I said, then turned to my wife and added, "In the meantime, Catarina, would you take Mama, Raphael, and Gramps down to the music room while I grab his things?"

When I returned, Catarina and Gramps were sitting on the piano bench. Raphael was perched on Gramps's lap. Catarina would hit a key, and Raphael would find the corresponding note an octave higher. After a few minutes, Catarina graduated to simple chords. She would play the three notes on her right hand, and Raphael would copy them an octave higher. She then shifted up one note to the next, thus changing the chord from C major, to D minor, then to E minor, F major, and so on. And after a few stumbles, Raphael picked up the exercise—C, D, E, F, and the like.

Gramps lifted Raphael up off his lap and said, "Okay, young man, hop down for a minute. Gramps has to fetch his fiddle." After tuning to Catarina's piano, Gramps played a four-minute "warm-up" exercise, Fritz Kreisler's dazzling cadenza closing out the first movement of Beethoven's violin concerto. Raphael stood a few feet away listening with rapt attention. When Gramps finished the fireworks, Raphael ran over and began pulling on his pant leg screaming, "More! More!"

"Whoa, boy, ya wanna wear Gramps out? I tell ya what, maybe ya could help him a bit. Ya like that?"

Raphael stopped screaming and nodded.

"Okay, come along then." Gramps took Raphael by the hand and led him over to the canvas bag. "What's in there, boy? It's okay. Open her up and see what's inside."

With a little of Gramps's help, Raphael managed to loosen the drawstring and drag out a small violin case. "Here, let me unlatch it for ya so ya can see what's inside."

Raphael lifted the lid, peered in, and then slowly withdrew a miniature silver masterpiece from the case. We all gasped at the beauty and the thoughtfulness of the gift. "You said he was big for his age," Gramps explained, "so I made it a hair larger—a quarter-size—usually recommended for a five-to seven-year-old." He looked over at me and asked, "Does she look familiar?"

I nodded and replied, "Yeah, same color as the six-string you built for me. Even has the black streaks like it."

"It's because I made the quarter-size here out of some of the boards I had left over after finishin' your dreadnought."

"Out of the thunderwood?"

"Yeah, out of the thunderwood ya dragged out of that pile. Remember?"

I nodded. "How could I forget?"

"Thunderwood?" Catarina asked.

"Yes. Trees that have been hit by lightning. Folks swear there's magic in the wood, and Gramps and I agree. There's an incredible balance between the bass, the midrange, and the treble." I glanced down at Raphael, who was now sitting on the floor, holding his violin like a guitar and plucking the strings. "Be gentle, son, that's not a toy!" I looked over at Catarina again and added, "Gramps won't let on, but he gets commissions from virtuosos in the finest orchestras in the land. Folks have compared his violins to Guarneri's and Amati's."

Gramps reached down and picked up the bow. "Enough of me now. Let's see how the boy takes to the fiddle." He sat down on the piano bench and motioned for Raphael to move closer. "Come here, son, sit here beside Gramps and let's play! Whatdaya say?"

After tuning the quarter-size, Gramps showed Raphael how to hold the bow and fiddle. He introduced him to open string rhythms, first on the E string followed by A, D, and G. With those exercises completed, Gramps looked over at Catarina and said, "I think that's enough for today. . . . Maybe tomorrow mornin' you could do forty-five minutes with him on the piano, and then I'll follow up with forty-five minutes in the afternoon after his nap. Okay by you?"

Catarina nodded. "Okay by me."

Later that afternoon we were stunned. Gramps informed us he was putting his own work on hold and was willing to stay a couple of weeks until we could find a suitable violin instructor. Everyone agreed Raphael should continue on this two-track schedule studying piano with his mother, who was an accomplished pianist, and receiving violin instruction from a professional associated with the local orchestra. Gramps even suggested and later vetted several violinists who were offering lessons at the Reinhardt Music Shop in the Peabody Hotel downtown. And only after Raphael's instruction became routine did Gramps express his desire to return home.

Since Gorman Hollow wasn't too far from Gramps's place, I took the opportunity to kill two birds with one stone. I had a lot on my mind and wanted to spend some time with Father sorting through the issues. So after accompanying

Gramps to Hollow Rock, I headed to Warfield by train.

As we drove to the farm from the Warfield depot, I asked my father, "Aren't you worried?"

"No, not really," he replied.

"I'm having trouble sleeping. Seems like every week another state ratifies the amendment. What are they down to now? A dozen or so states?"

"I think they're down closer to eight."

"And you're not worried that everything could go up in smoke? The wholesaler, the distilleries, the trucking, the bottling . . ."

Father smiled but then turned serious. "What did I tell you helped folks succeed?"

"Ah, anticipating."

"Okay then, start anticipating. So the states ratify the amendment repealing Prohibition. You have a drug wholesaler, five distilleries, a trucking company, and bottling operations here on the premises. Now what do you do? Shut it all down and sell as much of the real estate as you can to recoup a tenth of your losses?"

"I suppose not."

"Suppose? No, no, you don't. It's simple, son, you just slide everything over to the legitimate side of the ledger. Every one of these concerns can easily become legal and, most importantly, profitable. Legal and profitable wholesaling, trucking, distilling, and bottling. You see how it works? Anticipating."

"So you think we have nothing to worry about? Everything's secure?"

Father smiled. "Doubly so."

"Doubly so? Whatdaya mean?"

"The scenario I just laid out for you is the backup to the reality."

"The backup?"

"Yeah. You see, nothing's gonna happen here in Tennessee. Everything's gonna stay the same as before. We're not gonna have to slide anything over on the ledger for now."

"Why are you so sure? The state convention here's already ratified the amendment."

"Remember what you just said. 'The state convention ratified it.'"

"So?"

"This is the only amendment ever to be ratified by state convention rather than the state legislature. So I had no sway this time. But remember, the states can do anything they like about Prohibition. They don't have to follow federal dictates. And believe me, the influence I lacked at the state convention is more than made up for by the sway I have in the regular legislature." He removed his wallet from his breast pocket and pulled out some crisp hundred-dollar bills. "You see these? They talk, and the legislators listen. Politics is local, son. I have no doubt the ban that the General Assembly passed back in '07 will stay in effect for the foreseeable future."

"For how long, Father?"

"If you put a gun to my head, I'd say we have a good five years."

"And then what? Move over to the other side of the law, ah, the ledger?"

He smiled teasingly. "Not sure just yet. So ya better start anticipating, ya hear?"

"You doing some anticipating too?"

He nodded and stared out the window at the walnut trees bordering the property. "We sure have a lot of wood hanging around here."

"You're not gonna say anything, are you?"

He smiled and answered, "You never know how a cake's gonna taste 'til she comes out of the oven."

22

"I CAN'T BELIEVE the two of you are suggesting a voyage to Europe while my father's busy supplying rifle stocks anticipating a world war. What has gotten into y'all?"

Catarina tried to explain. "Grandfather says the boy no longer belongs to us. Even though he's only nine years old, he belongs to the world now; and we mustn't hold him back."

"So tell me then, who's this fella that Raphael would be touring with?"

"Now don't forget Raphael wouldn't be alone," Van rejoined. "Catarina and I would also be travelin' with him."

"I know, and for God's sake, Van, that means the three of you would be away from now until God knows when. Probably close to a year." I paused and spoke reflectively, "And that's a helluva long time to be away from home."

Catarina tried to soothe me. "But Grandfather says that that sacrifice is our gift to the world."

"With all due respect to both of you, I just wish y'all had never gotten Mr. de Terrant involved in raising our child. So, Van, tell me now, who's this fella your father recommends Raphael start touring with next month?"

"His name's Eugène Messier, a renowned French virtuoso, a prodigy who started performin' when he was five and made his debut at age ten with the L'Orchestre Lamoureux playing the Brahms Violin Concerto. And when he's not tourin', he teaches at the Paris Conservatory."

"What does this Mr. Messier have in mind for Raphael?" I asked.

"In his letter to my father, he suggested they perform together. Take the pressure off Raphael at the outset, playin' something like Vivaldi's *Double Concerto* or perhaps Bach's *Concerto for Two Violins*, that is, if Eugène thinks Raphael has progressed enough to master it. In addition, Eugène's offered to provide private instruction on their days off while travelin' between cities."

"So how did your father come to know this Mr. Messier?"

"Ah. He's a friend of the family on my mother's side," Van said. "Mama wasn't born here in the States, you know. She's a Parisian. Father met her there while travelin'; and after a lengthy transatlantic courtship, he proposed and brought her back home to his Louisiana estate. Well, anyway, Eugène visited our plantation after a successful tour playin' with all the leadin' American symphony orchestras. And like every young man in his twenties, he wanted to 'experience' the French Quarter in New Orleans. So he showed up on our doorstep and stayed for six weeks 'soakin' up the Creole culture.'" Van paused, smiled reminiscently, and continued, "He was such a striking young man then. In his twenties, dark curls, deep blue eyes."

I interrupted her reverie. "Where would the tour be taking y'all? I'm telling you I was serious about my father and the rifle stocks. You know, it could all blow up. It's not far-fetched."

"No worries," Van said. "We'll be safe. We're never steppin' foot into Germany anyway. So let's see, now—and help me out, Catarina—from New York we sail to Le Havre, then by train to Rouen, where we meet up with Eugène. He recommended startin' the concerts off in a smaller venue to acclimate Raphael to performin' in unfamiliar halls. Then it's on to Paris, then to, ah . . . ah . . ."

"Reims," Catarina filled in.

"That's right, Reims. Next we go to Brussels, then to Amsterdam, and from there we sail to Southampton and by train to Glasgow. Then a grand finale in London and"—she paused, smiled broadly, and concluded with a flourish—"and then we come back home to you!"

Catarina turned and gazed into my eyes. "Please, for Raphael's sake, please let us go."

Realizing I was outmanned and outgunned, I surrendered. "Against my better judgment, I'll agree to the tour, but with the provisos that you write often and that you abandon the tour if there's an immediate threat. Y'all promise?"

Both of them nodded and agreed in unison, "We promise."

So my stack of yellowing correspondence begins with a dispatch from New York City. Catarina writes: "Several hours ago we boarded the S.S. *Normandie* and will spend the next four days in the lap of luxury. Deluxe cabins appointed in rich palettes of blue with rare paneling and contemporary paintings; air-conditioned dining salons walled in molded glass; marble-lined foyers featuring wide sweeping staircases; and a 400-seat theater where tomorrow evening we'll see Ravel's acclaimed ballet, *Boléro*. . . .

".After disembarking at Le Havre, we traveled by train to Rouen, where we met up with Eugène. After an exquisite lunch at a quaint café, he guided us first along the banks of the Seine; next to the Place du Vieux Marché, where Joan of Arc was burned at the stake; then to Cathedral Square; and finally to the Musée des Beaux-Arts to enjoy masterpieces by Caravaggio, Rubens, Sisley, and Monet, including one of Monet's Rouen Cathedral studies in a cool mist of blues and grays. . . . The following morning, Eugène and Raphael rehearsed the Vivaldi piece and then played it flawlessly that evening before an overflow crowd at the Theatre Arts. You would have been so proud.

"During our first two days in Paris, Eugène and Raphael spent much of the time rehearsing the Bach piece with the Rameau Chamber Players. Since they could never completely iron out all the timing issues in the first movement, Eugène suggested they play only the slow second movement as an encore. All three thousand seats were filled for both the Wednesday and Thursday performances, which concluded with standing ovations. . . . Again, it would have given you the chills seeing our Raphael playing on the same stage where Stravinsky and Ravel conducted their own music at the opening of the hall a mere decade ago.

"With nothing scheduled on Friday, Eugène took us in the morning to the Louvre where we viewed da Vinci's portrait, *Mona Lisa*, Michelangelo's unfinished sculptures, *The Slaves*, and Alexandros's marble masterpiece, the *Venus de Milo*. Following a pleasant lunch at the museum, we traveled by taxi to Montmartre, where Eugène led us on an unforgettable walking tour of the bohemian neighborhood that numerous Impressionists had earlier called home. After passing by houses once owned by Renoir and Monet, we climbed a small hill to see the former apartments of an eclectic group of creative artists—the pointillist, Seurat; the composer, Eric Satie; and the controversial cubist, Picasso.

"Eugène's walking tour was full of surprises. He suggested we stop for an espresso and pastry at a small restaurant, *Aux Billards en Bois*, where he informed us we were sitting at the very tables once occupied by the likes of Pissarro, Sisley, Cézanne, Renoir, and Monet. After leaving the café, we descended into the seedy district of Montmartre, where we passed by Van Gogh's old apartment before ending the tour at a dance hall, the Moulin Blute Fin, which Renoir had captured so famously in his painting *Dance at Le Moulin de la Galette.*

"The driving rain curtailed the already limited amount of time we had for sightseeing in the ancient city of Reims. We managed to see the Saint Remi Basilica and the Cathedral of Notre Dame, both of which still bear the ugly scars of the German bombardment during that war to end all wars. Since the Reims venue was small and the Rameau Chamber Players would also be playing this concert with us, Eugène thought it worth the risk to play the entire Bach piece despite the difficulties they'd been experiencing during rehearsals. And his intuition was right on target. The pressure of the live performance caused everyone to focus on his timing and play almost to perfection.

"Brussels was all work and no play. Eugène was intent on Raphael increasingly spreading his wings. He not only wanted Raphael to play the Vivaldi and Bach pieces but to master two encores for violin and piano for the last two stops on the continent. Eugène first worked with Raphael on Elgar's *Salut d'Amour* and then Massenet's *Méditation* from *Thaïs*. The game plan was to perform the shorter Elgar piece for the encore in Brussels and then play both works at the famed Concertgebouw in Amsterdam. . . .

"We're currently sailing into the English Channel headed for Southhampton. The engagement at Amsterdam's Concertgebouw was memorable first because Raphael played all four pieces flawlessly and secondly because he received permission to attend a closed rehearsal of Richard Strauss's tone poems, *Ein Heldenleben* and *Death and Transfiguration*, conducted by the composer himself! After the run-through, Mr. Strauss agreed to meet privately with Eugène and Raphael. During the interview, the composer asked our son to play the Elgar piece and afterwards praised him for his genius.

"Right on schedule our train left Kings Cross Station en route to Glasgow Central. As we pass through the English Midlands, I stare out the window at the passing countryside. Everyone else has fallen asleep from exhaustion. I now have some rare time to myself to reflect on what the trip has meant for Raphael and me. As I've mentioned several times before, I believe the tour has been a blessing for him. He has grown so much in confidence, intellect, and artistic expression. You'll sense it right away.

"And as for me, our lengthy separation has helped me understand how important you are to my happiness. I know I've found the perfect man to share my life. You understand me as no one else ever has. When you hold me, I feel secure. My world of care disappears. I realize the sacrifice you've made while we've been traversing the globe. I miss your touch, your smell, your reassuring smile. And as the journey nears its end, I keep reminding myself that in only a few more days we'll all be going home."

23

LONG AFTER THE headlines and telegrams had been filed away, the letters continued drifting home like flotsam from some forlorn shipwreck settling to the floor of a sunless sea. For the longest time, I couldn't open the envelopes and bear witness to their final hours. But as Mama predicted, "Time does begin to heal all wounds." So on the second anniversary of their "passing at sea," I read the letters from beyond the grave and added them to all the others.

My stack of yellowing correspondence continues with a dispatch from Scotland. Catarina writes: "When we arrived at Glasgow Central, it was raining. A strong wind was blowing out of the southwest. It was cold for the end of August. Since we'd had an early lunch en route, Eugène suggested we drop our things off at the hotel and head over to the Willows for afternoon tea.

"One look at the Room de Luxe explained everything. Eugène hadn't suggested the Willows for the tasty sandwiches and scones but for the architecture, interior design, and decorative arts crafted by a leading proponent of the Art Nouveau—bay window, vaulted ceiling, a lavish palette of purples, white, and gray, silver-painted tables and high-backed chairs upholstered in a sumptuous rose. White walls as simple backdrops for a complex succession of colored and mirrored panels.

"We met that night at the Theatre Royal for the first of two rehearsals with principal string players of the BBC Scottish Symphony Orchestra. And there was a stark difference in focus and atmosphere between the run-through that evening and the one the next morning. The evening rehearsal was relaxed, upbeat, and all about the music, but that second session the following morning was tense, glum, and dominated by discussions of rumored troop movements near Germany's border with Poland.

"While all three thousand tickets had been sold for that evening's concert, only half the seats were filled. The stage manager speculated that folks who had suffered through the great war were nervously staying close to their radios listening to the latest dispatches about the growing crisis. Sad to say, the patrons who stayed away missed the finest performance of the entire tour. . . . But no time for regrets now. In the morning it will be off to the grand finale in London before heading home to you.

"We all piled into the taxi and headed for what Mother and I thought would be Glasgow Central, but ten minutes later we rolled to a stop near Queen's Dock at Stobcross. . . . Eugène handed Mother an envelope containing three tickets for the British ship, S.S. *Athenia*, sailing for Montreal via Liverpool and Belfast the next day. He apologized that while the accommodations were indeed first class, he expected the cabins wouldn't be anywhere near as opulent as what we'd experienced on our trip over via the *Normandie*.

"Why the ship and not the train? Eugène explained that the crisis was worsening by the hour, and he knew we had a promise to keep—if there was the slightest hint of danger, we were to set sail for North America at once. I admit I pushed back, asking about the grand finale in London. But Eugène said he expected a similar situation there as we'd experienced here, predicting half the audience would fail to appear. He reassured me, however, that he would carry on with the London concert before sailing back home to France.

"As Eugène had predicted, the *Athenia*'s first-class accommodations are nowhere near as luxurious as the *Normandie*'s. The cabins are smaller, the menu more limited, and the live entertainment nonexistent. But the prevailing mood on board is one of relief, realizing we're leaving Britain just in the nick of time. The radio dispatches are becoming more ominous by the hour; and in fact, just as we are now about to sail out of Queen's Dock, we hear the Germans have invaded Poland and a British ultimatum is most likely in the cards. . . .

"But looking on the bright side of things, we're safe; we're headed home to you; and romance flits about in the air! Raphael has made friends with a young Canadian girl, who of all things bears your mother's name, Margaret. But with all joking aside, it's good seeing him acting more like a boy than a child prodigy constantly trying to meet unrealistic adult expectations.

"Mother and I had plenty of time to talk while sailing to our intermediate stops in Liverpool and Belfast. In fact, we stayed up the whole night reminiscing and projecting the future! Since I don't want anything to get in the way when we arrive home, I am posting this final installment of our travelogue from Belfast before setting sail for Montreal. I want you to know what we discussed so you can adjust to the news before our arrival.

"While taking our tea on the upper deck, Mother turned and casually asked what I'd thought of Eugène. I responded honestly. I said I admired his talent, his intellect, and his desire to always put our safety and comfort first. I then turned the tables and said something to the effect, 'Since you're both unmarried and about the same age, perhaps it's more important we know how you feel about him.' Mother didn't respond immediately. She turned away, stared out over the railing, and took several sips of her tea. She finally turned and replied enigmatically, 'It's so much different now than it was back then,' which was her way of segueing to a revelation that Eugène is my father!

"I sat there stunned for the longest time. But as hurt eventually replaced numbing surprise, tears began streaming down my face. 'Why didn't you tell me? All that time on the tour together and nothing, no inkling he was my father.' Mother wiped the tears away and explained, 'Because . . . because he had no idea you were his daughter. My darling, when he returned to France, neither he nor I knew of my condition. And once I'd confirmed the pregnancy, I asked myself, what good would it do now telling him or anyone else for that matter? He was a friend of the family. Start a scandal, destroy friendships, and scuttle a promising career? No. . . . Steal away and abort the baby? Again, no. I was Catholic, and my father had the means to support the child and me.' She smiled and stroked my hair. 'And thank God I thought things through and didn't do anything rash.'

"When I had fully regained my composure, I probed naively, 'Any chance of the two of you ever getting back together again?' Mother smiled and shook her head. 'Couldn't you tell there was nothing romantic there? Oh, Eugène and I will never forget that summer, but we've both moved on now.' I asked, 'Moved on to other lovers?' Mother smiled and replied tenderly, 'We've both moved on, Catarina. Loving others safely from afar.'

"I must stop here. We're sailing soon, and I want to be sure this gets posted from Belfast. It won't be long now, my love. From Belfast to Montreal to Chicago and then to you."

Only ten hours after Britain declared war on Germany, the commander of U-boat 30 gave the command to launch two torpedoes. While one misfired, the other hit its mark, and the *Athenia* began to sink. Did they die in the after stairwell during the initial blast? Were they crushed trying to climb from a lifeboat to a rescue destroyer? Did they capsize in rough seas near the stern of the Swedish yacht, the *Southern Cross*? Or was their lifeboat of fifty souls sucked into the massive propellers of the Norwegian rescue tanker, the *Knute Nelson*? Of course, I'll never know for sure. The only certainty for me: the *Athenia* lies beneath six hundred feet of the North Atlantic two hundred miles west of the Hebrides cradling my wife, my son, and my lover.

24

"Did ya ever think you'd see the day?" Jesse asked.

I shook my head and replied, "I'll breathe easy only after we start rolling out of Les Pieux."

"Seems so long ago now since we volunteered. You said it was personal for you, that you couldn't stay home after losing Catarina and Raphael. Big step, I mean, selling your manor house and leaving the family business behind."

"And you said it was 'country' for you . . . and then you added with a wink, 'I also have to look out for my little brother.'"

"Looking back on it now, Todd, you were the one who sacrificed the most. Telling the world you and I were indeed brothers. Checking the box labeled 'Negro.'"

"Sacrifice? No. Just setting the record straight once and for all, Jesse. I pushed the guilt way down low hiding my color. But it was the only way I knew to make it in the world... Color and selling stocks and liquor just don't mix."

"But being a volunteer, if you had kept quiet, you could've gotten any assignment ya wanted. By declaring yourself a Negro, the best the recruiter could offer was armored. I recall you asking the sergeant, 'Armored?' He clarified for you, 'Yeah, tanks.'. You looked over at me and whispered, 'Tanks? Hell, I barely know how to drive.'"

We both laughed out loud and Jesse continued, "But the two years we've spent training to become tank commanders sure fixed that, didn't it? I'll never forget those long hot summers in Camp Claiborne and Camp Hood."

"Yeah, two years in hell," I said. "Especially for our boys from up north. Trying to figure out how old Jim Crow works. Oh, the stares when they wandered into town and crossed a line. Outrage from the white folk. Really hard for our boys adjusting."

"Maybe it was for the best, though," Jesse said. "Brought them together as a team. Made them a better fighting unit. Put a chip on their shoulder. Thinking, 'Give us Negroes a chance at fighting, and, by God, we'll show you what we're made of.'"

"Got a whole lot better once we got up to Camp Shanks in New York," I said.

"Yeah, but it wasn't long then until we were all boarding the troop transport for the haul over to England."

"Quite a send-off, though: the USO, the dancers, Lionel Hampton and the band. You remember what they were playing as we boarded the *Esperance Bay*?" I asked wistfully.

Jesse nodded. "Yeah, for sure. One of my favorites. 'Flyin' Home.' And I suspect that was Jacquet on the tenor sax too."

"And then from the fresh air and daylight of New York Harbor down into that oppressive, segregated hold. I remember catching up on my sleep. What'd you do?" I asked.

"Hearts and craps," Jesse replied lightheartedly. "It's not every day a man of the cloth has a chance to play. Took everyone for a ride too. But what good did it do me? We got to

England, and the next thing I know we're boarding the LST for the channel crossing."

"Yeah. Normandy. Impressive, huh? . . . Couldn't believe how much twisted metal and barbed wire was still piled up there beneath the cliffs. Been what now, some four months since the landing?"

"Yeah, something like that," Jesse said. "And I hear some three thousand killed and wounded right there along Omaha Beach."

"I'd like to have stayed a while longer and looked around, but Colonel gave the orders to start our engines; and we were off to this quaint place, Les Pieux, right in the middle of nowhere."

"And this too shall pass away," Jesse replied consolingly.

"Yeah, hopefully tomorrow morning bright and early. I guess we better get a little shut-eye. You wanna close the flap there? It's freezing, and it's only the end of October."

Just after sunrise our "bastard battalion" of seven hundred men, fifty-six Sherman medium tanks, and seventeen Stuart light tanks set off for Saint Nicholas-de-Port some four hundred miles to the east in the French Province of Lorraine. Our orders were to mark time there until called into action with the Twenty-sixth Infantry Division of the XII Corps in Patton's Third Army. These were the warriors who had earlier bled and died at the tip of the spear paving the way for our battalion's own "heroic" advance across northern France. Ironically, while the men of the Twenty-sixth had done all the fighting, we were the soldiers who were being cheered as heroes as we passed through every town and city on our way over to Lorraine.

Our six-day advance across northern France included two memorable stops, one for Jesse and the other for me. The first was Reims, where Catarina, Van, and Raphael had visited the cathedral and the basilica during their tour in '39. After my men had bivouacked for the night, I slipped away to walk where my family had walked and touch what they had touched.

The vast spaces of Notre Dame flickered in the enduring light of thousands of offertory candles animating the carved life of the Virgin and the martyrdoms of Saint Stephen and John the Baptist. Europe slept as I stood near the soaring nave listening to the mystical silences. From worlds away I sensed a prayer of intercession on my behalf. Among the midnight echoes I heard Van pray: "O Heavenly Father, whose majesty transcends all things, I beseech you surround him with your loving care until his journey's end. I ask these things through Jesus Christ our Lord. Amen."

Little more than a day later we made the second stop. Unlike the first, it was brief, and this time there were no boulevards, plazas, or cathedrals—only a dirt crossroad with a sign pointing north that read "Séchault 20 km." I watched Jesse climb down off his tank and walk over to the marker. He draped his scarf over the direction arrow, stepped back, and lowered his head in silent prayer. After several minutes of reflection, he saluted, climbed back up onto the turret, and gave the signal to proceed.

Two days later, on the twenty-eighth, we finally reached

our objective. While Saint Nicholas-de-Port greeted us unceremoniously with sleet, rain, and the distant thunder of heavy artillery, the Twenty-sixth Infantry Division commander welcomed our battalion: "I am damned glad to have you with us. We have been expecting you for a long time, and I am sure you are going to give a good account of yourselves. I've got a big hill up there that I want you to take, and I believe that you are going to do a great job of it!"

After establishing camp in a muddy field outside the village, we quickly fell into a routine. Our daily work: making minor repairs to the tanks, oiling the guns, and testing the equipment, including the radio and the six periscopes. Our occasional play: enjoying the creamy, rich French chocolates and cavorting with the local ladies of the night. Despite the low rumble from the front line, the war remained hypothetical and distant.

But this routine ended abruptly the following week when our entire battalion was directed to quickly assemble and form a semicircle. Several minutes later, five jeeps loaded with military police and .50-caliber machine guns raced in and took up positions at the front and sides of our formation. Then a lone jeep sped in and rolled to a stop directly in front of Jesse and me. As our battalion commander barked "Attention!," a three-star general stepped out of his vehicle and jumped up on the hood of a half-track. Jesse leaned over and said, "Look at those ivory-handled pistols. That's got to be Patton!"

I nodded. "Yeah, that's gotta be Old Blood and Guts, but he's a lot shorter than I thought."

After surveying our Black Panther Battalion, the lieutenant general shouted out in a surprisingly high-pitched voice, "At ease, men!" He paused and then exhorted us to greatness: "You're the first Negro tankers to ever fight in the American army. I would never have asked for you if you weren't good. I have nothing but the best in my army. I don't care what color you are as long as you go up there and kill those Kraut sonsabitches. Everyone has their eyes on you and is expecting great things from you. Most of all, your race is looking forward to your success. Don't let them down, and damn you, don't let me down! . . . They say it's patriotic to die for your country. Well, let's see how many patriots we can make out of those German sonsabitches!"

As he jumped down off the half-track, the men of the 761st yelled "Yes, sir!" and then began chanting the battalion motto they'd adopted from the boxer Joe Louis: "Come out fightin'! Come out fightin'!"

Patton walked over to one of my tanks, climbed up on top of it, and inspected its new high-velocity gun. He then climbed down and spoke directly to one of my tank commanders. "Listen, boy. This is war. I want you to start shooting. Shoot every gawd damn thing you see—church steeples, water towers, houses, haystacks. Whenever you see a German, if it's male, eight to eighty years old, you kill them because they'll kill you. Shoot every gawd damn thing you see. Ya hear me, boy?"

My man looked Patton straight in the eye and replied firmly, "Yes, General!"

Less than a week later we got our orders to proceed east to Athainville and prepare to attack on the morning of the eighth. By the time we reached the line of departure, the weather had turned to a freezing rain. The field where we bivouacked was a sea of mud. After getting our men squared away, Jesse and I sat down to eat supper. "Damn, my feet are freezing," I said. "The mud's so thick here it's gotten in over the tops of my boots."

"That ain't the worst of it," Jesse said. "Somehow it's gotten into my hash. I'm having to fish the meat out of the filth."

"Man, will you look at that," I said. "It's really beginning to pour now. Looks like we'll have to sleep in our uniforms with the hatches buttoned up." I paused and then got to what was really on my mind. "You think Patton will give the go-ahead for tomorrow morning?"

Jesse nodded. "I'd bet the farm on it. Since everything's stalled in Europe, we're the only game in town, and the general wants to stand out. He's hell-bent on breaking through the Siegfried Line and pushing on up into the Saar region where the Germans have lots of industry."

"So you think he's not concerned we'll get bogged down in all the muck?"

"No way," Jesse replied. "The lieutenant colonel told me a while back Patton's personal motto is, 'Don't take council of your fears. Demand the impossible.' So there's no question in my mind we're headed out at six o'clock sharp."

"Well, I guess we'd better check our grease guns again then and make sure we have enough .45-caliber ammo for them. If we get stuck in this shit, we'll be sitting ducks. We'll have to bail out and fire our greasers as a last resort."

A little before five o'clock the next morning Jesse's theory was confirmed. The battalion was yanked out of its restless sleep by the deafening roar of exploding shells. As planned, five hundred of our heavy artillery pieces began firing on German positions to shape the battlefield in preparation for our tank and infantry attack.

An hour later we started our engines and rumbled out of Athainville with the battalion commander leading the way in his jeep. We were headed east toward our first objectives, the village of Bezange-la-Petite and Hill 253. We hadn't been on the road long before trucked infantry and tank destroyers from the 101st and 328th Regiments joined us. And I recall the comfort I felt watching our numbers grow.

As we approached the front line, the horrors of war were fed to us in spoonfuls. First, I spotted the bloated remains of a horse, which had suffered a direct hit from an exploding artillery round. The force of the blast had literally turned the animal inside out. Intestines now framed the rest of the mare's body. A few miles on, we saw destruction similar to what we'd seen earlier while crossing northern France— pot-marked fields, wrecked trucks and tanks, and buildings reduced to rubble.

And then the war became immediate and real. A young officer swerved his jeep in front of our tank and jumped out. He shouted up that he was an artillery spotter assigned to our company. He then climbed aboard, took my position atop the turret, and ordered our driver to advance to the edge of a ridge so he could begin reporting back enemy positions for our howitzers.

Just as we began moving toward the ridge, the Germans opened up with machine-gun fire and artillery. An errant or lucky armor-piercing shell exploded nearby, and within seconds a torrent of blood began soaking the front of my jacket. I reached up and pulled the officer down by the legs. I recoiled in horror at the sight of a headless body with blood still gurgling up out of the neck.

While I wanted to vomit, I held it together for the sake of my men. I coolly ordered the driver to stop below the ridgeline. The cannoneer and I then eased the young officer up and out of the hatch and placed his body on the flat surface above the engine compartment behind the turret. The cannoneer and I jumped back into our blood-soaked Sherman and quickly buttoned up the hatch. And before ordering the driver to proceed, I calmly reminded him, "Remember our training now. When they zero in on us, the first artillery round usually goes long; the second is short; but the ones following the first two will be right in our laps. So keep changing speeds and directions while continuously moving forward. We've got to protect the infantry out there moving along beside us. Clear?"

"Clear, sir!" the driver responded confidently.

After fierce fighting throughout the day, our Black Panthers finally drove the enemy from the village of Bezange-la-Petite and off Hill 253. But it came at a high cost. Every company in the 761st had taken significant casualties, and ours was no exception. We had lost four of our fifteen tanks with five tankers killed and two wounded.

Once the town was secured, I radioed my men to gather outside the village church. And after offering up a brief prayer for the dead and wounded, I turned to the living and praised their courage in their first combat: "Gentlemen, you did us all proud today. Those weren't just any German troops you were facing. That was the elite Eleventh Panzer Division with a whole host of reserve troops, big guns and top-line tanks. The Eleventh Panzer has a well-deserved reputation as one of the finest fighting units in the *Wehrmacht*. They have a lot of notches on their guns fighting in Russia and North Africa. But you carried the day, and we're one step closer to pushing the bastards back into their own country. So congratulations and now it's on to the next victory! God bless you and keep you safe!"

After mingling with a few of the men gathered at the church, several volunteers and I drove back up the road toward Athainville to collect our dead. It was difficult opening the hatch of the wrecked tank and peering in at the carnage. I had tried steeling myself earlier before beginning the search for the crew. I recalled the whispers about the havoc the white-hot fragments of an armor-piercing shell could wreak once they had penetrated the interior of an "iron coffin." But nothing could have prepared me for what I saw when I opened the hatch and stared down into the tank: a thick swirl of flesh and blood coated the white interior.

As a tank commander, I knew I had to take the lead and climb down into the slaughter. What was once a team with youthful hopes and dreams was now a scramble of body parts. I did my best; but it was almost impossible to match up the arms and legs with a torso, that is, when I was lucky enough to find one. I loaded the pieces into plastic containers, handed the boxes up to a volunteer, and then arbitrarily called out the name of one of the crewmembers who had been on board. And when the awful task was done, we returned to the village, where I spent the night alone staring up at the sweep of indifferent stars through my tears.

25

"I LOST COUNT, Todd. How long has it been now?" Jesse asked.

"Forty days and forty nights," I replied, grinning at the coincidence.

"It'll be good to finally get a few days off the front line. Hot baths, mattresses, and new uniforms. Getting tired of washing my things out in gasoline. The clothes are rotting right off my back."

"Don't count your chickens before they hatch, Jesse. That rumor's not set in stone yet. Remember what happened just a week ago. We were gonna rotate out with the Twenty-sixth Infantry, and here we are still pushing east toward the German border with the Eighty-seventh. Things can change pretty damn quick around here."

Jesse looked around to ensure no one was listening and then said, "And just between you and me, it's galling having to protect those greenhorns. Did you see the way they marched in here? Cheerful and raring to go."

"Ignorance is bliss," I said.

"Sure is. But that's not all that's burning my shinny. You hear what those white boys in the Eighty-seventh are calling us behind our backs? We're not warriors to them. We're just black."

"How ironic," I muttered.

"Yeah, and how many Panthers have we lost so far?"

"Twenty-seven through November," I replied. "And of those, fifteen alone died at Morville-les-Vic and Vic-sur-Seille."

"Yeah, and those numbers have names too. Rivers, Turley, Coleman. Friends first, and now heroes forever. And those white boys of the Eighty-seventh think we just magically appeared here only two miles now from the German border."

I reached into my jacket and pulled out a piece of paper. "Maybe they should read this."

"What do you have there?" Jesse asked.

"A note from the XII Corps commander. Just got a copy an hour ago from the captain. You'll be getting one too. We're supposed to share it with our troopers."

"What's it say?"

I held out the piece of paper. "You wanna read it for yourself? It's special."

Jesse raised his hand. "No, no. My hands are freezing. How about you doing the honors?"

"Okay, then. Here goes. 'I consider the 761st Tank Battalion to have entered combat with such conspicuous courage and success as to warrant special commendation. The speed with which they adapted themselves to the front line under most adverse weather conditions, the gallantry with which they faced some of Germany's finest troops, and the confident spirit with which they emerged from their recent engagements in the vicinity of Dieuze, Morville-les-Vic, and Guebling entitle them surely to consider themselves of the veteran 761st.'"

Jesse smiled but then shook his head. "Nice getting re-spect from the top like that, but I have a gnawing feeling this wouldn't mean beans to the white boys here. To them we're black, and nothing's gonna take those blinders off."

"Maybe so, but we're gonna have to learn to get along with them just as we did with the Twenty-sixth. And who knows, maybe we'll gain their respect once we've saved their bacon a time or two."

So this time, it was my turn to be right. The good news: we did get the rumored R&R. The bad news: —the R&R last-ed hours, not days. Patton decided to keep pushing forward and force the Germans back on their heels. He planned to cross into Germany and attack their defensive positions along the Siegfried Line. He ordered the Eighty-seventh Infantry and our 761st Battalion to prepare to lead the charge into Germany.

But as I told Jesse earlier, things could change pretty damn quick; and just before we were to launch our attack, the Germans beat us to the punch, unleashing a massive counter-offensive to the north in the forested regions of Belgium and Luxembourg known as the Ardennes.

"Well, so much for that attack on the Siegfried Line," Jesse said. "Looks like we're gonna have to hold the fort down here in the south while Patton's Fourth Armored and the Twenty-sixth and the Eightieth Infantry Divisions make tracks up north. They'll have to shore up defenses where the Germans are threatening to break through."

"Yeah, but I hear the Eighty-seventh and our battalion will be heading north too," I replied. "We'll be heading back up to Reims once the units of the Seventh Army get here from Alsace and take over our positions defending the Saar region. Makes sense, Jesse. We don't want to lose what we fought so hard to win down here in the south."

And just before Christmas the Eighty-seventh Infantry and our 761st Battalion were pulled off line and ordered to move first to Weidesheim and then to Wuisse where we were to spend Christmas Day and await further orders. We had finally caught a break, a respite from the front line to enjoy a "peaceful" holiday. Adding to the festive spirit, the company cooks got right to work preparing our first hot meal in weeks: turkey, dressing, and all the fixings. Before we could sit down to eat, however, we got orders to move out. As we climbed up onto our tanks, the cooks tossed us large steaming chunks of half-baked turkey to eat as we sped past Reims on our way to our revised destination, Offagne, in the Belgian forest.

"Damn, it's cold!" I said. "Woke myself up shivering!"

"Yeah, I feel for all the troops out there having to trudge through that knee-high snow," Jesse responded.

"You got a read on the plans yet?" I asked.

"Rumor has it we're supporting the Eighty-seventh in pushing the Germans back from Bastogne. Jerry had the 101st Airborne and the Ninth Armored surrounded in the town. Our men had been told to hold Bastogne at all costs. I hear it was the Fourth Armored with the help of the Twenty-sixth and Eightieth Infantries that rushed northward from our position in the Saar that finally broke through. Established a lifeline to the town, but they say it's so thin you can spit across it!"

"Hold it at all costs? What's so important about this Bastogne?" I asked.

"Strategic crossroad. Seven paved highways intersect there. Germans need them for quick movement of their troop carriers, armored vehicles, and supply trucks as they continue their counterattack to the west. You know what they say in the manuals . . . 'When you own the roads, you own the war.'"

"You hearing anything about when we're moving out?" I probed.

"No, but if I had to bet, I'd say day after tomorrow. On Sunday, New Year's Eve."

Sure enough, Jesse nailed it. We got the word late that evening we'd be giving our equipment the once-over on Saturday and then we'd be moving out northwest of Offagne on the thirty-first. Our objective was to provide cover for the Eighty-seventh Infantry as they attempted to cut off supply lines for the Germans still surrounding Bastogne and for the German counteroffensive raging to the west. And despite sleet, drifting snow, and subzero temperatures, we advanced steadily, loosening the German grip—that is, until heavy resistance abruptly stopped us outside the town of Tillet.

So it was now our battalion's time to do the heavy lifting—to take the lead into this German stronghold, which had earlier almost destroyed a complete battalion of Sherman tanks from the Eleventh Armored Division. The elite 113th Panzer Brigade took everything we threw at them, and then immediately returned fire with deadly accuracy, destroying tanks and ripping infantrymen to shreds. Metal and body parts hurtled away in every direction. Men and machines just seemed to vanish into thin air. Witnessing the carnage, the young soldiers of the Eighty-seventh dropped their rifles and started running back up the road from Tillet. Without infantry support our Shermans couldn't advance, so we had to back out of our positions one tank at a time while still trying to provide cover for the medics who were evacuating the wounded.

After countless attempts on succeeding days, we finally managed to inch down the narrow road and enter the heavily fortified town. But within minutes of establishing a foothold, Jesse's tank broke down and the turret of my Sherman was blown sixty feet into the air. In the heat of the battle, we tankers seized our grease guns, exited our Shermans, and joined the infantry in deadly house-to-house combat. And once we'd emptied our submachine guns into a house filled with forty to fifty Germans, Jesse and I grabbed a couple of M1 rifles from the dead and dying and continued our charge with the Eighty-seventh.

The last thing I recall about our battle for Tillet is the flash of light, the sensation of being swept up into the air, and Jesse's face screaming, "You'll be all right, Todd! Stay with me! You'll be all right!" And in my morphine-induced stupor, the only thing I remember about heaven is clutching my M1 and gazing into the eyes of a Negro angel who stroked my cheek and prayed for my recovery.

26

AFTER AMPUTATION OF my right leg at the knee, I was shipped out of Bastogne to Calais and then across the channel to Portsmouth, England. Throughout my rehabilitation, Jesse managed to find time to write occasionally, keeping me updated on the 761st Battalion's progress. His first letter arrived at the hospital toward the end of January 1945: "After taking Tillet," he wrote, "we cut the Marche-Bastogne Road choking off the key German supply line. Next, working with the Seventeenth Airborne near Houffalize, we blocked the Liege-Bastogne Road. And after capturing the towns of Gouvy, Hautbillan, and Thommen, we cut the road from Saint Vith, which effectively relieved the siege of Bastogne for good."

His next letter detailed more of the battalion's movements: "We cut the Richmond Julich railway near Milich, entered the Reich, and mopped up resistance along the way to Schwannenberg, Germany. . . . After reaching our intermediate objective at Klingen-Munster, we crossed the Rhine at Oppenheim and headed for Austria. . . . We then struck the Salzburg-Vienna Highway and turned southward toward Steyr on the Enns River where it's rumored we'd be shaking hands with the Russians!"

And on May 6 he wrote triumphantly, "Today, after 183 days in combat, we achieved a milestone for our people; but as usual it wasn't easy reaching the goal! As the easternmost *American* troopers, we met the First Ukrainian Army in Austria! So our Black Panthers were the first *Americans* to rendezvous with the Russians! But as I said, Todd, it wasn't easy. And if it hadn't been for some quick thinking, our meeting with the Russians would never have happened at all!

"Since rumors were flying that the war was coming to an end, we were told we wouldn't be getting our regular supply of gasoline for our tanks. But all of us Panthers knew it was a charade. Higher-ups didn't want us Negroes being the first American soldiers to meet the Russians! That distinction would go to the white boys in the Thirteenth and Fourteenth Armored Divisions.

"But a creative sergeant in the 761st Supply Company drove trucks over to the Kohlrube Depot and discussed the situation with Negro troops in the quartermaster unit. They agreed to help us out by 'requisitioning' thirty thousand gallons of gasoline from a nearby airstrip. We returned to our bivouac, fueled our tanks, and headed off to Steyr! . . . Can you believe it? After a hundred and eighty days on the frontline, two thousand combat miles, eleven Silver and sixty Bronze Stars, four battlefield commissions, a Medal of Honor, thirty-four killed and three hundred wounded, they had the gall to deny our battalion the honor because of our color!"

Over the next two years I received occasional letters, which became fewer and farther between. In them Jesse described the battalion's occupation and training duties in

Germany and how much he looked forward to getting back home and resuming his ministry. While he tried painting a positive picture, it was easy to read the boredom and increasing frustration lurking between the lines. So it wasn't really a shock when the letters finally dried up in the spring of '47. But Gramps and I took that as a good sign, an indication he was finally headed home. We speculated that Jesse wanted to surprise us—get back to the States, sign his discharge papers, and then make a beeline back to Hollow Rock.

And as we learned later on, that's exactly what he had planned. But something bad happened between Louisville and Nashville. Decked out in his decorated uniform, he boarded a bus at Fort Knox, Kentucky, the day after receiving his honorable discharge from the service. Everything was going according to plan until the driver pulled into Mount Pleasant for a rest stop. When Jesse returned to the bus after using the "colored" bathroom, the driver excoriated him for taking too much time and getting the bus off schedule. Taking exception to the cursing and vile epithets, Jesse responded aggressively.

When the argument escalated, the driver called the police. And when the local sheriff arrived, the driver asked the lawmen to arrest Jesse for public drunkenness. Jesse objected vehemently to the charge, explaining he was a minister and a teetotaler. When the sheriff tried handcuffing him, Jesse spontaneously pushed away, infuriating the officer. The sheriff reached for his billy club and beat Jesse mercilessly. He then threw the unconscious war hero in the back of his cruiser and hauled him off to jail. The next morning, the sheriff dragged Jesse before a corrupt judge who found Jesse guilty and fined him a hundred dollars plus court costs. After his rigged prosecution that morning, Jesse stumbled out of the courthouse and collapsed in the street. The curb became his stone of destiny.

Later that week Gramps received a phone call from authorities informing him of Jesse's death. The official indicated Gramps could retrieve the body and effects at a Mount Pleasant funeral home on Main Street. Since neither of us could drive, Gramps asked Pastor Dives of the Mount Nebo Church to drive us up to Kentucky. After claiming the body at the funeral home, we stopped to talk to a number of town folk, who honestly didn't want to give us the time of day. They all shrugged their shoulders and said they had no idea how "the Negro passed away." They speculated he'd just taken ill and "up and died." None of the townsfolk dared mention the beating, the jailing, or the sham prosecution.

So we took Jesse home to his people. Pastor Dives conducted a moving sermon in the same church where Jesse had served as assistant minister. After the service we transported Jesse's body out to Gramps's property and stood in the same semicircular space where Jesse and I had stood on that first auspicious January morning. Pastor Dives offered up a prayer: "Lord, grant the spirit of faith and courage to us who grieve today that we may have strength to face the days to come, not mournful as those without hope but in joyful anticipation of eternal life together."

The minister then placed his right hand on the coffin and spoke directly to Jesse: "And now as you depart to carry on the fight, may the Lord bless thee, and keep thee. May the Lord make his face shine upon thee, and be gracious unto thee. May the Lord lift up his countenance upon thee, and give thee peace, now and forevermore. We ask for these things in Jesus' name. Amen." And after tucking him in next to his "Mama" and "Granny," Gramps and I walked down the forest path to the hollow rock where we hammered out a flat marker and inscribed it simply "Jesse."

We returned to the house and sat down at the kitchen table. Gramps held up the plain manila envelope containing Jesse's effects. "Pretty light. Doesn't seem to be much in here."

"Yeah and his duffel bag's gone missing too," I said. "The vultures in that hellhole picked him clean."

Gramps opened the envelope and dumped the contents out on the table. "What do we have here? . . . Three things worthless to them I guess: his comb and these two, ah, medals."

I picked up the first medal. It was a bronze cross with crossed swords extending out between the arms. The medal was suspended from a green ribbon with thin vertical red stripes and two bronze palm branches. I turned it over, read the inscribed date, 1914–1918, and looked up at Gramps. "Thank God this didn't get away."

"Whatcha got there?" Gramps asked.

"The French Army's Croix de Guerre awarded to Jesse's father for bravery in battle. Jesse must've carried it with him throughout the war."

I picked up the second medal and examined it. The only differences in the two medals were the thickness of the stripes on the ribbons and the dates inscribed on the reverse. While the first medal read, "1914–1918," the second was dated

1939–1945. I glanced up at Gramps, smiled, and said, "That's just like Jesse Lockwood."

"Whatdaya mean?" Gramps asked.

"This may be the first and only time a father and son have received the Croix de Guerre. This must be Jesse's medal, Gramps. Got it after the war and never told us a thing about it. My way of thinking, the thieves got away with the valuables but left us the true treasures!" As I handed Gramps the medals, I said, "I'm sure his father would've been proud of Jesse, if he'd only lived to see the day."

Gramps held the medals up in the palms of his hands, smiled, and shook his head. "These boys were heroes."

I nodded. "Yes, heroes in every way."

27

LOOKING BACK ON it now I'd have to say there were three truly memorable shows at the Shanghai. The first was my inaugural concert where I introduced the Delta blues to the club via Son House and his young protégé and harmonica wizard, Robert Spencer.

The second was the W. C. Handy concert coming on the heels of the unforgettable night I had just spent with Van. For that show I performed my usual opening monologue about Mr. Handy hearing Henry Sloan playing the Delta blues on the railway platform in Tutwiler, Mississippi. But for this special concert I added a twist. I had folks upstage behind me acting out the scene as I described it to the audience. Spotlights streamed down on the figures of the two men. But unbeknownst to anyone, it wasn't an actor playing Henry Sloan this time. It was *the* Henry Sloan, the father of the Delta blues. I had sneaked him into town as a surprise for Mr. Handy. Later that night Mr. Sloan played several encores with him. The review in the *Commercial Appeal* the following day ran with the headline, "And the Crowd Went Wild!"

The third concert, the pièce de résistance, was the return visit of the young harmonica player, Robert Spencer. Only this time he wasn't Robert Spencer, he wasn't playing the harmonica, and he wasn't playing duets. He was now Robert Johnson, and he played solo guitar. Yes, that's right. The same boy who Son House earlier said "couldn't hold a tune in a bucket playin' a guitar" was front and center at the Shanghai.

Now, I wasn't crazy booking him as a solo guitar act. I'd gotten word from club owners on the Hog Belly Circuit that young Spencer-Johnson had miraculously become one of the most talented Delta blues guitarists on the tour. To a person, they used the word *miraculous* to describe this burst of talent, and then they'd undercut their argument by explaining Robert had gone to the Mississippi crossroads of Highways 49 and 61 and worked a deal with the devil. That Faustian explanation has refused to die even up to this day. Everyone now agrees there are three ways to become a great musician: you can be born with it; you can practice until your fingers bleed; or you can go to the crossroads in Clarksdale and sell your soul away.

But I'm here to set the record straight. Folks transferred that Faustian tale from the guitarist Tommy Johnson to Robert. As Jacque explained to me, Tommy would get a little drunk and start boasting anyone can play the guitar, "Take a seat at the crossroads around midnight and start a'playin'. Won't be long. Some tall fella will come up on ya from behind. Won't say a lick. will just take your six-string. tune it. play a piece or two. and then give her back to ya. From then on, ya can play anything ya want." So first it was Tommy and then it became Robert who had visited the Mississippi crossroads and dealt with the devil at midnight.

There were three things I never told Gramps: first, how

disappointed I was he couldn't teach me the blues; second, that I had quit playing guitar; and third, that I had given Gramps's special gift to me, my thunderwood six-string guitar, to that young harmonica wizard, Robert Spencer. And when Robert returned to the Shanghai for that third memorable concert, it was the only guitar he played. The spotlights reflected off the brilliant silver soundboard. And for us sitting upfront, we could detect the flecks of lightning etched into the gleaming wood. As for the sound, it was as dynamic as ever—the booming bass, the mellow midrange, the bell-like treble, and the mystical shimmer in the overtones. And I have to tell you now, I've known for some time where the magic really lay in Robert Johnson's transformation. So don't talk to me about Johnson, crossroads, and the devil. Talk to me about a shy young man, Gramps, and the regifting of a thunderwood guitar.

Let's see now. It's been twenty-five years to the day since Van and I shared that night. Every year on the anniversary of our tryst I take two books down off the shelves—Woolf's *To the Lighthouse* and Stevens's *Harmonium*. They are Van's personal copies. Her brother had graciously asked me if there was anything of hers I wanted as a keepsake. I told him I only wanted the two books, which meant so much to her and me.

After enjoying her favorite part of Woolf's novel, the "Interlude," I open the Stevens volume to her favorite poem, "Sunday Morning," and begin reading aloud:

> Complacencies of the peignoir, and late
> Coffee and oranges in a sunny chair,
> And the green freedom of a cockatoo

Upon a rug mingle to dissipate
The holy hush of ancient sacrifice.
She dreams a little, and she feels the dark
Encroachment of that old catastrophe,
As a calm darkens among water-lights.
The pungent oranges and bright, green wings
Seem things in some procession of the dead,
Winding across wide water, without sound.
The day is like wide water, without sound. . . .

And, in the isolation of the sky,
At evening, casual flocks of pigeons make
Ambiguous undulations as they sink,
Downward to darkness, on extended wings.

Every year I ask myself, could Stevens have had a premonition when he wrote this back in 1915 long before Van and I met. After all, we lived his poem that Saturday night and Sunday morning—two lovers sharing breakfast, the peignoir, the rug, the fruit, the coffee, the Matisse, and for God's sake, even the religious doubt. I then focus on the words Van had added next to the text. Near "pigeons" she writes "Matisse"; near "water-lights" she has penciled in "Woolf's Lighthouse"; and near "coffee and oranges" she has printed "TODD."

As I write today, I'd describe my situation as alone surrounded by throngs of well-intentioned people. The last time I spoke with Jacque, he said he was heading home to Charleston. He said he spent so much time dreaming about going home he might as well just do it. Everything changed after Van died, he said. He was quick to add, though, that that was no knock on her brother, who had taken over the club after her death. Everyone just understood that Van was irreplaceable. She was the soul of the Shanghai.

Thankfully, Gramps continued his labor of love into his nineties, producing what experts say are some of his finest violins, violas, and guitars near the end of his life. For me it was like a religious ritual. I would rise on Sunday morning, strap on my leg, and head out to spend the Sabbath with my adopted father. We went walking every Sunday regardless of the season or the weather. Two places were always on the itinerary: the tiny graveyard near the stand of birches and the enigmatic hollow rock. But surprisingly, those were the only places where we reminisced. Our conversations were usually dominated by the future. One Sunday morning after our walk, Gramps said unexpectedly, "I think I need to lie down for a spell. The strings seem to be loosenin' and the joints are comin' unglued." He added jokingly, "This fine instrument's in need of some serious repair." I checked in on him a little later in the afternoon. The expert was right. Gramps was lifeless but smiling.

The customized calendar I had ordered from the stationer listed the days of the week as "Monday," "Tuesday," "Wednesday," "Thursday," "Friday," "Mamasday," and "Grampsday." That's right. If Sunday was "Grampsday," then Saturday was "Mamasday." Unlike Gramps, Mama's focus was mostly on the past. She was the family historian. She had the incredible knack of remembering exactly what happened on a certain day at a certain time. But the one thing that was off-limits during our conversations was any mention of my father or his whereabouts. As the years passed, discussion of him had dwindled to zero.

So we'd be having Saturday lunch, and I would say something that would trigger a memory in Mama's mind. And then out of nowhere, she'd pipe up with some comment like, "You remember our first Thanksgiving here at Hollow Rock?"

I would respond distractedly while focusing on Mama's home cooking. "Uh-huh."

"Well, after you'd consumed three turkey sandwiches for supper the following Saturday night, we sat down near the Crosley 51 and passed the headphones back and forth between us. Remember?"

With my mouth full of ham, beef, potatoes, corn, or what have you, I'd reply, "Uh-huh."

"You remember what was on at eight o'clock that night?"

"You better refresh me, Mama. It's been far too long."

"Uncle Jimmy Thompson and his niece, Miss Eva. He played his fiddle—he called her 'Old Betsy'—and Miss Eva played the piano. Remember?"

"Yeah, Mama, I vaguely remember a pianist and a fiddler."

"Uncle Jimmy said he was inching up on eighty and started playing fiddle before the Civil War. Said he had a thousand songs in his repertoire and encouraged us to tell our neighbors to send in their requests. Remember?"

Knowing I was sorely outgunned by her encyclopedic memory, I would look up patiently and respond, "I vaguely remember sending letters to that radio station. W . . . uh . . . W . . ."

"WSM!" she would interject. "It was in the National

Life and Accident Building in Nashville on the fifth floor. I'd memorized the address. We must have sent in over a hundred requests while listening that first year. And Uncle Jimmy would keep on encouraging us to write in. He'd yell out, 'I want to throw my music out all over the Americee!' You remember, Todd?" she would ask excitedly.

And I would nod and reply, "Uh-huh, I kinda recall the yelling, but I do definitely remember helping you write the letters, Mama."

"Now who woulda thought that Uncle Jimmy's show, the WSM *Barn Dance*, would expand and eventually become the *Grand Ole Opry*."

I looked up truly surprised where the narrative had taken us and said honestly, "Wow, I didn't know that."

"Yes, sir, Todd, you and I listened to the very first broadcast of the *Grand Ole Opry*!"

And that was always Mama's hidden agenda—finding an entertaining story to illuminate a long lost fact about the past. One Saturday I would say something, and she would consult her museum of memories and then be off and running with the life of Marcus Aurelius and his impact on stoicism. The next Saturday I would say something and she would be off to the races discussing Zoroaster and the human struggle with truth and deception. And God only knows if there was hidden personal meaning buried beneath that particular conversation.

So Mama loved teaching. She had taught all of her life. In fact, she had met my father in a classroom. I would ask her occasionally if she ever thought about doing anything else, and she would shake her head and reply, "I want to keep teaching until the day I die." And Mama got her wish. One fine spring morning I got a call from the school principal. He advised me to get over to the Warfield Hospital as soon as possible. Mama had collapsed in the classroom, he explained, and was in "a very bad way." I rushed over to the emergency room and learned she had died "peacefully" ten minutes before I arrived.

Over the years while visiting with Mama, I sensed a slow physical decline. But with my father it was entirely different. He seemed to be picking up steam healthwise as the years passed. I realized he wouldn't live forever, but I felt it would take an act of God to tear him from this earth. His approach to life—absorb, adjust, attack, and anticipate—made him virtually invulnerable to health and environmental threats. He always reminded me that anticipation was the key to long-term success.

And I'm sure he had done his usual homework before boarding TWA Flight 891 from Milan to Paris's Orly Airport. I could imagine him checking off the variables: a reputable carrier, a safe aircraft with a spotless accident record, and four reliable Wright R-3350 engines. I could see him confidently belted into his seat sitting next to his latest lover as the Starliner lifted off the runway at Malpensa Airport. I could hear him reliving the two-week holiday the lovers had just shared at his hillside mansion on Lake Como.

But that's where my confidence ends and the questions begin. Did the pilot announce they had just passed through ten thousand feet? Did my father feel the lightning strike? Did he sense the explosion in the seventh fuel tank? What about the one in the sixth? Did he survive the explosions? If so, did he realize the plane was breaking apart? Did he see the open field near Marnate fast approaching?

But the one thing Father clearly anticipated was the passing of the torch. He and his lawyer had earlier drawn up plans detailing precisely how my father's estate would be divvied up. While he bequeathed a substantial lump sum to me, he expectedly left the estate in the hands of Mrs. Burrows's elder son, whom Father had adopted as a condition of marrying her. The irony of all this was while a stranger inherited my father's fortune, I inherited a "stranger's" farm. Since Jesse had preceded his grandfather in death, Gramps had quietly named me sole beneficiary of his property and possessions.

When I first returned home after my rehabilitation in England, I was still using a crutch. The military had offered to fit me with an artificial leg, but I had something far different in mind. Throughout the ordeal—from Bastogne to Calais and then to Portsmouth—I had refused to surrender the wrecked M1 I was firing when the blast splintered my leg. No one, not even the black Belgian nurse who had bravely saved my life at the aid station in Bastogne, could wrest the rifle from me. I kept it by my side until I could hand deliver it to Gramps, who fashioned a peg leg out of the singed walnut stock, which now looked strikingly similar to thunderwood.

Mama always said, "Boy, you make lemonade out of the lemons life throws you." And I did just that. I stepped back into the limelight. I donned my uniform, strapped on my "M1" leg, recalled all the oratorical and sales skills I'd honed over the years, and launched my evangelical career first in the revival tents, next on the radio, and finally on the burgeoning networks of television. The recent memories of a victorious war, my highly decorated uniform, my peg leg, and my reliance on Bible stories and hymns related to war and the military helped launch a successful career offering attendees and radio listeners eternal life if, as the old hymn says, they:

> . . . put their armor on,
> Strong in the strength which God supplies
> Through His eternal Son. . . .
> From strength to strength go on,
> Wrestle and fight and pray,
> Tread all the pow'rs of darkness down
> And win the well-fought day.

Father had taught me that to survive at any endeavor you have to change with the times. As the positive memories of a victorious war faded, I sensed the military theme, the uniform, and the "M1" leg would have to be jettisoned. After a lot of thought, I replaced the khakis with a fashionable business suit, swapped the peg out for a lifelike leg, and radically overhauled the theme of my ministry. Soldiering was out, but property ownership was in! Everything—the sermons, the hymns, and the overall thrust of the ministry—now centered on owning property in heaven.

I launched my transformed ministry at an outdoor revival standing on the mossy heights of the hollow rock and surveying the massive crowd that had gathered that fine Easter morning to first celebrate the resurrection and then spend the rest of the day following the town's decades-old tradition of welcoming in the spring. We began the service with a prayer and a hymn, "I Need No Mansion Here Below":

> When Jesus comes to claim his own,
> I will move to my new home.
> I'll walk and talk with him upon the streets of gold.
> A mansion is waiting me soon.
> It's beauty I will see.

I opened the Easter sermon reading from the book of John, chapter 14:

> Let not your heart be troubled: ye believe in God, believe also in me. In my Father's house are many mansions: if it were not so, I would have told you. I go to prepare a place for you. And if I go and prepare a place for you, I will come again, and receive you unto myself; that where I am, there ye may be also.

And then I spent the lion's share of the sermon explaining the concept: as weekly tithing members of the church they would receive fractional shares in acreage and a house in heaven. Members who regularly tithed would receive actual parchment deeds with embossed gold seals indicating the size of their current property. The more they tithed, the more shares they were awarded and the larger the acreage and the house grew. I ended the stirring sermon reminding them there would be no set limit on the size of either the house or the land they could own.

Once I had established the concept locally, I rolled it out nationally with a weekly church service broadcast on television called *Celestial Properties*. During the shows I encouraged viewers to support our worldwide charities with generous donations to our ministry; and in return, they would be receiving through the mail embossed parchment deeds indicating the current size of their mansion and the acreage surrounding it.

When I read stories now about the birth of jazz, the mutual fund industry, or broadcast evangelism, I usually laugh out loud. About jazz the critics usually write something to the effect that "if it hadn't been for that joint concert of W. C. Handy and Henry Sloane in Memphis that night, the Delta blues and the Memphis blues might have never gotten together and forged what we now call jazz." About mutual funds the economists write, "Although they got off to a rocky start with the market crash and the subsequent depression, credit must be given to pioneers like T. J. Cavanaugh, who single-handedly introduced the concept of open-end mutual funds." And about television evangelism, the clerics write, "Credit must be given where credit is due. The Reverends Wyrtzen, Crawford, and Sheen must be praised for bringing weekly religious services into our living rooms."

In my mind's eye I leap up and object, "Wait one minute there, sirs! It was I who brought Sloan and Handy together! It was I who introduced Mr. Cavanaugh to the concept of open-end mutual funds! And it was I who labored right alongside all those good reverends you like to praise! And as a parting shot, sirs, I want you to know here and now, I won more awards than the three of them combined!" But as I said it's all in my mind's eye. I close the newspaper or the journal, smile, and acknowledge that while it sure didn't feel much like success at the time, I can take pride now in knowing I played the hands pretty damn well just as they were dealt.

I walk over to the frosted window and gaze out at the starlit stand of birches swaying in the strong January wind. I nod and whisper, "For the first time, I believe I value the mist of that first morning at Hollow Rock. Yes, I agree now. We're all thunderwood. And despite the endless buffeting and the occasional fiery strike, our scarred branches reach higher, and our roots drive deeper into the rich, nurturing soil of our beloved South."